THE
GRANDDAUGHTER
AND THE
MONKEY SWING

THE GRANDDAUGHTER AND THE MONKEY SWING

HELEN GUMIENNY GLOWACKI

To order additional copies of this book:

Visit the author's website at:
www.helenglowacki.com

For wholesale or multiple copy information:

Send inquiry to helen@helenglowacki.com

Contents

Dedication

To those who were our roles models, those who never gave up on us, those who were perfect because they allowed the Lord to shape and guide them, and then shared the blessing this created with us.

> *Cannot I do with you as this potter? saith the Lord.*
> *Behold, as the clay is in the potter's hand,*
> *so are ye in mine hand.*
>
> *—Jeremiah 18:6*

Novels by Helen Gumienny Glowacki

When God Broke Grandma's Heart
When God Took Grandma Home
When Grandma Chased the Spirits
The Granddaughter and the Monkey Swing
Grandma's Little Book of Poetry: The Story of God's Plan of
Salvation
Abiding Faith, Hidden Treasure
And Then They Asked God

Why God Why Series by Helen Glowacki

To What Purpose?
Why God Why?
Why Trust Scripture?
What Should I Know About Life after Death And The
Coming Tribulation?
What Does God Want Me To Do *RIGHT NOW*?
Do The Little Sins REALLY Count?

Other non-fiction Books by Helen Glowacki

Politically Incorrect: The Get Some Gumption Bible Study
When Enough is Enough
What No One Is Telling You about Addictions
The Many Faces of Depression: How to be Happy
****

Authors Website: www.Helenglowacki.com

Face book: http://www.facebook.com/pages/The-
Grandmother-Series/155300907853909?ref=ts

Acknowledgments

To my husband, Wally, who painstakingly helped with the edit; to my children, Julie and Joe, and daughter-in-law, Debra, who believe in me and gave me the wonderful gifts of David, Michelle, Scott, and Samantha;

To friends who shared my vision and never doubted: Barbara, Lisa, Sue, Becky, Dina, Fred, Anna Mae, Ben, Linda, Debbie, Tom, and Herold;

To Richard Levinson, whose kindness gave me the courage to try;

To Dr. John Sullivan for sharing his incredible knowledge of alternative medicine;

To the ministers of the New Apostolic Church who pray for me and strengthen me spiritually;

To Lynnel Landerito, submissions representative; Tiffany Arranguez, author representative; Kevin Desabelle, editor; T. Gomez, artist; and Vanessa, Sherry, and Jackie, marketing representatives, who all contributed to a great experience and helped me make it better;

And most of all, to my Heavenly Father, who guides my life, gives so much, loves so much, and made all this possible!

MY HEARTFELT AND HUMBLE THANKS

Note to the Reader

The King James Version (KJV) of the Bible, which is public domain in the United States, is used throughout the books of The Grandma Series. However, for further study, the author recommends the New King James Version (NKJV) of the Bible for easier reading and less usage of the old-world language while remaining true to the original text.

The books in The Grandma Series are works of fiction. References to real people, events, locale or organizations are intended only to provide a sense of authenticity and are used fictitiously. All other characters, incidents, and dialogues are drawn from the author's imagination and are not to be construed as real. Resemblance to actual persons, living or dead, is entirely coincidental. No part of the books may be used or reproduced in any manner whatsoever without written permission except in the case of brief quotations embodied in critical articles and reviews.

This book contains a scriptural index. Instead of assembling this index according to the *Chicago Manual of Style*, the author has developed a format that might be more useful to the reader. The chapter and verse identification of the scriptures are found under key word categories that highlight a specific concern or interest. This index style may also better support a teaching program based on this book since all verses pertaining to a specific subject are listed together.

Practical applications of interior design, developed by the author, are also included in this book and may be employed by the reader. The endnotes contain additional examples of properly proportioned room sizes as well as examples of room sizes that require the illusion of elongating or shortening two of their four walls so the room appears properly proportioned. Finally, there are examples of room sizes that can obtain proper proportions by being divided into two sections.

BOOK REVIEWS
The Grandma Series

From Dallas, Texas: "I have just read one of the most inspiring books I have read in a long time! The story and characters reveal real life situations in a remarkable and inviting form. I am certain that such a riveting story can also serve as an effective supportive tool for pastoral and mental health counselors. Ms. Glowacki described the stages of grief and God's comforting plan in an extraordinary way and through characters that really grab the heart. She is an author I expect to see on the bestseller lists very soon and for many years to come. I look forward to the next books in her wonderful, inspiring series. A pleasure to read, a masterful idea, *"When God Took Grandma Home"* by Helen Gumienny Glowacki is filled with the most beautiful insight into God's plan for us!

Reverend Fred Krueger,
retired Lutheran Minister of 12 years and
Clinical Social Worker for 26 years.

From Sea Cliff, New York: Helen Gumienny Glowacki is a magnificent writer, who is truly able to weave a story that will make the reader become emotionally involved in the character's lives. It was a joy to read this book and the reader will appreciate the strong Christian values portrayed therein. This book will certainly whet the appetite for the other books in the series. *"When God Broke Grandma's Heart"* by Helen Gumienny Glowacki is a certain bet to be a best seller.

Reverend Richard C. Freund,
President, New Apostolic Church USA.

Once again, Helen Gumienny Glowacki enthusiastically presents a scenario, which will delight readers and bring comfort to anyone who is grieving. This book *"When God Took Grandma Home"* will inspire all readers and give them a deeper insight into the after-life. This book is a masterful portrayal of young people searching for the truth. It is sure to be a great success.

Reverend Richard C. Freund.
President, New Apostolic Church USA.

From Odenton, Maryland: As a counselor to many who struggle with challenging circumstances in their lives, I found *"When God Broke Grandma's Heart"* an inspirational story of hope. Despite cruelty and betrayal from those she trusted, and the multiple adversities Grandma endured, she was able to find strength and understanding through her faith in and love of God. Helen Gumienny Glowacki beautifully portrays the phases that individuals move through and the transformation that can occur when one is able to let go of negative events in their past and strive towards the understanding that regardless of how unjust, none of the pain was for naught.

Tammera L. Shelton, M.S. Psychology.

From Clifton, New Jersey: I am the wife of a retired minister. Many times during my husband's ministry I was aware that a parishioner was living through a difficult circumstance, but because of my husband's responsibilities to provide assistance and counseling, I was not always able to help in the matter. Helen Gumienny Glowacki's *The Grandma Series* are a wonderful way to provide help and support to someone in need when other avenues of communication are closed. These books are inspiring, uplifting, educational, and heartwarming. Every story ends with a beautiful example of how God explains our pain, renews our hope, shows us the way out of our situation and creates a miracle for our lives. I love this series.

Edith Stier, 32 Years as the wife of a Minister.

From Brookfield, Wisconsin: Wow! I've just finished reading the third book in this series of great novels and can't find words great enough to describe them. At a time when there are so many troubles in the world and so many people who suffer, these books are a real eye opener about God's plan of salvation and why bad things happen to good people. They remind me of Jim LaHaye and Jerry B. Jenkins "Left Behind Series". These books are a MUST READ!"

Ben Lodwick, Avid Reader.

FROM ONLINE BOOKSTORE WEBSITES:

Reader Reviews

5 star rating: ***When God Broke Grandma's Heart***: (A) well-written, heartwarming story of Grandma's struggle to overcome heartbreak and tragedy through her belief in God. This story will touch your heart. A worthwhile read for all generations. I look forward to reading more from this author.

A reviewer, a reader in Kentucky

5 star rating: ***When God Took Grandma Home:*** Remarkable for someone looking for answers! Found it extremely inspirational and deeply moving. A fascinating storyteller with a real message.

Fred D'Alauro

5 star rating: ***When God Broke Grandma's Heart***: This book is written from the heart with such thoughtfulness and grace. The author provides the reader with a meaningful experience. The messages are gentle yet powerful to the soul even through experiencing grandma's struggles and grief throughout the novel. The author shares the ideas of strong beliefs in ourselves, carries our faith, and shelters us in times of need and guides us home. Transformation and courage are profound themes of this novel to find truth and faith within all of us. The reader will be captivated at the book's end and will want to read what comes next. Thank you Grandma.

Debra Forman

5 star rating: ***When God Took Grandma Home***: Heartwarming! This book touched my heart. It is both heartwarming and very spiritual.

Debbie Espeland

5 star rating: ***When God Broke Grandma's Heart:*** Fantastic! A must read for all generations.

A Reader

5 star rating: ***When God Took Grandma Home***: Must Read! Touching story of life's tragedies and heartaches and how lesson learned from these heartbreaking events can turn into blessings.

A reviewer, a Kentucky reader

5 star rating: ***When God Broke Grandma's Heart:*** What an outstanding writer! I chose this book because throughout my life, (my) Grandma was always there for me making things become rosy. This book kept me riveted – there are many valuable lessons. Helen is an angel sent to help us through our trying days. I am now reading her second book. Thank you for helping me find some peace in this world.

Robert W. Rothe, USMC 1970-1976, a reviewer

5 star rating: ***When God Took Grandma Home***: A very captivating book, keeps you moved from the beginning.

A reviewer

5 star rating: ***When God Took Grandma Home***: Wonderful, Inspirational! I enjoyed reading this book. It is well written . . . .

Patricia Robinson

Message from the Author

In the beginning of a relationship there is often what is called the "honeymoon period". It is a time when we are so happy with that relationship that we do not notice normal faults and failings, only attributes and strengths. It is a time of wonder and joy, a time when life seems especially good and any difficulties we have seem to fade. How wonderful it would be if we could keep this first impression always.

Eventually however, as we encounter faults, mistakes, real or imagined slights, or a slacking off of responsibilities, the relationship is tested and, based on this new information, we draw a conclusion or make a decision about the relationship. That decision is a judgment that determines whether or not we want to continue to nurture the relationship. It is also the moment when we can make our own mistakes.

Our human nature easily finds fault, easily believes that what we perceive as a fault, failing, or lack of responsibility is a deeply ingrained character flaw rather than simply a mistake or a misunderstanding. When this occurs, we've not only judged, but we've perhaps lost a potentially good relationship and the opportunity to help someone learn from their mistakes.

There is an old adage that reminds us that for every fault we see in someone else, we need to remember that they see one in us; for each fault we overlook, perhaps someone will overlook a fault in us; and for every mistake we forgive, we too might gain forgiveness. The Bible tells us that the small sliver of fault we think so huge in someone else can't compare with the much larger number of faults in ourselves.

Hypocrite! First remove the plank from your own eye,
and then you will see clearly
to remove the speck from your brother's eye.

—*Matthew 7:5*

This point in scripture is a profound truth, and over the years I have learned to look for and admire those people who, by taking these words to heart, provide Christlike love and forgiveness, and offer an example to us through their patient teaching. They are a treasure to us and are the role models God wants us all to be. Because we are His children, God *expects* us to be teachers, role models, and examples, and to practice forgiveness, gentleness, understanding, and compassion.

Once we have become aware of our responsibilities as a child of God, we *must* become the teachers, role models, and counselors to those who strive but fail in various situations. We need to perfect our ability to do this because as children of God, this will be our major role during the thousand-year-kingdom of peace. God tells us:

For unto whomsoever much is given,
of him shall be much required.

—*Luke 12:48*

This verse also lets us know that we need to know what God says so we can discern what is right for us to do in any given circumstance. Sadly, when we do not know what God says, or what He asks of us, mistakes are easily made and we can lose not only the blessing God offers, but we also risk our soul's salvation.

The Pharisees allowed themselves a self-righteous, hurtful, and dismissive attitude toward the errors of judgment and the mistakes or oversights they believed existed in others. If we allow this attitude to be active in us, we may destroy the benefit we have reaped from the good we have done in the past.

Perhaps we should ask ourselves if the circumstance that made us question a relationship could have been a simple and innocent mistake, an error in judgment, or even a trap laid by Satan to distance us from a relationship. Perhaps we should also ask ourselves if we believe we are "owed" something and, not obtaining it, justify our decision to withhold support to someone we could help. This can be a sign of self-righteousness and retaliation. At that moment, what Christ taught us about the gift of forgiveness and compassion is lost, as is our opportunity to be a teacher and role model to those who made an error.

Sadly, so many in today's world enjoy focusing on what is wrong. This behavior is a far cry from Christ's example of how He forgives us and teaches us. God asks us to be teachers, to be an example, and to lead all souls to higher standards of conduct wherever we can. When we gently teach others to be more circumspect, by being less impulsive ourselves, and by our example of knowing and teaching what God asks of us, we touch God's heart and bring a blessing into our own lives as well as the lives of others. But through our self-righteous nature, when we find fault, complain, or lash out, we can lose this blessing. These actions are not the fruits of the Holy Spirit.

With clearer hindsight, we might discover that we'd been wrong in our quick judgments and dismissive attitudes, and we'd been the one who made the error and jumped to a conclusion without the facts, losing the trust of those we so quickly judged. When this happens, we have caused harm, and as those who should have known better, this could harm our relationship with God. Further, we will have to account for the harm we've caused.

While God does tell us that there are circumstances where we have been unequally yoked, should distance ourselves from certain relationships, and not throw "pearls to the swine," more often, God tells us to forgive and teach, so we are an example to others in a manner that helps others see Christ in us.

> *Give not that which is holy unto the dogs,*
> *neither cast ye your pearls before swine,*
> *lest they trample them under their feet,*
> *and turn again and rend you.*
>
> —*Matthew 7:6*

> *Let your light so shine before men,*
> *that they may see your good works,*
> *and glorify your Father which is in heaven.*
>
> —*Matthew 3:16*

In the first book of The Grandma Series, *When God Broke Grandma's Heart,* Grandma was unequally yoked and needed to remove herself from a situation where sin was rampant. Despite her pain and heartache, she tried to make all other things in her life perfect. But God began to show Grandma that she had to let go of the past and forgive those who had and still sought to harm her. Through her second husband, Grandma realized that she had painted a picture in her mind of the perfect house, the perfect child, and of perfect relationships, and he explained that this would bring her disappointment because this world, and all in it, offers no constant perfection.

This was excellent advice. The fairy tales of happily ever after can only be achieved through adjustments, compromises, teaching, and most importantly an understanding of and patience with the imperfections of others, knowing we too carry imperfections. If striving for godly pursuits drives someone's heart, then the errors of poor judgment can more easily be forgiven, and opportunities for change pursued. Scripture teaches that we must recognize the imperfections in one another as a part of the human condition, the consequence of inherited sin, and work through God's word to help one another make changes and grow in faith, understanding, and responsibility. These changes, however, start with us.

When Grandma was young, the perfect house wasn't necessarily large or expensive or located perfectly, but it was perfectly maintained with fences painted, ivy trimmed, lawns edged, no spider webs on the gutters or eaves, and flowers always perfectly pinched. She'd thought that one should do whatever was in someone's power to do to make life as orderly as it could be. She thought that this brought happiness, but she was wrong. She needed to learn that a Spirit-filled peaceful heart is the ultimate happiness.

As she moved toward this understanding, Grandma realized that she hadn't considered that even good people didn't always do what was expected of them. Some wanted to and couldn't, some could but didn't want to, some didn't take the time to learn, and others simply did not have anyone to teach them. It was a hard lesson for Grandma to accept, but when she finally understood, she learned that the one constant in life was God. He gave warnings, examples, promises, and directions. His advice was always perfect, and His promises exquisite.

Grandma learned that if she listened to God's word, and followed as best she could, He would direct her, so she would avoid many of the disappointments of life. God would also help her develop a heart that had the capacity to love, understand, and provide the empathy that would allow her to accept the faults she would inevitably encounter. Through this development, she found happiness, not in the form she had originally imagined, but a happiness that filled her soul. She learned that she did not need what she'd imagined she did. Through this understanding and her striving, her heart found peace. She wrote her journal because she now wanted to pass this understanding to her grandchildren.

God does want us to have the best of everything. Throughout scripture, God tells us that first must come our striving to create the best within ourselves. This is our work, a work we must accomplish on ourselves so we can appreciate what God gives us now, which in turn will help us to appreciate what He wants to give us in the future. He wants us to share this wisdom with others and be ambassadors of Christ by loving, forgiving, teaching, supporting, and helping those whom God loves. He is preparing us for the larger work in the thousand-year kingdom of peace.

We are blessed when we find these attributes in another, and especially so when we find it in our ministers. They can often be our best role models because they know the word of God and, through this wisdom, meet the responsibility to act according to those words God speaks, and teach this to their congregation. We should support one another to uphold this standard of conduct, not only to help one another, but also because there is a serious danger when one causes another child of God to stumble.

> *But whoever causes one of these little ones who believe*
> *in Me to stumble, it would be better for him if a millstone were hung*
> *around his neck, and he were thrown into the sea.*
>
> —*Mark 9:42*

The easiest way to test ourselves is to ask "Would Jesus have acted in the way that I have just acted in this circumstance?" If we do this, then the Holy Spirit is a force that is alive in our hearts. Without seeing its effects, we cannot assume that it is an active force within us. When we examine what the Holy Spirit allowed Christ's apostles to accomplish we can see its incredible power, and as we read further into scripture, we can also see that this power is still available to us today. We can recognize its strength by our daily actions and by understanding and looking for the fruits that an active Holy Spirit produces. "What would Jesus do?" is a wonderful question to keep in our hearts to guide our behavior.

> *But the fruit of the Spirit is love,*
> *joy, peace, longsuffering, gentleness,*
> *goodness, faith, meekness, temperance.*
>
> —*Galatians 5:22, 23*

When we find ourselves judging, abruptly dismissive, jumping to conclusions, hurtful in any action, we should ask ourselves if this could be the very circumstance that could hold us back from developing a noble heart or undo the refining process we need in order to be a part of the Bride of Christ. As we practice the things God asks of us, as we help others mend, God may mend what was broken in our own lives. But if we do otherwise, we need to ask ourselves if this grieves the Holy Spirit.

As we demonstrate that we have made the decision to allow the Holy Spirit to work in us to help us practice humility, empathy, and forgiveness, and strive to be a role model, God can bring into our own lives the joyful change we've longed for. He brings miracles, small and large, into our lives. Though circumstances may be difficult or painful, if we trust God and not blame Him for the pain or disappointment we experience, and if we thank Him for what these circumstances can then create within us, He can change hearts, change relationships and lives, and bring us understanding.

Only through the gifts of the Spirit can we detach ourselves from our own self-righteousness to consider the extenuating circumstances that may cause people to act or react in a certain manner. Illness, fear, insecurity, and misplaced trust may all play a part in how someone acts. Here, too, these may be circumstances God uses to create a stronger faith, a nobler heart, a deeper understanding of His love, not only in us, but also in those we have thought to dismiss or be angry with. God demands we give second chances, forgive, understand temporary failures, continue to be a friend, and teach by example.

This book, *The Granddaughter and the Monkey Swing*, is the fourth book in The Grandma Series. It is a novel that addresses the transition God requires of us as we give our "Yes" word to follow Him. It is a novel that speaks of the repercussions of misjudgment, the amazing impact believers can have on one another, and the journey from youth to adulthood. It also addresses the incredible manner in which God can use illness, loss, errors and fear to bring about an unshakable faith, not only in one who may experience these tragedies, but also in those around them. God's miracles are not only huge earth-shattering experiences that the first three novels in The Grandma Series describe but are also smaller day-to-day miracles that bring changes to our lives that bring us joy.

This story also provides some interesting insight into the practical application of interior design by explaining how God has provided us with the gifts of Divine Proportion and given us information about how we can obtain His blessing on our decorating projects. It is an incredible and refreshing look at how God, through both scripture and nature, shows us His all encompassing love by providing us with everything we need.

As the granddaughter Sarah, and her fiancé Matt approach their wedding day, their friends and relatives come together to help in preparation for this special event. As the story unfolds, the reader encounters the heartaches relating to the pain of an impulsive act, insecurities and misconceptions secretly harbored, and the anger that growing up without a good role model can cause. Eventually helping them triumph over these problems is yet another of Grandma's legacies, a manuscript for creating a beautiful and godly home. Through her unending love and faith once again she is able to help her family and the friends with whom they share her gift.

And once again, by struggling to live by Grandma's legacy of faith, and mimic her ability to use the Bible as a resource to answer their questions, the characters experience how God steps in to bring about incredible changes for people they love. Grandma's example still provides the glue that holds an ever-growing family together.

The manuscript that Matt and Sarah discover in Grandma's old trunk helps her family develop a godly and beautiful home according to God's extraordinary teaching on this subject. It not only is filled with wonderful interior design ideas, nor only about designing a comfortable and beautiful home, but also explains that making the right choices for the right reasons can touch the heart of God.

God has provided us with insight into His own creativity and design interests, through both scripture and nature. From these we find instructions about design, proportion, adornment, and how to approach our own design projects. It is amazing to learn that even in this, God provided a way for us to have the best.

We can see with our own eyes that through every flower and color, every variety of tree and snowflake, the majesty of mountain and sea, God is the ultimate interior designer. In scripture, God shares His thoughts about both exterior beauty and the inner beauty He sees in our souls. Both need nurturing to blossom.

This, like all the novels in The Grandma Series, is a book for those who seek answers through scripture. *The Granddaughter and the Monkey Swing* contains a thought-provoking treasury of scripture that offers a new viewpoint about our home environment, provides step-by-step instruction for gaining God's blessing on our home, and also contains wonderful hints for decorating a home. But it is primarily a story of how God gives us the final triumph if we follow His admonition not to prejudge, to bear each other's burdens, and to help each other in life and in faith.

Let's embark on a wonderful journey where amazing promises and guarantees abound, where God is the ultimate interior designer, and Noah and King Solomon His design apprentices. Let's explore what God asks of us in return for those gifts He wants to give us. Then let's culminate our journey learning more about the wonders of our loving Heavenly Father and, as an added bonus, a step-by-step design method for a well-decorated home that also guarantees God's blessing as well. Here is the ultimate promise, one that allows us to create our own Bethany, a place of replenishment where we leave behind the cares and concerns that we find out in the world and one that brings us the joy of knowing that God has provided for every aspect of our lives.

Description of Characters

Grandma

Grandma, whose life story of sibling betrayal and marital abuse was told in the first book of The Grandma Series, *When God Broke Grandma's Heart*, remains a constant throughout all the novels as a source of incredible inspiration. Her legacy of faith, her interest in alternative medicine and interior design, all work together to help Matt and Sarah and they in turn, share these treasures with friends and family.

Sarah

Sarah, the granddaughter, helped Grandma write her journal and through this learned even more about the power of God, His unwavering love, and His desire to help. She has also learned who her enemy is and how to fight him; and in the second novel, *When God Took Grandma Home*, she struggled through a period of grief and uncovered her long-held suppressed anger. She and Matt are to be married soon. They have just purchased a house, which they are renovating with the help of family and neighbors.

Matt

Matt, Sarah's fiancé, has a rocklike faith in God and the ability to see problems with "the glass half full" rather than half empty. He suffered from the loss of a loved one and had to overcome his anger at God for taking someone so young, but in the process Matt learned about God's incredible plan of salvation and the role God wants him to take in that plan. He loves their new home and looks forward to their wedding.

Mary

Mary and Kevin are Matt and Sarah's new neighbors, and the two couples have become close friends. After struggling through a dangerous need to seek good luck by any method, in the novel *When Grandma Chased the Spirits,* Mary and Kevin learned about Matt and Sarah's faith in God and now joyfully share that faith. Mary has just been reunited with the child she had when she was fourteen years old and is planning the renovation of their carriage house to bring the child and her adoptive mother to live near them.

Kevin

Kevin, Mary's husband, is delighted to have Matt as a friend and neighbor and wants to learn from him how to be the kind of husband who can lead by example. Matt has shown him what God asks of him and how to keep an unscrupulous enemy from harming his family. He is happy with Mary's plans to bring her child and adoptive mother to their home and looks forward to working on the carriage house renovation with Matt once Matt and Sarah are married.

Elizabeth

Elizabeth is the adoptive mother who sought to bring Mary and her child together. She is twenty-five years older than Mary. Through her unselfish, loving, and down-to-earth nature, she becomes to Mary what Grandma was to Sarah. Everyone who meets Elizabeth comes to admire and respect her for her strength and her unwavering faith in God. Very few people know how desperate Elizabeth is in fighting her own battle.

Rebecca

Rebecca is the child that Mary had when she was fourteen years old and had to give up for adoption. She, like Mary, is an artist. She is struggling to accept the many changes that have occurred and are now occurring in her life. The incredible example that Elizabeth has been to her has given her a maturity far beyond her fourteen years, and this will prove to help her in her despair. But for now, Rebecca can only express her fears to her friend Jayden and has yet to acknowledge her anger at God for what her mother must endure.

John

John is Elizabeth's new friend whom she meets while attending a health seminar. Many years ago he lost his wife to a debilitating illness and has worked to help others through the same ordeal. He enjoys spending time with Elizabeth's new family. His faith in God comes from a lifetime of service as a deacon in his church. He uses this wisdom to help his daughter and grandson cross the rock-strewn bridge from the devastation of divorce to the joy of God's love and also to help Elizabeth regain her hope.

Jayden

Jayden is John's grandson and becomes a friend to Rebecca. Jayden has grown up in the church and knows a great deal about approaching God with personal problems from listening to his elders speak of their own difficulties and seeing those problems solved through prayer. He is active in the youth group at church and invites Rebecca to join him. Their friendship blossoms, and they both open up to one another and talk of the heartaches they have experienced. But as Rebecca tells him her real feelings, he finds that he has to warn Rebecca about trying to fool God.

Joshua

Joshua is Sarah's younger brother. He adores Sarah and considers her the epitome of what a woman should be in life. But Joshua's expectations of people are too high, and he has become demanding and judgmental. This attitude begins to affect his relationship with his fiancé, Debbie. He and Debbie are in Sarah and Matt's wedding party and begin to face many serious issues that need to be resolved. He thinks it's unmanly to show his pain or to give in to Debbie, and only Caleb can finally reach him.

Debbie

Debbie, Joshua's fiancé, is excited about being in Matt and Sarah's wedding. She has grown up without a good role model and looks happily to Joshua's family to fill that void in her life. She learns quickly and gladly but needs to learn how to curb her impulsiveness. The insecurities she developed during her childhood and her inability to communicate well under pressure bring her into a situation that may ruin her relationship with the whole family. When Joshua breaks their engagement, she finally sees that only with God's help will the relationship mend.

Caleb and Ann

Caleb is Sarah's older brother and has been a source of strength and protection to her since their mother died when Sarah was only eighteen years old. They both looked to Grandma during that time, and through Grandma's love and faith in God they learned to accept what happened and continue the education that their mother wanted for them. Caleb has grown so much in Spirit over the years that the family now looks to him as they once did to Grandma. Ann, Caleb's wife, is always willing to lend a helping hand. Unrecognized except by God and Caleb, Ann gives incredible spiritual gifts to this family she loves through her fervent prayers for them day and night. She is a rock providing strength to those she loves, but there is a secret sadness in her heart that needs to be addressed.

Barbara and Jim

Barbara is Matt's sister and a close friend of Sarah's. She has excellent communication skills in addition to being talented, down to earth, able to sew beautifully, create unusual craft projects, and garden. She gladly takes efficient charge of family gatherings and has the ability to do this without anyone feeling left out. She is now directing the wedding plans. Her husband, Jim, has never been willing to join the church because of a bad experience he and his mother had in another church many years before he'd met Barbara. He does listen carefully to and is secretly impressed by the family's discussions of faith. He is very family-oriented, hardworking, smart, and up-to-date on every issue. He loves to play devil's advocate when the family gets into the debates they love to have.

Chapter One

ELIZABETH

But let all those rejoice who put their trust in You. Let them
ever shout for joy, because You defend them;
Let those also who love Your name be joyful in You.

—*Psalm 5:11*

Elizabeth stood between the bay window of Mary and Kevin's kitchen and the table and chairs that sat in the bay. She looked out to the exquisite blues of the sky highlighting the lush green foliage of the tall oak trees that lined both sides of the street but reached across to embrace one another and form a canopy of dappled light. The light and shadows fell on the ground in patches that both enriched and softened the myriad colors in the flowers Mary and Kevin had planted along their walkway. Elizabeth loved this old house and felt at home here. It helped quell her fear for Rebecca.

She was thinking of the past and how much her life had changed in just a few years. She and her husband had had a happy life, ordinary perhaps, but probably like most other lives that were relatively free of trauma or drama. *It was when my husband got sick,* she thought, *that everything began to change.* She'd been so proud of him, so filled with awe as she saw into his heart, witnessed his faith, and listened carefully to his words when he spoke with Rebecca. She'd known him since she was a child, loved him all that time. She had never thought she would be so lucky that he would love her back. That had been a wonderful surprise to her.

Elizabeth had been an only child and grew up mostly in the company of adults. Music, politics, and philosophy were often topics of conversation, as were deep and open discussions for problem solving. As she reflected on those times, Elizabeth realized that the conversations had been steeped in years of accumulated and hard-earned wisdom. Only now, so many years later, did she realize it was through these open adult discussions that she had developed an early insight into human nature and the psychology of dealing with difficult situations.

Her husband often told her that he so admired her common sense and her insight. He said that he'd never known anyone filled with so much wisdom regarding such diverse circumstances. She had been flattered by his remarks, but never quite believed that what he said was really true. Now, of course, she hoped he had been right. She would need those skills in this new and most difficult phase of her life. She wished he was still with them; she missed him, his calm, his strength.

He was always so good with children, and when they had adopted Rebecca, he immediately took her into his heart. For many years they'd longed for children, but none came. They had tried so hard, and for so many years to have children, even visiting a number of doctors and fertility clinics, and enduring test after test. No reason could be found for why they didn't have a child. Finally, they accepted the fact that it was not to be and began to talk about adopting.

They were already in their late forties before they applied to the adoption agency. They worried that because of their age, they would no longer qualify as adoptive parents, especially for an infant. They hoped that having a nice home and a good income to provide for a child would matter more to the agency than their age. They hoped and prayed the agency would make a favorable decision about them.

It had taken longer than they wanted, but it worked out, and they were finally approved and told that they were on the waiting list. Elizabeth could remember, even all these years later, how excited they were to hear that news. From that point on the process moved quickly. Within a span of only six weeks, which at the time seemed an eternity for them, they were told a child awaited them. Elizabeth recalled how happy they were when they saw her tiny face and circle of coal black hair for the first time. Rebecca was the best thing that could ever have happened to them. They knew instantly that the delay had been God's plan to bring them to Rebecca.

Elizabeth loved to listen to her husband talk with Rebecca. When Rebecca was little, they would sit at the kitchen table and talk while she prepared their meal. When Rebecca was a little older and helped her in the kitchen, her husband would sit at the counter on the dining room side and look into the kitchen as they talked together. He was always so gentle, but in everything he said, Elizabeth was able to recognize the teaching, the moral, the reasons he'd said what he did. Her heart always overflowed with pride at what a fine man he was, what a wonderful role model he was, and what great wisdom he had in the way he presented his stories to Rebecca.

He had been raised in a mixed-faith family, his mother Jewish, and his father Lutheran, and he always felt that he had had the best of both worlds because he'd learned so much about two different cultures, two forms of faith, and about respecting both. He'd listened to many a heated debate when the families got together, and yet he'd always come away admiring their respect for one another and the courtesy with which they could disagree. He said that this gave him an advantage in life. It also gave him the freedom to determine how he wanted to live his own life of faith.

Elizabeth loved him with all her heart, always felt safe and secure with him, always felt she had a true and loyal friend in him, and was joyfully astonished when he proposed. They'd known each other since childhood, but she always thought that he saw her only as a gawky kid, just a friend. She never knew how he watched her, and listened to her, and came to respect her honesty.

Rebecca too loved him with all her heart. Although she knew they had adopted her as an infant, Rebecca loved them both as completely as any child could. To her, they truly were her mother and father, loving, wise, good, loyal, perfect. Rebecca knew it would always be that way.

One day when Rebecca asked her father why he thought God allowed his illness to be so terribly painful, Elizabeth listened for his answer as if her life depended upon it. He told Rebecca that it was for the benefit of all three of them, and for their future. He explained that God was refining them, creating a noble soul in them, and teaching them compassion, patience, and trust. He looked up some scriptures to read to Rebecca and cited the following:

> *I will bring the one-third through the fire,*
> *will refine them as silver is refined,*
> *and test them as gold is tested.*
> *They will call on My name, and I will answer them.*
> *I will say, "This is My people"; and each one will say,*
> *"The Lord is my God."*
> —*Zechariah 13:9*

Her father also explained that when we allow God to refine us, it becomes His joy to also bless us and care for us in every way. He told them that even through illness and sadness and loss, God is there to help, even when we might believe He no longer hears our pleas. "Some things have to be as they are for our benefit and soul's salvation," he said. "When a situation seems impossible to accept, impossible to understand, God will show us that He has never left us, and will comfort us if we can accept His decision in certain things, and someday we will see that He was right in all His decisions." Then he showed Rebecca another scripture that supported his words, saying, "When you question God's plan, when you think it is impossible for you to accept His will, pray that He will help you find peace and accept His decision. And pray that He will strengthen your faith in His decisions."

For with God nothing will be impossible.
—*Luke 1:37*

"Once we understand what God plans for our eternal future, and give him our 'yes' word," he continued, "God will then mold us into the image of Himself, and provide us with the Holy Spirit so we can become a part of His royal family."

For as many as are led by the Spirit of God,
they are the sons of God.
—*Romans 8:14*

Elizabeth was filled with wonder as she listened to her husband speak with Rebecca and saw in his heart the depth of his understanding of and his love for God.

He died two years ago, when Rebecca was twelve years old. He'd battled his cancer for two years without a single complaint, fully trusting that God's plan for his life . . . and theirs . . . was perfect. He rejoiced in what came, fully believing that it was for good reason and that God never made a mistake, was always at his side. Despite his strength of faith, both Elizabeth and Rebecca struggled at times to retain their own trust in God as they watched him weaken and suffer such pain. He'd always been such a good man, so kind to others and so faithful to God, so when they saw he was in so much pain, it certainly tested their trust in God.

He had died with dignity despite his suffering because he died still praising God and praying for Elizabeth and Rebecca, knowing beyond a shadow of a doubt that in the twinkling of an eye by God's time, they would all be reunited again.

Now, two years after his death, Elizabeth's heart raced as her mind wondered about possible future events. Her husband had been such a good role model for her, even more so in his illness. Elizabeth silently asked God to give her the same faith and courage her husband had had. She longed to be a blessing to those around her, those she loved with such passion, those she so appreciated, those God allowed her to know and be blessed by.

She'd felt such relief to learn how wonderful Mary and Kevin were and was immensely delighted to meet Sarah and Matt and witness their kindness. She could see that both these couples lovingly practiced their faith and had a close relationship with God. Knowing that this would be good for Rebecca set Elizabeth's mind at ease, making her content with her decision to contact Mary and Kevin in the first place. It had been a difficult decision at first. She'd been afraid that Rebecca's birth mother would try to take Rebecca away from her.

Rebecca was only fourteen years old and legally might not have been able to choose for herself if there'd ever been a custody battle over her. She'd worried about that. She'd also been afraid that they might be the kind of people who would have a bad influence on Rebecca. She'd commiserated over the decision to ask the adoption agency to find Mary and ask if she wanted to make contact with the child she had had when she herself had been only fourteen years old. But she'd held on to the promise her husband had given her before he died. He'd said, "Elizabeth, you must promise me that you will not worry. You must hang on to God's assurances that He will care for you and Rebecca. There may be lots of glitches on your journey, but He has promised that He will never leave your side, will bring you and Rebecca through life to the glorious goal of our faith." She'd kept faith with God and her promise to her husband, and so had Rebecca, despite their grief.

Elizabeth thought of the beautiful poem that Rebecca had written for her father a few weeks before he died. Elizabeth had framed it and stood it on his bedside table so he could read it often. He loved the poem and told Rebecca that she had touched his heart with her words. He also told her that he could see through her words how much she trusted God even though she sometimes doubted that her trust was good enough. He told her that she too must reread her poem often so she could see that the Holy Spirit had given her these words as insight into her own future. He said, "Hang on to the wisdom in those words for God inspired them in you."

After her father died, Rebecca kept the little framed poem on her own bed stand so she could reread it as her father had asked her to do. She wanted to learn from it when her tears still came from missing her father. She took the little frame with her when she traveled, so she could read it whenever she spent a night away from home. Elizabeth often walked into Rebecca's room to read the poem again herself.

Elizabeth could recognize, in the words within Rebecca's poem, what her husband had taught Rebecca. She remembered a conversation they had about how diamonds were formed by nature's application of great pressure and heat to carbon. They spoke about what was required after the diamond was brought from the earth, the process of cutting and polishing the diamond, and then fitting it into a certain setting. She also remembered their conversation about searching for gold inside rock and extracting it from the earth, then processing the gold by heating it intensely so the impurities could be removed. Then they spoke of designing and forming the gold to develop it into something beautiful. Rebecca's poem had certainly demonstrated that Rebecca had listened and remembered.

To Dad from Rebecca

When I Ask Why

Dad has taught me that gold is highly valued,
beautiful, durable, and sought by many.
Yet pure gold comes into being only after suffering under intense heat.
Diamonds are also highly valued, durable, and very beautiful.
And these too come into being only after much
intense pressure and shaping.
Our Heavenly Father is creating a Heaven, which He wants to fill
with beauty, with perfection, with things durable and valued
and those things God believes valuable are us, especially you Dad.
So we have to learn compassion, understanding, and
love to gain our greatest value.
We too have to be molded and developed in patience,
but because of sin, we are difficult to mold and cannot do it alone.
Rather, we can only be developed by the grace of God.
When God directs the intense heat and the
pressure we need to be perfected,
we can rest assured that He never gives us more than we can bear.
He gives us victory over the situation we have carried,
therefore we can be thankful for our times of pain, knowing we grow.
And we can ask Our Heavenly Father to help us learn quickly.
Then we can say, "I'm thankful" for the pain, the lesson, the growth,
the hope we have, the opportunities, the failures, especially the victories.
For without these things would we be the person we are today?
Perhaps, without these experiences of pain and the test of our faith
we would not have needed, and would not have sought and found God.

Tears welled in Elizabeth's eyes as she again understood the inner struggle to accept God's will that Rebecca's words portrayed, and her heart filled with wonder to read the great wisdom in Rebecca's words. Yes, at times our circumstances were hard to understand, even harder to accept sometimes. Our human nature clamored to ask *Why? What did I ever do to deserve this?* "But it wouldn't be called faith if it were perfectly seen and understood," Elizabeth said aloud.

When she heard her words, she thought of a scripture that her minister had given her to hold on to as she struggled to accept what was to come.

> *Show me Your Ways, O Lord; Teach me your paths.*
> *Lead me in Your truth and teach me, For You are the God*
> *of my salvation; on You I wait all the day.*
> —Psalm 25:4, 5

As she stood by the window, Elizabeth silently prayed, *Please God, let me handle this with dignity, let me be an example of faith, let me leave behind a legacy of faith like my husband did, like Sarah's grandma did. Give me courage. And doggone it, don't let me cry!*

Elizabeth was fairly tall, about five eleven, and slim. Lanky was how she would describe herself. Her hair was gray, actually close to white now, and she wore it long, always either pulled up into a chignon or forming a thick braid hanging loose down her back or to one side. Wisps of softly curling hair that escaped her chignon or braid outlined her oval face making her look windblown and youthful. Her cheekbones were high, made more prominent by her slender jaws. Her teeth were large and straight and her smile beautiful. She wore no makeup at all. She always wore dresses and stockings, even when she worked in the yard. You would never find her in slacks. No one ever thought to ask her why.

Her arms and legs were long and straight, and her walk was lively and her gait long. Her feet were big. *There was no getting around that ugly fact*, she thought, for she always wished her feet were smaller and she could wear a fancy shoe. But she never did. Ever practical, her shoes were always practical too. And yet, despite the fact that Elizabeth wasn't the epitome of high fashion, what she wore fit her somehow, was right for her, and added to her aura of strength and kindness, wisdom, and endurance, gave her a sort of no-nonsense, loyal-to-the end aura too.

Her fingers showed the beginning of the gnarls of arthritis, and she sometimes would rub them when they proved painful. Elizabeth had sharp, see-all eyes that demanded one acknowledge that she was intelligent. The set of her mouth clearly said that she would not take too much guff from anyone. That is, until she smiled. Then her eyes would crinkle, and the incredibly beautiful character lines around her eyes and mouth would light her face with benevolence, and you suddenly knew you could easily win her heart. Her sometimes gruff-seeming manner was merely a bluff!

Elizabeth never thought of herself as pretty or even particularly attractive and often wondered why her husband had chosen her to marry. She was wrong though. She was attractive physically because her kindness and her strength of character encompassed her. It was that strength of character and her no-nonsense answers that had first attracted her husband to her. He'd told her that he loved that she'd tell him in no uncertain terms when she thought he was wrong . . . and why. And to his chagrin, she was usually right.

It was her faith and stubborn determination to serve God that brought them together initially when they met at a youth function at a church concert. He loved her stubborn nature and felt that it had brought them through many a crisis. Because he'd told her this, she too was proud of that stubbornness. It had served her well when her husband died. It had held her together, and held her tears in check.

Now, Elizabeth faced her own crisis. As she continued to stand in the bay window, she looked at the beauty of nature as it lay before her and made up her mind to engage her stubborn nature to fight this fight, and to project the person she wanted to be. *I've faced many challenges in my life, and I'll face this one too.* With this thought firmly in place, Elizabeth determined to make sure Rebecca's future was secure, and then make sure that both of them kept their faith intact! *And that was that!* she thought.

> *Be strong and of good courage, do not fear nor be afraid of them;*
> *for the Lord your God, He is the One who goes with you.*
> *He will not leave you nor forsake you.*
> —*Deuteronomy 31:6*

At just that moment the phone rang, and Elizabeth moved away from the window to answer it. It was Debbie, Joshua's fiancé, and Elizabeth could tell that she'd been crying. As Elizabeth listened, her heart went out to Debbie. She liked her so much and could see how hard she was trying to please not only Josh, but everyone else in the family, too. She was thoughtful and considerate, and Elizabeth believed that she would make Josh a good wife.

As they talked, Elizabeth realized that Debbie had to begin to stand up to Josh, but not in a confrontational way. Somehow she instinctively knew that to stand up to him would be a good thing. As Elizabeth learned about their breakup, and saw how much Debbie loved Josh, she determined to do her best to help. She told Debbie that to win him over, she would first have to be patient, act with dignity and grace, act as if she was impervious to his orders to break up, or even to get back together again.

She suggested that perhaps they both needed counseling, together and apart, so Debbie could express her side of things too and better understand what it took to make a good marriage. Finally, Elizabeth told Debbie that she should pray and ask God to do with their lives what He deemed best, telling her that only with God's blessing could the longing in her heart for their happiness be satisfied. Then Elizabeth prayed with her over the phone and gave her a verse from scripture to hang on to and read when she was upset. When they hung up, Elizabeth felt that she'd given Debbie good advice for the moment.

Elizabeth also recognized that she suddenly felt good to be needed again and hoped that she really could help without interfering. She was good at resolving this kind of situation because she grew up listening to how her parents counseled the many people who came to them for advice. This is what her family had taught her since she was a little girl.

Elizabeth continued to sit at the table for a moment and prayed for Debbie and Josh, then, trusting God to take care of it, began to think about how she was going to approach her needs about the carriage house.

Grabbing the little portfolio that Mary had so thoughtfully made up for her with tape measure, a pen, and notepad, Elizabeth began to skim the two lists of decorating suggestions Mary had copied from Sarah's grandmother's manuscript. She was fascinated. *How wonderful,* she thought. *How amazing that Sarah's grandmother could discern these things from the Bible. I will definitely do this!* Then Elizabeth, intrigued by this unique approach to building or decorating a house, made her way to the backyard and walked along the path to the carriage house.

Mary and Kevin had asked Elizabeth for her ideas about what she and Rebecca might want in the apartment they planed to build in the lower level of the carriage house. Elizabeth thought that to do this, she'd start with a floor plan of the size of the space and note where the current plumbing and other immovable objects might be so she could begin to assemble some ideas. She had thought that once she had some facts and figures, she'd also ask Sarah for help since she loved Sarah's decorating skills. But now, she was also going to seriously consider everything Sarah's grandmother had outlined to be sure to gain the blessing on her endeavor.

As Elizabeth walked through the garden to the carriage house, her thoughts of Sarah's grandma led her mind back to last night when she had seen Sarah and Matt across the street. She smiled to herself as she remembered glancing out of the window and looking across the street toward their house. She had seen them silhouetted in their window appearing to be laughing and dancing together and thought, *They are such a lovely couple and so perfect for one another. I am so happy for them and so pleased that Rebecca has met them.*

Then she realized that although her mind had been elsewhere, her eyes must still have been on the window across the street because her attention was directed back to them when she saw Matt answer his cell phone. He began to pace back and forth across the large bay of his turret room seeming to be excited by whatever the caller was saying. She saw Sarah, hands on hips, appear to confront Matt, but then, hands still on her hips, begin to sashay around him gypsylike, coaxing and teasing. Elizabeth had wondered who could have phoned, what this was all about.

Suddenly, she laughed at herself, feeling like a busybody, but knowing her reaction was, in reality, only that of a mother hen. She felt as if all these friends of Mary and Kevin were her own children and she wanted to look after them, be sure everything was okay. *Make everything okay? Ahh,* Elizabeth thought, *sometimes we just can't make everything okay, most of the time circumstances have to play themselves out.*

As she looked toward the carriage house from her position on the path, Elizabeth could feel the excitement in her heart about the upcoming renovation. The prospect of being with these wonderful people as the carriage house was being renovated was so uplifting. Listening to their banter and being a part of their daily routine when they got together for this project would be good for her and Rebecca. It would help take their mind off the past and hopefully off the worries they had about the future.

Rebecca will learn so much about building projects, about families, about people working together, she thought, *and I will enjoy every minute of it too. Even before the construction starts, working together on the plans will be such an educational experience for us both, and an enjoyable and exciting one as well. We'll be creating our very own home, working together to do it. We'll have the expertise of Matt and Kevin's building skills and Sarah's exquisite decorating skills! What more could we ask for?*

The carriage house was a two-story building, thirty-four feet deep and sixty-two feet wide. It had been used as a barn when it was first built, then later as a carriage house. It had one bathroom on the lower level, but Kevin thought it would be no problem to install a second bathroom on the lower level and another one on the upper level where they planned to create a studio for Rebecca and Mary's art projects.

The interior of the building had thick, exposed ceiling beams and wide plank wood walls projecting the sense that the building had been sturdily built. Many years ago, the exterior of the building had been covered over with wood shingles that had now aged to a natural brown patina. Kevin found that the outside walls had first been framed and insulated, then covered with exterior plywood to which the wood shingles were attached. This had also made the building very attractive from the outside and helped it blend with the main house and garden. The roof was also covered in wood shingles. This gave the building the look of a New England cottage by the sea. Kevin had been delighted to find this because it meant that, except for the skylights, he only had to tackle the inside for the renovation. Mary wanted skylights put into the roof to provide abundant light for the art studio.

The ceilings were high, almost eleven feet, except where the heavy, hand-hewn overhead beams extended into the room. The beams were beautiful and Elizabeth hoped they could remain exposed. *This will add so much character to the décor,* Elizabeth thought. The floors of the lower level were of stained concrete, and the upper level, which had its own entrance by way of an outside staircase, had floors of the same wide wood planks as were used on the walls.

As Elizabeth looked at the carriage house, she saw that the windows on both levels were fine as they were and, while rectangular in shape, they looked more like arched windows on the exterior of the building, by virtue of a wood insert placed above each window. These inserts were painted the same color as the window frames and thus contrasted to the patina of the surrounding wood shakes. Each window consisted of many panes of glass held in place by the wood mullions that divided the window into a dozen separate areas. Elizabeth loved the way they looked but wondered how she would ever keep them clean.

Currently there were double barn doors through which to enter the lower level. Elizabeth noted that these should be removed and that perhaps a double-door entry with sidelight panels could fill this space, maybe with an arched wood insert above the doors to match the inserts above the windows. Elizabeth loved the quaintness of the building, the woodsy setting of the yard, and the prospects of a little garden she could tend. She also looked forward to having a say in choosing the interior construction and finishing materials. This would also be a great experience for Rebecca too.

As Elizabeth took her measurements and transferred these to the rectangle she had drawn on her notepad, she began to feel an excitement about planning their little home. She would make a drawing of the floor measurements and window placement on graph paper in their exact dimensions and make several copies of it. Then she would ask Sarah and Rebecca if they could spend some time with her to look at the drawing and discuss some ideas for the inner walls, doors, and furniture placement.

Maybe she could also sketch some plans onto tracing paper, and they could move these across the fixed floor plan to see what arrangements worked best. Then, once they'd thought of all the little problems and nuances that would have to be addressed, they could bring their plan to Mary and Kevin to see what they thought. *Between the five of us, and Matt too,* Elizabeth thought, *we will create something wonderful. Not only will we have fun doing it, but we will be in fellowship together while we do it too!*

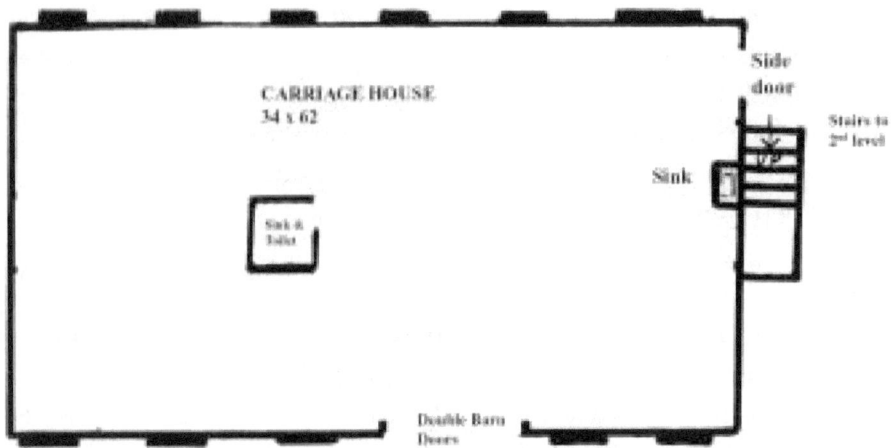

Elizabeth ran back to the kitchen and made a list of what she and Rebecca might need to make the big building into their home. *Hmmm,* she thought, *two bedrooms, two bathrooms, a living room, and a dining area and kitchen should do it for us. And I need to think of parking, of how this would benefit, not take away from, the main house. And I'll need to think of storage space . . . closets for our clothing, how many kitchen cabinets I'd need, how much storage for linens, things like suitcases . . . oh and a computer and desk . . . maybe two, or maybe a double desk so Rebecca and I could work together. I wonder if I could have one of those little arched niches built into the wall like the one Sarah put in her new house? Gosh, is this too much, will all these things fit? Will Mary and Kevin be okay with me making all these suggestions for* their *carriage house?* Her thoughts flew in many directions at once, threatening to pop out of her head as corn pops in a microwave.

Trying to capture these thoughts before they escaped, her pen flew across the paper with her ideas for the carriage house, and her mind forgot her troubles. She wanted to see Rebecca settled and wanted

Rebecca to have her own space. She couldn't have asked for a better transition for Rebecca. *God is good,* she thought, *He worked it out so much better than I could have imagined.* And Elizabeth's heart was content for the moment, filled with the wonder of how God had done so much for them.

As this thought filled her heart, she forced thoughts of the renovation from her mind so she could again take the time to thank God for bringing Mary and Kevin into their lives and thereby providing them with a loving family and so much joy. She asked God to allow her never to forget how He always had provided for them, in the past and now again in this. She wanted to hang on to that when the future seemed difficult. *How awful,* she thought, *that we forget so quickly how God helped us endure, even triumph, in the past, and yet when we are faced with a new worry we panic. Why do we forget our blessings so quickly?* Elizabeth asked herself; then she suddenly knew. *Ahh yes, the wily mischief of our cunning enemy and all his ugly cohorts! Please, God, let your gifts stay fresh in my mind always.*

She looked at her watch and realized that she still had about two hours before the women would be back from their shopping marathon and the men from moving Matt's furniture. The women had made an appointment to have the bridesmaid gowns fitted; then, with the promise of a swatch of the gown material, they planned to shop for shoes, perhaps getting them dyed to match the gowns. They also planned to go to the florist to look at their options for flowers that would match or complement the gowns.

Matt, Kevin, Sarah's brothers, Caleb and Josh, and Matt's brother-in-law, Jim, would be arriving about 5:30 after they finished moving Matt's things from his apartment to the house. They planned to rest for an hour after the move was complete, then freshen up and meet here, so that together they could create a scrumptious salad to eat with the four huge dishes of lasagna Elizabeth had prepared this morning. They would open some fruit flavored zinfandel wine to toast their successful day.

Elizabeth loved to watch them together and enjoyed listening to the wonderful camaraderie between these young people. Her own lack of siblings and aunts and uncles made her marvel in their banter and in the double and triple conversations going on all at once. Some of them seemed able to listen to two or three conversations at one time and would occasionally comment on something that had been said in a far corner of the room. This amazed Elizabeth since she always had to look at someone and concentrate to listen well. *This is a good environment for Rebecca,* she thought, *good people, faithful people, loving people, noisy people.*

Elizabeth decided to make herself a cup of tea since she still had a few hours before everyone would arrive back at the house; and never having to worry about her weight, she thought that she would also have that last piece of almond coffee cake left over from this morning. After placing the cake and a fork on the table in the bay window, Elizabeth sat with her tea and began to eat, again with her thoughts thanking God for the events of the past month when she first met Mary and Kevin. She marveled at how close they'd become in such a short time and how, well, natural it seemed to be with them. *But then again,* she thought, *children of God all across the world should have an immediate rapport with each other since they share the same values, carry the same heart's attitude. Everything will be okay, after all,* she thought, *Rebecca has a family now and we will have a new home with them where we can feel truly welcomed and loved.*

When she finished the last bite of the delicious cake, she was surprised because she hardly remembered eating it. Her mind had been so filled with plans for the carriage house, Matt and Sarah's wedding, and Rebecca's future that she didn't even remember what the cake had tasted like! *The next time I eat some cake, I will stop thinking so much and simply enjoy every last bite!* Elizabeth placed the dish and fork in the sink to await her teacup before placing them all in the dishwasher; and since the cake was gone, and she couldn't remember eating it, she decided to at least savor the remaining tea in her cup by sipping slowly and not thinking of so many things. She picked up her cup, leaving the saucer on the table, and walked around the table to the window to look across the street to where some of the men could be seen carrying furniture and boxes into Sarah and Matt's house.

See, she chided herself, *the tea tastes so good when I pay attention to it and not just gulp it down without knowing!* But as she brought the cup to her lips for the last sip, suddenly the cup slipped from her fingers and shattered loudly as it hit the ceramic floor, sending shards of porcelain in a half circle around her. Shocked, Elizabeth looked down at the mess and thought, *Oh no, please, God, don't let it be happening yet, please not yet.*

> *Some trust in chariots, and some in horses;*
> *but we will remember*
> *the name of the Lord our God.*
>
> —*Psalm 20:7*

Chapter Two

MATT AND SARAH

But as for me and my house,
we will serve the Lord.

—Joshua 24:15

Matt had awakened at 6:00 a.m. He'd been too keyed up to sleep. Today he would be moving into the house! Finally! This made the wedding day, and the day Sarah would also move in, seem close, seem real. Their special day was almost here! *I might as well get up,* Matt thought, *and I might as well drive to the house to wait for the guys. I can bring a few of the boxes with the more fragile items in them and maybe I'll stop by Dunkin' Donuts. I can get my own breakfast there and bring it to the house to eat. Yeah, and I think I'll pick up coffee and donuts for the guys.*

Sarah's brothers, Caleb and Josh, Matt's brother-in-law, Jim, and Kevin were scheduled to arrive at the house to help him with the move today, and he was grateful for their help. As he dressed, he remembered how excited he and Sarah were yesterday when they had finally finished the last of their chores in preparation for the move today. Anyone looking through the window and seeing them yesterday would have thought they were behaving rather oddly. Well, they had been! Matt remembered with a soft smile how they were holding hands, and with their bodies spaced apart as far as their arms would allow, they were dancing in a circle, laughing, and smiling into each other's eyes.

They were so happy! "Matt is going to move into our new home . . . *this* house . . . tomorrow!" Sarah had exclaimed.

He had given his landlord notice last month and today he and Caleb, Joshua, Kevin, and Jim would be moving the furniture and personal items they planned to keep from his apartment to the house! Matt was relieved that he'd already delivered to the hospital thrift shop the boxes of items they would not need, and those that would duplicate what Sarah had. That would save them a lot of time and effort today.

Matt had planned that today in addition to the items from his apartment they would also pick up some of Grandma's smaller furniture and boxes from the storage unit. Whatever they didn't get today from the storage unit, they would get the following weekend when professional movers would be moving Sarah's furniture from her apartment to the house.

Sarah had planned to keep her apartment until a week before they were married; then after the movers came to her apartment to take the furniture to their new home, she would be staying that last week with Caleb and Ann. But soon, very soon, this would be the home they would share! Matt recalled with a smile how happy they both felt to know that they were on the very brink of beginning the life they'd planned for so long.

They had worked hard yesterday; they had finished washing all the floors and everything that had any Sheetrock dust or floor-sanding dust still on it. Now, the house was shining, and the only thing left to do was to have the kitchen counters and two of the bathroom vanities installed, and this would be done next week. They had finally reached the end of their hard work on the renovation, and they were both ecstatic! The house looked great!

Winded from their silly dancing and all their laughing, Sarah and Matt had dropped to the window seat still holding hands and moved into an embrace. Matt kissed Sarah's cheek and whispered her favorite words, "Hi, my dearest-darling-sweetheart-love . . . my soon-to-be *wife* . . . How are ya . . . and do ya know how much I love you?" Sarah had laughed, loving his use of Grandma's special endearment, and she hugged him fiercely, answering, "Well . . . lemme think about it for a minute . . . hmm, if I said no, you might leave me and I'd never get to live in my beautiful house . . . so . . . yeah, I guess I do luv ya!"

Matt had laughed at Sarah's words and told her she should worry about the gorgeous woman who could live in the house if she didn't love him. Sarah had guffawed, warned, "Better not even go there," and grabbed his hands again, pulling him up from the window seat, continuing, "Matt, let's take another tour of the house and see if we have missed anything, and we can comment once again on our favorite parts of the house, and I can leave the Post-it notes for where to place the furniture tomorrow!"

Matt groaned remembering their conversation, knowing this was a "girl" thing to look at the house again, but he hadn't wanted to dampen her excitement. However, given the fact that he would have to endure yet another tour, he decided to tease her and said in a very high-pitched falsetto voice, "Ohh, Matt, I just love the crown molding, isn't it just soooooo pretty!" Matt chuckled to himself remembering that Sarah, not to be outdone by him, had retorted in a deep gruff voice, "Hey, Sarah, take a look at the strength of those huge storage shelves I put up in the garage, and didja notice that the screws all have their slots facing the same direction!" And they both broke down into gales of laughter knowing how different things please the different sexes, and that they really were happy with every aspect of the house . . . and how well they got along despite their silly antics.

Matt's cell phone rang just after they had broken into their laughter, so Matt had to struggle to answer the phone in a normal voice. He was incredulous when he heard who was calling and why! He knew that Sarah was looking at him questioningly, but he couldn't respond to her and listen to what was being said at the same time.

To allow himself better concentration, he turned and began to pace in front of the bay windows of the turret. He did not dare to look at Sarah. As he listened, his mind raced to what he'd already said aloud. He hoped that he hadn't said anything that would give away who was on the phone and what they were talking about.

Matt knew instantly that Sarah would want to know who had called and what had been said. Obviously what she'd heard would have piqued her curiosity, and she'd be all over him to tell her everything. Yet the caller was asking, almost demanding, that Matt keep both the caller's name and purpose completely secret. Matt agreed, conceding that for many reasons this request was proper. But how was he going to handle this? Matt's mind was going a mile a minute as he listened and at the same time tried to play back his part of the conversation to remember what Sarah had heard.

As best as he could recall what Sarah heard was "What a surprise! How are you! Wow, it's been a long time! Yes, that's right, yeah, we are. Yes, at five. Really? Wow, that's great! You'll *what*? Oh, wow, that is great, really great. Of course! Well, uhh, I'll try. That's going to be a tall order, but it's so super . . . she'll be so surprised. Yeah. Okay. Good. Okay. Okay. Okay. Goodbye."

Sure enough, when Matt hung up, Sarah was all over him demanding, "Who was that? What will be 'so great'? Why will I be surprised?" Matt stumbled for a moment. His mind dancing upon different stories he could tell Sarah, but then he chose exactly the right thing to say when he told the truth. "Sarah, it's going to be a surprise, so I can't tell you. I promised that I wouldn't spill the beans, so I just can't . . . but I can promise you that it's a good thing and you will be happy. Will you please trust me on this one?"

Sarah then danced around him, smiling like a little pixie, swinging her hips like a gypsy, trying to get more from him. "Come on Matt, just give me a few hints . . . Was the person a male or female?" Matt smiled, noting how cute she looked trying to cajole him into an answer. "Come on, Matt, just a hint . . . was the person older or younger? Is it someone I know?"

When Matt just grinned and didn't answer, Sarah went into a slight crouch, feet apart, bouncing on her toes, her hands folded into little fists, arms raised and the thumb of one hand brushing against her nose. She was trying to look like a prize fighter, just as Grandma used to do when the family wouldn't listen to her and she wanted to get their attention. "Okay, then, if you're not going to tell me anything, let's fight, and the winner gets the answers," Sarah said, grinning.

Matt grabbed her in a bear hug and laughed as he told her she was the cutest fighter he'd ever seen. He was just aching to tell Sarah, knowing she'd be thrilled, but he'd been asked to give his word that he would keep what he'd just learned a secret. He simply could not tell her even if he wanted to. He was bursting with it though and thought they'd better get on to another subject before he broke down and gave her a hint.

Matt loved her with all his heart and really didn't like keeping anything from her. He hoped he could be strong for the next two weeks. Matt tried to be positive about the call, thinking, *Sarah will be so pleased, so honored, and so exquisitely surprised!* Sarah, sensing that Matt felt torn and knowing that he had given his word, decided that even though her curiosity was killing her, she'd better back down. She realized that Matt probably wanted to tell her, but could not, and she didn't want to tempt him any more.

Everything that happened last night was still so clear he could remember it all. He remembered how, suddenly serious, still holding Sarah's hands and still in front of the window seat, he had looked into Sarah's eyes and quietly said, "Sarah, I'd like you to pray right now that God will always bless our union and help us remain faithful to Him all our lives. We both acknowledge that that is the most important thing to us, not the house, not the furniture. I really want to do this. The world is so full of pitfalls that we need to be sure to protect our love. If you will pray, then I will follow your prayer with mine. Then we'll go on your tour!"

Sarah told him that her heart swelled with pride by her soon-to-be husband's incredible example of faith. She said that she loved him so much that sometimes she thought her heart would burst. And she'd said that he was right, they needed to make sure that the house did not rule them and did not become more important to them than their faith. She told him that it was so easy to think of him as the head of the household when he always thought of the blessing for them, when he acted like a loving minister looking after every detail of his flock. She'd said that even though Matt's flock was one, just her right now, she could just imagine the care he'd someday give to the spiritual welfare of his children too. Matt hoped she would always feel that way.

Sarah had told him that when she folded her hands to get ready to pray, she'd suddenly thought of the time, when she was just a little girl, that Grandma tried to pray with them and Sarah kept interrupting her. She and her brothers had been on Sarah's bed, and Grandma was sitting on the edge of the bed and had folded her hands to pray. Grandma had rested her folded hands in her lap when she began her prayer. After the first few words, Sarah pulled on Grandma's sleeve, and Grandma told her not to interrupt anyone in their prayer. Grandma started again, but once more Sarah pulled on Grandma's sleeve. Grandma just said, "Shhhh," and kept going. Sarah pulled on Grandma's sleeve more persistently this time. Finally Grandma stopped, opened her eyes, looked at Sarah, and asked her what was wrong.

Sarah explained that Grandma was holding her hands in the wrong position to pray. Grandma had been surprised by what Sarah said and asked her why she said what she did. Sarah replied patiently in her sweet little girl's voice, "Well, Grandma, you are supposed to hold your hands up here like this, close to your heart when you pray." Grandma looked at her for a moment and gently asked, "Can you tell me why I should do this, Sarah?" Sarah replied, somewhat exasperated by Grandma not knowing, "Grandma, you are supposed to hold your folded hands close to your heart because that's where Jesus lives . . . Mommy said so!

Sarah had remembered how Grandma's eyes filled with tears as she told Sarah that she was right and that Grandma had forgotten for the moment. Grandma thanked Sarah for helping her do it correctly. Later Sarah saw Grandma hug her mom and say "Thank you" to her and tell her the story of what had happened when they began to pray. Grandma had said that she was so proud of her daughter for what she laid into the children's hearts, and over the years Grandma never forgot that wonderful experience.

Then, as Matt had requested, Sarah brought her hands to her heart, folded them, bowed her head, and began to pray.

Dear Heavenly Father,
We wish there were more ways in our language to say "thank you"
so we could express this sentiment more eloquently,
but please know that our thankfulness lies deep within our hearts
and that we long to show you this by how we conduct our lives.
Please help us, Father, because we keep on making mistakes,
and every day we need the grace
that You and the Lord Jesus so lovingly have provided for us.
Please help us remain faithful, help us to bring joy to Your heart,
help us to be an example of Your love wherever we go.
Father, Matt and I ask you to bless us in our marriage
and allow us to always share our faith with one another
and all who enter our home,
and together strive to become a part of the Bride of Christ.
Let our home and our hearts and our union be filled
with your Holy Spirit and the angel protection.
And this, Father, we ask in Jesus' name, Amen.

Matt had said, "Amen," then began his prayer saying,

Dear Heavenly Father,
Help me to be strong in my faith and in learning Your words and ways
that I may always help my family and be the kind of man You wish me to be.
I know I falter from time to time, Father,
but I yearn to be all You would have me be and need Your help to do so.
Thank you for giving me Sarah as a wife. Let me protect her with my prayers
and with the strength of faith,
and if You grant us children, Father, let us be an example to them
that they will always know You and love You as well.
Bind the forces of Satan, the powers and principalities that he sends against us,
and let our home and our hearts always be our Bethany.
We love You, Father, and ask these things in the name of Jesus Christ,
Amen.

Sarah was crying by this time, so filled with emotion about their longing to remain connected to God and the knowledge of how blessed they were to soon become husband and wife. She told Matt of the thoughts that ran through her mind about Grandma before she began to pray and that those thoughts had moved so quickly, that while it had taken her about three minutes to relate the incident to Matt, it had moved through her mind in seconds.

"Can you imagine, Matt," Sarah had said, "how it will be when Christ returns and we are given celestial bodies? Look how fast my mind covered that memory of Grandma, and God gives us so many other examples of what we will be able to do in our celestial body when He shows us how beautifully some people can sing, or dance, or leap, or balance, or run so fast. Some have even lifted heavy cars in an emergency, some have learned to swim underwater for long periods, some can do difficult math problems instantaneously in their head, and others can speak many languages. The celestial body can do all those things and more!"

Now, recalling Sarah's words, Matt thought, *Yeah, it will really be something to experience. God's plan is truly a wonder! How super not to have a tired old body that wants to rest after a hard day's work! Today will be lots of hard work to move all that furniture with my imperfect body, so I'd better get moving and mustn't forget to tell the guys that there are Post-it notes that Sarah put up to let them know where to place which piece of furniture.*

He and Sarah had taken a tour of the house before they left last night, so Sarah could place her Post-it notes. They had started from the top of the house at the bedroom in the back of the house. The walls and ceiling had been touched up where needed with new plaster and repainted. The old woodwork was freshly stained and varnished to a beautiful patina. With its crown moldings and its new closet with doors they had so painstakingly searched for in the antique stores, and then stained and varnished to match the other woodwork, the bedroom looked wonderful.

Matt and Sarah had given this room their stamp of approval, and Sarah placed her little Post-it notes for where the furniture should go when it arrived. This room would be their main guestroom since it was the second largest and closest to the extra bathroom. As they walked from the bedroom to the hall Sarah had asked him if he thought they should revisit all the rooms after their furniture was in place to make sure that they had incorporated those suggestions they had read about in the manuscript they'd just found in Grandma's old trunk. Sarah had said, "I can't believe that we keep finding things so important to our lives, it's as if Grandma is still helping us. We never even knew that she had so many other writings in that beautiful old trunk."

And Matt had replied, "Yeah, Grandma seemed to be born to teach, it's as if God endowed her with so much information and no outlet for it except through her writings . . . and now look what it does for so many! She helped Mary and Kevin with that Feng Shui stuff, she is helping us with our own home, and hopefully will help Elizabeth and Rebecca with the carriage house. She's been such an inspiration and fount of knowledge. We'd better go through everything in that trunk of Grandma's very carefully after our honeymoon. There are still many papers there, something titled 'Human Behavior,' another about world religions, even one about acupuncture, and another about nursing, maybe there were others that I didn't even see."

Sarah sighed, and said, "It breaks my heart to see that because of the way the world is now, children do not get to sit at the feet of their elders and listen to the wisdom of their years, of their experiences. We're just too busy nowadays and when we're not, it's television, e-mail, iPods, or something else. We never just sit quietly to listen to our parents, grandparents, or others who could share so much wisdom with us. We lose so much. How can we avoid this with our own kids? Should we place limits on TV and computers and such?"

Matt had replied, "Absolutely! In fact, we should set aside one night each week for a special family evening, a fellowship that encourages the sharing of our experiences of faith, of our daily struggles, and how God has helped us. That way our kids will learn about God, see how we address life, and this will teach them what to do when they are older and don't have us anymore."

And Sarah had wondered, "Do you think that Elizabeth will want to incorporate the things we saw on Grandma's lists? Do you think Mary and Kevin might even revisit some of their own rooms?" "Yeah, I'm sure they will, both of them," Matt replied. "This is stuff we should even discuss as a family, in a fellowship, because it's interesting, it's a healthy conversation, it makes you think, . . . and it brings us closer to God to understand how much He cares for us, and in such incredible detail."

"I never would have believed anyone who tried to tell me that God tells us how to decorate and how to get a blessing on the decorating and planning of a house," Sarah added. "In fact, I'd almost be embarrassed to tell anyone this because it seems so preposterous."

"Yeah, but again it shows us that God addresses everything we need in scripture, and that this is the real and ongoing miracle of the Bible," Matt said. "It's what teaches us that the Bible is something that is alive. I am amazed at how Grandma caught this stuff. God really did lift the veil from her eyes and give her understanding, show her the mysteries of the Bible."

Sarah had said that she liked his idea about the fellowship and discussing what they'd found and asked him to talk to Kevin and request that he bring this up after he had a chance to digest all that Grandma had written. Matt had agreed, but at that moment he'd wanted to get on with their tour because he was really beat and wanted to get home.

They had looked at the guest bathroom next and except for the installation of an antique-looking vanity cabinet and sink, this room was also finished. They had installed crown molding in here too, and it looked quite elegant. But Sarah felt that it might be nice to add another of their arched niches in the hall opposite the bathroom door to break up any pictures they might hang on the long wall of the hallway. Matt had looked at the long expanse of wall in the hallway and agreed with Sarah's assessment, and put this note on his to-do list.

The next room was another, but smaller, bedroom which would also be a guest room. They gave this room the same approval as the first, and placed their Post-it notes around the room for the placement of the furniture. This is where Matt would sleep until they were married since this room would be filled with the bedroom furniture from his apartment. They planned to use Sarah's bedroom furniture, which had originally been Grandma's for their master bedroom. This wouldn't arrive until next week.

When they came to the door of the room that would be their bedroom, they tried to imagine how the room would look if they put one of Grandma's love seats, with a table on one side, into the turret space. This would give them a little place to sit and would look nice since it was the first thing to be seen from the doorway that led into the bedroom. Matt thought that they might even use a tiny coffee table in front of the love seat since the turret was so deep. Sarah placed the proper Post-it notes for the love seat and said that she would have to see what tables might be left over to use next to and in front of the love seat when they were done.

They looked carefully at the new walk-in closet that they built by taking away some of the space in the adjoining fourth and now smallest bedroom which they hoped would become a nursery some day. For now, it held miscellaneous items that they weren't sure they would keep or where they would go, so the room had become their temporary storeroom.

As they looked at the new closet, Matt thought that on his side of the closet he ought to hang two rods since he would be tall enough to reach both and the ceilings were high enough to accommodate them. "This way," he joked, "I can have twice as many clothes as you."

"No, Matt," Sarah had replied, "don't you recall seeing those decorating shows on TV where the woman *always* gets three quarters, and sometimes *all*, of the closet space for her clothing?"

"I guess I'm lucky not to get just the garage . . . but," Matt retorted, "I get to put my clothes in here before you do . . . my dearest-darling-sweetheart-love, because I move in tomorrow . . . so . . . maybe you'll only get what's left over!"

Sarah laughed, knowing Matt was joking because he always put her first and they had already decided what part of the closet she would get and what part he'd have for his own shelves and rods. Grinning, Matt took a few notes about the length of the extra rod he'd need, and they began to walk down the stairs to look at the other rooms.

As they stood on the landing, three steps above the rooms on the first level, Matt and Sarah discussed the need to employ the suggestions on Grandma's lists and the incredible "monkey swing" technique she'd created. They wondered if they'd be able to fully understand the, ugh, math stuff Grandma mentioned. But they knew that they'd need some kind of special technique to decorate the unusual layout of both the turret room and the parlour, so made no immediate plans for furniture, except for Grandma's desk and chair which would be almost in the center of the turret room. They hoped the monkey swing technique Grandma mentioned would help them solve the problems they had envisioned in the turret room. They hoped Kevin would go over these puzzling solutions in another week or so and perhaps during a future fellowship he could help them explain it. Everyone would be so amazed!

Next, they walked through the kitchen, admiring the gleaming cherry cabinets, the beams, carved corbels, and small square-faced spice drawers. Sarah opened one of the large drawers that made up the base cabinets and said, "I'm so glad we did this, Matt, look how easy it will be to see and access what's in here without getting down on our hands and knees." "I don't know why someone didn't think of this years ago." Matt replied, "It really is so much easier, and the fact that the drawers pull all the way out makes everything that will go into them totally accessible. I'm glad we did it too."

Suddenly, Sarah gasped, remembering something of utmost importance. "Matt, I never thought about lining the kitchen cabinets and the pantry shelves! I don't have the materials yet. Do you think you can wait to put your kitchen stuff away until we have time to do this?" Matt, knowing that Sarah needed this, agreed, even though he wondered if it was really important. But he didn't have much in the way of kitchen stuff, and they could leave Grandma's kitchen stuff in boxes until Sarah decided what went into what cabinet anyway. Sarah's stuff wouldn't be coming to the house for another week, so they were okay. *What do women need shelf paper for anyway?* Matt silently wondered.

The dining room and living room were also finished to their satisfaction, and the furniture would be placed on the walls they naturally fit, so Sarah quickly posted her little notes, and they were done for the day. Matt made a note to purchase two or three matching trash bins on wheels for the garage, ones with solid locking lids and hopefully easy to wrestle to the curb. They did not have any furniture for the screened porch, but that could be purchased later. They both wanted to create a sort of tropical garden there with large jardinières and a double chaise lounge where they could lie back, read the paper, listen to the birds, and be surrounded by nature . . . without the mosquitoes!

As he was locking up, Matt's cell phone rang for the second time that evening. It was his sister Barbara asking to talk with Sarah. She sounded upset, and this was unusual for Barbara. She was the one who was the organizer, never worried, always had everything under control, and usually could fix anything at the last minute. *What could be wrong?* Matt had wondered.

Matt heard Sarah responding to Barbara by saying, "How could that happen?" and, "Well, who actually placed the order?" then "Can it be fixed?" There was a heated discussion about polka dots and plaids. Matt had no idea what they were talking about, so he continued to lock up the back doors, the porch door, and garage. When he came back to Sarah's side and they were ready to leave, Sarah grinned and teased, "Unlike someone I know, I will not keep secrets from someone close to me." Then she explained that when Barbara went to make a last-minute check on the gowns before the women arrived for their fittings tomorrow, she found that the men's cummerbunds and bow ties and the women's sashes and belt bow colors had been mixed up. The original sash fabric had been used on the cummerbunds. Barbara also explained that the tablecloths they ordered from the caterer were the wrong color, and the style of the chairs, which they ordered by number, was incorrect.

Barbara said that she spoke with the dressmaker and the caterer and they'd said there was still time to correct these things. She explained that they would be in tomorrow to iron it all out. She had also spoken with Ann who had suggested that they leave the sashes as they are, and choose a coordinating color for the cummerbunds since that would entail the least amount of work and would still look great. Barbara said that she was perplexed by all the items that needed correcting, and asked Sarah if she could think of what could have gone wrong. Barbara said that when she realized that the items were incorrect, she'd checked the numbers that the retailers had written down when the items were ordered, and they didn't match the list that Barbara had, the one that they had all agreed upon. Barbara didn't know how that could have happened.

But Barbara was on top of it, and as long as Sarah didn't mind the polka dots being where the plaid was, and the plaid being where the polka dots were supposed to be, Ann could make that problem go away. Tomorrow they would correct the other two problems. Sarah thought everything would work out too. She trusted Barbara's choices and knew it was best to be flexible at this point and that by tomorrow they would have everything back on track. Sarah had told Matt that she felt so lucky . . . no . . . blessed . . . that Barbara and Ann were there, and that Barbara had thought to check on everything so early.

When Sarah hung up the phone, they walked across the street to lend Mary and Kevin Grandma's manuscript, and Matt asked Kevin to look at the math and monkey swing stuff so he could, with Matt's help, try to explain it to everyone in a week or so, preferably before the wedding. This way while they were on their honeymoon, others could help with the planning of the carriage house. Then they left for the restaurant and, when finally seated, began to talk about what problems the men might encounter when moving Grandma's beautiful things from the storage unit.

Matt said that Caleb and Joshua had borrowed some thick moving quilts with which to wrap Grandma's things. They were originally going to use their own smaller pickup trucks, but Caleb had gotten a closed truck with straps attached to its sides and ceiling with which to fasten the furniture and keep it from moving when they were driving. Caleb felt that this would be the safest way to move some of the larger and more delicate pieces of furniture. He knew their sentimental value and didn't want anything to happen to them.

Sarah had suddenly become very quiet, and Matt had asked her what was wrong. She asked Matt if he thought they were too obsessed about the house and getting everything just right. She knew that God frowned on anything that stole their heart, and right now the house was of such importance to them. She asked Matt what he thought, and he'd felt that God knew that they were trying to create a home that they intended to use not only for them, but also for their future children and for fellowship with family, friends, and maybe even strangers who they'd invite to become children of God. Matt told Sarah that while they might be a little obsessed right now, and maybe they'd even shortchanged God a little bit right now, he felt that they were still on the right track and would be okay. He also assured Sarah that they would use the incredible list they'd found in the newest manuscript of Grandma's so their home would best serve others.

Amazed by all his thoughts of yesterday, Matt began to focus on today, the moving day that had finally arrived. While the men were moving furniture, the ladies were to have their gowns fitted for the last time, buy their shoes, and choose their flowers! It was hard to believe, but here it was . . . the wedding would take place in two weeks, and most of the work was done on the house. Their wedding plans were moving along on schedule . . . thanks to Barbara's efficient planning.

Matt, now dressed and walking out the door of his apartment with two large boxes in his arms, headed toward his truck. He'd go directly to Dunkin' Donuts and then to the house. He chuckled to himself as his mind again moved to yesterday and he suddenly remembered their silliness in the restaurant last night. They had been talking about how difficult it was for the elderly or infirm if they had to get up and out of a very low chair or had to try to move closer to the dining room table if they were sitting in a very heavy chair.

Sarah imitated how Grandma had struggled when she was seated in a huge, heavy dining-room chair. Once she was in place, she couldn't move without help because the chair was so heavy! She didn't have the strength in her hands to move the chair back to get up, or move the chair in to get close enough to the table to eat properly. She was too polite to say anything, but because of her own experiences, she had taught Sarah to be aware of what others needed. That included little children too. She'd told Sarah that by making provision for these things, they would be pleasing God because they were looking out for the comfort of others.

At the restaurant, Matt had laughed aloud as his mind filled with an image of Grandma struggling to get the chair close enough to the table to reach her soup! As he shared this image with Sarah, he howled with laughter and pretended to be trying to inch his chair closer to the table and unable to get it to move. Sarah had joined the antics by moving her restaurant chair far from the table, and pretending to try to cut her meat from this distance. She could not get the knife in the right position with her arms fully outstretched, so she too started giggling, and those sitting close to them in the restaurant began to look at them.

"Try it, Matt," she said. "It's close to impossible to cut your meat! And can you imagine the soup you'd spill?" "What about peas?" Matt roared. "And gravy," Sarah exclaimed! "How would you ever reach a wine glass that had been placed all the way across the dinner plate? And . . . and . . . remember when Grandma sat in that one huge chair and her feet didn't even touch the ground? How uncomfortable she was!" And the tears began to stream down their cheeks from their laughter and the memories they shared.

After recovering from their silly giggling, knowing it wasn't funny to the one living through such a challenge, they acknowledged the enormous difficulty the aged could have with everyday things, especially those who were ill or weak. "See how loving God is, and how He sees everything we need, and wants us see this also?" Sarah said. "Let's try to look at our home as if we were weak or old or sick, and see what accommodations we can make for others, and still have the house look beautiful."

"See, Sarah," Matt said, "we are okay with our house, not obsessed in a bad way since we want to make it right for others to share." And with that, they had agreed to look for ways to make the house suit others as well as themselves. They finished their meal and drove to Sarah's apartment where Matt had stayed for only an hour because he was so tired and wanted to get home and rest for the big moving day.

Matt also thought of the dining room chandelier that Sarah had taken from Grandma's house and reminded himself to be careful when moving it because of its tall, fluted, amber globes. One globe already had a crack in the bottom, which at present could be hidden by the cup it would sit in. They had to be careful not only in moving it, but also with installing it. They had decided not to put it up until they had the dining room table ready to be placed under the chandelier so no one would walk into the low hanging fixture.

Matt recalled how he had reminded Sarah that there were many, many verses in the Bible where God speaks about the adornment of the temple that Solomon was to build. But that it was still important to first adorn themselves with godly thoughts and actions. "As long as we first prepare our hearts with the adornment God wants to see inside us, we'll be okay in planning to adorn our home," Matt had assured her, reminding her of the verse Grandma mentioned to them about decorating their hearts before they decorated themselves or their home.

Do not let your adornment be merely outward—arranging the
hair, wearing gold, or putting on fine apparel—
rather let it be the hidden
person of the heart, with the incorruptible beauty of a gentle and
quiet spirit, which is very precious in the sight of God.
                                        —1 Peter 3:3, 4

Sarah had remembered another verse Grandma always mentioned about the choices people have in life. There are just two. They can choose to work toward a blessing or a curse.

Behold, I set before you today a blessing and a curse:
The blessing, if you obey the commandments of the Lord your God
which I command you today; and the curse, if you do not
obey the commandments of the Lord your God, but turn aside from
the way which I command you today, to go after other
gods which you have not known.
                                        —Deuteronomy 11:26, 27, 28

Sarah also remembered Grandma's advice to them to watch and examine what was important to them so they would always be able to recognize where their heart was.

For where your treasure is,
there will your heart be also.
                                        —Matthew 6:21

Matt reminded Sarah that although these were warnings we all had to be aware of, God nevertheless did love beauty and had created beauty for us in nature. God also included His own decorating requests right in scripture when he directed a number of various structures be built.

And I have filled him with the Spirit of God,
in wisdom, in understanding, in knowledge, and in all manner
of workmanship, to design artistic works, to work in gold,
in silver, in bronze, in cutting jewels for setting in carving wood,
and to work in all manner of workmanship.
                                        —Exodus 31:3, 4, 5

You shall overlay the boards with gold,
make their rings of gold as holders for the bars, and
overlay the bars with gold.

—Exodus 26:29

Moreover you shall make the tabernacle with
ten curtains of fine woven linen, and blue, purple, and scarlet
thread; with artistic designs of cherubim
you shall weave them.

—Exodus 26:1

"These verses show us," Matt had said, "that as long as we put God first, and put those He loves next, we can ask for a lovely home and decorate it in a way that brings everyone joy. We can make our home a Bethany for us, and for our loved ones."

Sarah had explained to Matt that sometimes she really got scared. "Things are going well for us right now, but life isn't like that and I just dread what trials we might have to go through. I still make so many mistakes, I have thoughts I shouldn't have, I get exasperated with people at work, . . . and in traffic, sometimes I *really* lose my cool." But Matt assured her that God tells us not to worry about tomorrow. As long as we strive, stay faithful, whatever it is that we need to go through, or whatever comes our way that is difficult, God will see us through it, not only to it, but through it . . . and that God forgives our sin when we are remorseful.

For there is no one who doesn't sin.

—2 Chronicles 6:36

Now no chastening seems to be joyful for the
present, but painful; nevertheless, afterward it yields the peaceable
fruit of righteousness to those who have been trained by it.

—Hebrews 12:11

But if we walk in the light as He is in the light, we
have fellowship with one another, and the blood of Jesus Christ
His Son cleanses us from all sin.

—*1 John 1:7*

But God demonstrates His own love for us,
in that while we were yet sinners, Christ died for us.
. . . we shall be saved by His life.

—*Romans 5:8, 10*

Suddenly Matt realized that here he was, at the house, the boxes he'd brought from his house were placed in the living room, the chandelier carefully tucked into a corner of the room, and the coffee and donuts were on the folding table. He had been so engrossed in his thoughts of yesterday that he'd been on automatic pilot, hardly aware of his actions.

Now, as he sat in the window seat slowly savoring his steaming coffee, bacon, egg, and cheese croissant followed by a French cruller, he was amazed by how his mind had wandered to his conversations with Sarah yesterday. He hardly remembered showering, dressing, carrying boxes to his truck, driving to Dunkin' Donuts, then to the house, or even unloading the boxes.

I guess it's just that such a big change is coming up for me today to finally move in here and know that soon, so soon, Sarah and I will be married and living here together. Please, God, help me to be an example to her, help me to be what You want me to be, help me to keep learning of You, and to keep my faith uppermost in my life.

Chapter Three

MARY AND THE CARRIAGE HOUSE

*Delight yourself also in the Lord, and He shall
give you the desires of your heart.*

—*Psalm 37:4*

Mary had gotten up early to prepare the lasagna noodles so Elizabeth would have a little less work to do for tonight. They'd made their sauce last night. Today, all Elizabeth had to do was make her wonderful ricotta filling, assemble everything to form the lasagna, and put it in the oven at just the right time. They'd planned for Elizabeth to make four large pans of lasagna because they expected twelve people tonight for dinner and felt that the men would be very hungry after all their hard work that day. Except for the salad, the others would bring everything else, the Italian bread, the wine, and the desserts.

Mary had purchased all the makings for a great salad. But rather than have Mary prepare it, they'd wanted to gather around her huge kitchen island and all work on the salad together. That way, they could have a close-knit fellowship by talking about their day. The men and women would be pitching in to make the salad together and this would be a perfect venue for "catching up" on what had been accomplished today by the women and by the men. This would also allow Elizabeth to be brought up to date on what they'd accomplished. So much was planned for the day that they knew there'd be a lot of experiences to share.

With the wedding just two weeks away, today would be one of their busiest days. The men would be helping Matt move into his house, while the women would be having the final fitting for their gowns. Elizabeth was going to make the lasagnas and take some measurements of the carriage house so she could begin developing her ideas for its renovation. It would be an active day for everyone, but Mary felt the day's plans were perfect, and she smiled thinking of their day and of the carriage house as she made the coffee.

Mary and Kevin were hoping to get some rough plans of the carriage house to the architect before the wedding so that by the time Matt and Sarah returned from their honeymoon, the architectural plans could be close to finalizing and the permits applied for. Mary was excited with the prospect of Elizabeth and Rebecca moving here. While they would have their own home in the carriage house, they would be so close to Mary . . . right in the backyard . . . that she would get to see them often. She wanted so much to become a part of her daughter's life and was so grateful to Elizabeth for wanting that too.

Mary and Rebecca would take on the job of designing the art studio that would be created on the second floor of the carriage house. The architectural plans would include some skylights for the studio so the lighting would be appropriate for their work. What a joy it had been for Mary to learn that her daughter shared her talent in art. And now, together, they would plan their studio. They would also plan for the addition of a bathroom in the studio. Mary would leave the first floor design to Elizabeth and Rebecca so it could really be *their* home.

As she thought about the events of the past few months, Mary was once again enthralled by the love, power, and intervention of God. She had been in despair just a few short months ago. She had been controlled by her fears, lived only to find ways to draw good luck into her life, and never dreamed she would find her child again. *How could life turn around so completely in such a short time?* she wondered. Then she answered her own question saying aloud, "God is the worker of miracles. He loves us so much that His plan to bless us is way ahead of our simple thoughts."

Mary had been raped when she was only fourteen years old and been forced to give her baby up for adoption. These two events left her with constant panic attacks and a desperate need to feel safe. Because of her fear and the secrets she felt she had to keep, as well as the suppressed anger she had, she had never been able to get close to anyone other than Kevin. She'd been lonely and isolated. She couldn't find joy in simple pleasures, find the energy, muster up the trust, or suppress the fear needed to make friends. For fourteen years she had been on medication to help her through the panic attacks.

Feng Shui, the ancient Chinese method of decorating, had come into Mary's life because she had heard that this decorating method would guarantee good luck and prosperity. It had become an obsession with her. She began to leave Kevin out of the process, and over time he became terribly concerned about the Feng Shui, its accompanying astrological charts, lucky numbers, chants and divination. *Why did I never recognize how involved I had become with these parts of Feng Shui?* Mary wondered. *It had slowly trapped me and I hadn't realized it.*

Mary glanced over to the little chest Kevin's sister had refinished and given them as a gift. She remembered how her refusal to allow the chest in the house for fear of its "poison arrows" almost destroyed her relationship with Kevin. She'd been terrified to have those poison arrows in her home.

Mary's Feng Shui master had told her that all sharp corners in a house send out poison arrows that cause bad luck or bring illness to the occupants of the house, and had to be eliminated or offset in some way. Kevin had gone along with all the Feng Shui recommendations until it came to refusing to allow his sister's wonderful and thoughtful gift to enter their home. Mary was thankful now that Kevin had stood his ground. How foolish she had been. How blessed they were that Matt and Sarah had come into their lives just at that crucial time and become such a wonderful example to them. How incredible was God's timing, how perfect His engineering of events!

Matt and Sarah had become their best friends. Mary and Kevin were so grateful for their friendship and for what they taught them about God. Mary had no idea that God promised to protect her, had no idea that Satan existed and could cause such heartache, had no idea that she would see a miracle take place if she had the courage to give up Feng Shui and place her trust in God. How glad she was that this change had come into her life. She'd never felt this degree of peace and joy before. She'd never felt this was even possible.

Whenever she thought of what Matt and Sarah called "her experience of faith," Mary was humbled. She never knew that miracles still happened today. She'd thought that they had only happened back in biblical days so God could show the people who He was. But now that a miracle had actually happened to her, and Matt and Sarah had shared some of the miracles that had occurred in their lives, she knew she'd been wrong . . . miracles *do* happen today. Mary was free of her fear. She no longer had panic attacks and no longer needed any medication. What further proof did she need? Ahh, how much she'd learned about how Grandma recognized, then chased, those awful spirits!

When Sarah first told Mary to begin praying for the child she'd given up for adoption but still hoped to find someday, she'd also told her to drop something extra, even if a little bit, into the offering box as a thank you for what God would provide. Mary had to take a leap of faith to give up trusting in the luck from Feng Shui and trust God instead, and she never could have done it without the support of Matt and Sarah and Kevin. They had stuck by her even when she'd been so wrong in her actions. She was so grateful for that. She knew that many people coldly turned away from those who made mistakes. But Matt and Sarah had stuck by them and taught them and won them to God by their example.

And look what it had brought her! She and her daughter were reunited! And they could call these wonderful people, Sarah and Matt, such true examples of a godly nature, their friends. What an extraordinary gift, not only for Mary and Kevin, but also for Elizabeth and Rebecca.

Mary recalled that Sarah had promised her that God was loving, all-knowing, compassionate, and already was working on solving her problems. To convince her, Sarah had given Mary a list of verses from the Bible that showed where God promised to help her if she would trust Him and learn and follow His words. Mary still carried some of those verses in her wallet so she would never be without them if the fear ever tried to come back.

For He Himself has said,
"I will never leave you nor forsake you."
—Hebrews 13:5

When you pass through the waters I will be with you;
and through the rivers, they will not overflow you.
—Isaiah 43:2

Call to Me, and I will answer you,
and I will tell you great and mighty things.
—Jeremiah 33:3

The angel of the Lord encamps around those who fear Him,
and rescues them.
—Psalm 34:7

And Mary still practiced what she called her "Grandma No's" as Sarah had taught her to do whenever a spirit of fear started to attack. Sarah said that Grandma had learned the trick of yelling the word "NO!" aloud whenever a bad or fearful thought came into her head. When she did this, the thought immediately vanished. At first Grandma had to yell this frequently, but as the years went by, seldom did she have to do it. "The spirits that wanted to attack Grandma started to learn that it wasn't worth it . . . she was prepared to do battle with them . . . and they gave up," Sarah had said.

Mary longed to have her thought pattern changed and admitted that she hadn't known about evil spirits before she'd met Matt and Sarah, and that she was amazed by what she'd read in Grandma's journal *When God Broke Grandma's Heart.* She was fascinated by what she'd learned in the journal about Satan and the powers he had, and about the spirits that helped him with his attacks. She hadn't known about the Holy Spirit and how we needed to have this Spirit live in us so we could understand the Bible and learn God's word and what to do to touch the heart of God. It was the work and power of the Holy Spirit that brought about miracles in today's world.

All these experiences provided the spark that ignited Mary and Kevin's desire to work to gain God's blessing on their lives . . . in their hearts and in their home and family. But they realized that to do this to the best of their ability, they needed to learn more. They now believed that through fellowship with Matt and Sarah, regular attendance at their church services, and praying, God would lift the veil from their eyes and give them an understanding that really worked. *So many don't understand the Bible, yet God tells us He will give us understanding when we ask for it with a pure heart and pure motive.*

> *But their minds were blinded:*
> *for until this day remaineth the same vail*
> *untaken away in the reading of the old testament;*
> *which vail is done away with in Christ.*
> —*2 Corinthians 3:14*

Then He opened their understanding;
that they might understand the scriptures.

—*Luke 24:45*

Mary had also learned a lot from Grandma. Sarah had said that through Grandma's life and the journal, and other writings she had left for them, a wealth of wisdom and a legacy of faith had been provided for those she'd loved, as well as those they would love. Now, Sarah and Matt willingly shared these with Mary and Kevin, and as they also shared their faith, the friendship deepened.

Sarah and Matt had recently given Mary another of Grandma's little manuscript's to read. Sarah found it in the trunk that had once belonged to Grandma. This one was about decorating according to the will of God. They felt that it might help Mary and Kevin with their plans for the carriage house. They knew that when Kevin and Mary had been reunited with Rebecca and uncovered the circumstances that had led Elizabeth into trying to bring Mary and Rebecca together again, Mary had thought of creating a weekend place for Elizabeth and Rebecca by renovating the carriage house. These plans had joyfully expanded into making the move full-time and permanent. Mary was thrilled with this idea. So was Kevin. Matt and Sarah had been so happy for them.

Kevin had been wonderful through all these changes in their life. He'd always given so much to Mary, supported her need to feel safe, wanted her to have her own art studio, encouraged her to find her child, and assured her that he would accept that child as his own daughter. When he'd finally met Rebecca, he was astonished and delighted by her maturity, her beauty, and her talent. He'd felt that she was so much like Mary. He'd welcomed Elizabeth and willingly took her into his heart as well. Mary knew she was blessed to have Kevin and now, free of her fears, she loved him with a greater understanding of what love really is. Now, he too was excited to think of the carriage house becoming a home to Elizabeth and Rebecca.

Last night Mary and Kevin had been delighted that Matt and Sarah had dropped in before they left to go back to Sarah's apartment. Their friends had been excited when they arrived, both babbling at once about their discovery of the new manuscript they'd found in an old trunk that had belonged to Sarah's grandmother. Apparently Grandma had written it. They said that it was about renovating and decorating in a manner that would please God, and there were concepts in it that they'd never known existed. Sarah and Matt wanted Mary and Kevin to look at it and to share the information with Elizabeth. They'd even asked Kevin to learn the concepts well enough to help Matt explain them to the rest of the family in another week or so.

Matt and Sarah hadn't stayed long because they were headed out to dinner; then would each head home. Matt had some more packing to do at his place. They both had to get up early for the big moving day for the men and the dressmaker outing for the women, so they decided that it was important to get home so they could get enough rest for what they wanted to accomplish the next day.

Before they left, Sarah teased Matt by asking him to tell Mary and Kevin about the mystery caller who had talked about a surprise for her. Mary and Kevin had pressed Matt because they both loved surprises and were curious as well. But Matt explained that he'd given his word to keep both the caller and the surprise a secret. "However," he said, "you will all know soon, and it will make Sarah very happy. And that's all I'll say." They were all very curious now. *Who could have called? What could the surprise be?*

After Matt and Sarah left, Mary and Kevin skimmed through the yellowed manuscript that Grandma had written, and enjoyed what they read, realizing that they'd never before heard or read anything like it. Every word was a gem that seemed so perfect for all of them to utilize in their homes, not just for the carriage house renovation.

Mary and Kevin had been amazed by what they read. Grandma had started off by listing the things God wants us to do. This list made it so easy for anyone about to decorate a house to take those instructions into account. *What a great idea*, Mary thought, *I'll bet only a handful of people would think of that.* Mary too wanted to share these thoughts with Elizabeth so she could consider them in her own plans. *Perhaps*, she thought, *I'll make her a copy of the lists so Elizabeth can start to envision what she might want to do to incorporate them into the carriage house right away. She can read the whole manuscript later!*

As Mary continued with her chores, her mind was running a mile a minute. *How can we know what God wants*, Mary thought, *unless we want to know? The answer is clearly in scripture. In Grandma's manuscript she proves this by examining the verses that tell us what to do. Then she explains how these verses impact us, and what we must do to gain the blessing. She was so organized that she even began with a list of some of the things we should do and identified the verses that supported this.* To impress Grandma's words into her memory, Mary began to read aloud.

"The first step is to list those activities that we are asked to do according to scripture. When this is complete, we are ready to make a floor plan for the room that will allow these activities to be carried out with ease and in comfort. In other words, we determine what we need to do, which functions our rooms should serve, and what furnishings help make God's instruction easier to fulfill. When these considerations are complete, the design process can begin with God's blessing, for He is sure to bless all that we do in His name when we understand how He wants us to care for others."

When Mary read Grandma's list of what God wanted her to do and what would come from doing them, she quickly ran to her copier so she could copy the list for Elizabeth. Grandma's first list was:

STEP 1: KNOW WHAT WE ARE ASKED TO DO

1) Teach our children the ways of God (Ephesians 6:4)
2) Pray in the morning and at night (Deuteronomy 11:19)

3) Keep the Sabbath holy (Exodus 20:8)
4) Cover the transgressions of others (Proverbs 17:9)
5) Don't provoke one another (Colossians 3:21)
6) Be kind and tenderhearted (Ephesians 4:32)
7) Be overcomers (Revelation 2:7, 11, 26 and Revelation 3:21)
8) Care for widows and orphans and revere the elderly (Proverbs 16:31)
9) Have fellowship with one another, speaking of our faith (Acts 2:42)
10) Do good and share (Hebrews 13:16)
11) When we pray, pray without repetition (Matthew 6:7)
12) Set the right example and don't be hypocrites (Matthew 7:15)

Grandma went on to say that God wants to make a bargain with us. He doesn't just ask us to do something arbitrarily, He always has a reason, and He offers us something in return. The special beauty of God's love for us is manifested in the wonderful promises He gives us if we do our best to follow His ways. To support this Grandma included another list to show some of those promises.

Step 2: WHAT GOD PROMISES IN RETURN

1) We will obtain the peaceable fruit of righteousness (Hebrews 12:11)
2) It will go well with us and our children (Deuteronomy 12:28)
3) We will get good things (Matthew 7:11)
4) We will be given the desires of our heart (Psalm 37:4)
5) We will be blessed (Deuteronomy 11:26), (Proverbs 8:32)
6) Our children will be faithful to God (Proverbs 22:6)
7) We will live and multiply (Deuteronomy 30:16)
8) We will gain understanding (Proverbs 15:32)
9) God will not leave us (Deuteronomy 31:6)
10) God will clothe us (Matthew 6:30)
11) Our cupboards will always be filled with food (Proverbs 3:9, 10)

12) We will receive an inheritance from God (Deuteronomy 12:9)

13) We will be forgiven (Matthew 6:14)

14) We will not have to worry (Matthew 6:34)

15) We will have strength against the devil's wiles (Ephesians 6:11)

16) We will be granted wisdom (James 1:5)

17) We will not be condemned (Luke 6:37)

18) God will make an everlasting covenant with us (Isaiah 55:3)

19) The Lord will recompense and reward our work (Ruth 2:12)

20) We will be safe and secure (Proverbs 1:33)

The manuscript continued in instruction by explaining that these were only a few of the promises found throughout scripture, but they demonstrated the magnitude of what God longs to provide for us. *How can we miss,* Mary thought, *we will be wise, will escape the ploys of Satan, we'll always have enough to eat, our children will be faithful, we won't have to worry since God will bless us and care for us, and to top it all off, after we die we will receive a crown and an inheritance. That's incredible!* Then followed, at the bottom of this list, some of the promises God gives for our eternal life when we are faithful to His word.

STEP 3: THE PROMISE'S GOD MAKES ABOUT OUR ETERNAL LIFE

1) There will be no death, sorrow, tears, or pain (Revelation 21:4)

2) There will be no hunger or thirst (Revelation 7:17)

3) There will be no defiling, abomination, or lie (Revelation 21:27)

4) There will be no more curse (Revelation 22:3)

5) There will be no more night (Revelation 22:5)

6) There will be fruits, fountains, milk, honey, roses, and lilies (2 Esdras 2:18, 19)

7) We will not be ashamed: neither be confounded, nor put to shame (Isaiah 54:4)

8) We will go with joy and be led in peace (Isaiah 55:12)

9) Whoever gathers against us will fall (Isaiah 54:15)

10) No weapon or tongue against us will prosper (Isaiah 54:17)

11) We will receive a crown in Heaven (1 Peter 5:4)

12) We will sit on God's throne (Revelation 3:21)

13) We will not be hurt by the second death (Revelation 2:11)

14) God will sup with us (Revelation 3:20)

15) We will have power over nations (Revelation 2:26)

Once again, Mary thought, *If we could only remember these gifts every day, if every waking hour of our life we could know, really know, and understand what we are working toward, it would be easy to keep our eye on the ultimate goal of this life. Sadly, though, we forget so easily and slip into complacency. We work to get our paychecks every week, and are often very careful not to jeopardize that, but we so seldom work to get these eternal benefits. Why?*

Since Mary was now a parent of one and would soon be a parent to two, she wanted to do the things God asked of her and wanted to discuss what these were so she and Kevin could be assured that they had incorporated them into their own home. She was so blessed that Kevin would gladly work toward this goal with her. She was so blessed that Sarah and Matt would too.

The manuscript went on to say that there were certain decisions that a family had to make before they could incorporate the actions God wanted them to take. Grandma had also quoted a passage from scripture that gave good reason for them to want to do things God's way.

> *Observe and obey all these words which I command*
> *you, that it may go well with you and your children after you*
> *forever, when you do what is good and right*
> *in the sight of the Lord your God.*
>
> —*Deuteronomy 12:28*

Grandma's manuscript went on to explain that in order to implement the word of God in their homes, they'd need to list some of the rooms in which these godly activities would flourish and what should be placed in the rooms to fulfill those activities, and she gave some examples.

STEP 4: DETERMINE WHICH ROOMS BEST SUIT WHICH ACTIVITIES

1) The Living Room (fellowships, outreach)
2) The Family Room (family time, faith-based games)
3) The Den or Office (private talks and prayer)
4) The Kitchen (experiences of faith, our daily lives)
5) The Dining Room (thankfulness, sharing experiences)
6) The Child's Bedroom (communion with and about God)
7) The Adult's Bedroom (parents' time to talk and pray together)

Mary felt that most of the activities Grandma listed would provide parents, grandparents, and children with the opportunity to learn what really lives in the heart of one another. She knew that she wanted to start right away to foster this type of closeness between her and her daughter. Mary realized that through this we learn how to be an example and support to one another. *Whether discussing how someone's prayers were answered, or how they responded to a difficult circumstance in life, or how they speak of their concern over a person who treated them badly, each of these conversations can become not only a learning opportunity but also a teaching opportunity,* she thought.

Grandma's manuscript pointed out that when parents demonstrate a kindness, when they show their effort and ability to forgive, when they speak of how God created a miracle in their lives when they were exposed to a threat or danger of some kind, children remember. They carry into their adult lives those experiences that they heard their parents and grandparents speak of or saw them do. Events of everyday life, such as how they might have dealt with an unkind employer, or dealt with a traffic tie up, or a long line at the supermarket, all became teaching opportunities showing whether or not they responded in a God pleasing manner. These things are part of the experiences from which children learn. It is often these very experiences that guide them and strengthen them when they become adults and must face difficult and painful times themselves. Grandma said that scripture tells us exactly what to do.

> *Seek ye the Lord while He may be found,*
> *call ye upon Him while He is near.*
>
> *—Isaiah 55:6*

> *Come, eat of my bread and drink of the wine*
> *I have mixed, forsake foolishness and live,*
> *and go in the way of understanding.*
>
> *—Proverbs 9:5, 6*

Mary thought, *God wants us to follow the guidelines He has provided us through scripture because this opens the pathway for Him to provide us with His protection and for us to avail ourselves of grace and the angel service at all times, and in the end become a part of the Bride of Christ. Shouldn't we pass this legacy on to our children? Isn't it a far better way of life than Feng Shui? Certainly life after death holds such promise when we follow the word of God. What does Feng Shui offer after death? Shouldn't then our home be laid out in a way that makes accomplishing this goal easier for us, and more a natural part of our lives? How wonderful to think that we bring this into the lives of others when friends enter our homes and join in what we simply 'do' every day.*

Mary realized that to develop the things Grandma suggested, she would have to assess her home and what areas would be best suited for those activities. She would also give these lists to Elizabeth so she could plan the carriage house according to God's will, and thus encourage these activities in her home as well. *By doing this*, she thought, *we can discover how we can best use our homes to fulfill what God asks of us . . . and ohhh what a wonderful lesson for Rebecca!*

> *See, I have set before you today life and good,*
> *death and evil, in that I command you today to love the*
> *Lord your God, to walk*
> *in His ways,*

and to keep His commandments, His statutes, and
His judgments, that you may live and multiply; and the Lord
your God will bless you in the land which you go to possess.
—*Deuteronomy 30:15-18*

Mary knew that by examining scripture, she could find many verses that specify parental duties. She didn't yet have any parenting skills and hoped to learn from Elizabeth. But she did want to talk with Elizabeth so when they planned the carriage house and were seeking God's blessing on that home, the goal would be to enhance and facilitate the godly activities they might plan for their home. *Decorating should not be simply a matter of satisfying our pride or 'keeping up with the Joneses,'* she thought.

May He grant you according to your heart's desire,
and fulfill all your purpose.
—*Psalm 20:4*

Mary now realized that while the living room, family room, or den may be the relaxation areas of the house where conversation and interaction take place, so too was the kitchen, dining room, and bedrooms. These are all important areas for conversation and instruction. Once she fully understood God's instructions, she could explore how each room could be made to meet those needs and obtain the promises God gives for implementing them. By providing a special place for the family to meet to share the tenets of their faith, read the word of God, exchange their experiences of faith, and express their thankfulness to God, she understood that the family would then begin to meet God's requirements. She and Kevin, Elizabeth and Rebecca could explore what these rooms may require in order to support those activities. *We can tackle our decorating projects, and especially the carriage house, knowing that because we truly desire to serve God and we have placed Him first and foremost in the decorating of our home, He will bless us in our projects. And we will have fun doing it!*

As Mary thought about the things she looked for in a home, she began to see how specific elements could also serve to support each activity

God asked of us, and also make the room become better suited to each member of the household and each guest.

Armed with this information, Mary understood that Elizabeth would now be better equipped to determine what functions she and Rebecca would want each of their rooms to provide. As a result, they would take a slightly different look at what pieces of furniture would help them meet their new goals. Whether they decided on little stools tucked under a console table for extra seating, or floor pillows for children, or higher and firmer side chairs in the living room for elderly members of the family, they would now be making a conscious decision for God's way in their decorating choices. *We will also be showing our children not only how to be considerate of others and meet the needs of the family, but also that we are followers and doers of God's word,* she thought. *These may be little things, but they show a heart's attitude of consideration for others, of loving others as ourselves, which is what God asks of us.*

Never before had Mary considered that it was important to strive to create a home life that is so conducive, supportive, and encouraging to family gatherings where family communication about God is a natural consequence. If she'd first thought in these terms when she planned her decorating projects, she and Kevin would have had the blessing of God on their home, and on them, as a couple, a lot sooner. *This is a better promise than that of Feng Shui,* she thought. And Mary decided that she and Kevin would also take a new look at their own home and incorporate God's direction wherever they could.

> *And you shall teach them the statutes and the laws,*
> *and show them the way in which they must walk*
> *and the work they must do.*
>
> —*Exodus 18:20*

Grandma also mentioned that God wasn't pleased with people who were with Him today and with another spirit tomorrow. He didn't want fence sitters. He didn't want someone who was lukewarm about Him. He wanted those loyal to Him, those committed to Him and to learning what He asks of us, and striving to do those things! And . . . once someone had been made aware of these things, they would have no excuse before God when the day of reckoning came!

> *Beware lest any man spoil you through philosophy*
> *and vain deceit, after the tradition of men at the rudiments*
> *of the world and not after Christ.*
> *I know your works, that you are neither cold nor hot.*
> *I could wish you were cold or hot. So then,*
> *because you are lukewarm, and neither cold nor hot,*
> *I will vomit you out of my mouth.*
> —*Revelation 3:15, 16*

Grandma ended this section of her manuscript by saying that this understanding of God's word provides us with the freedom to love beauty and creativity, and the revelation that God is the Ultimate Designer and King Solomon had been His willing apprentice!

Mary and Kevin had read Grandma's manuscript together in bed last night. Kevin too had been impressed with it, and Mary had to hold him back from jumping up and measuring their bedroom. Mary smiled to herself remembering how absolutely thrilled he was with the section on Divine Proportion and the monkey swing concept. She knew that he was already planning how he would explain all this to everyone in another week or so when he himself understood it more fully.

Mary's thoughts came back to the moment as she heard Kevin coming down the hall toward the kitchen and she quickly placed his coffee on the table so they would have some time together before the day's activities began. *What a fun day this should be,* she thought as she turned to Kevin's kiss.

Chapter Four

KEVIN AND THE CARRIAGE HOUSE

Today would be a busy day, but Kevin was looking forward to the camaraderie the men would have as they worked together during the day and shared the fellowship with the women tonight. The men would be moving Matt out of his tiny studio apartment and into the house and then would get some of Grandma's furnishings out of storage and move that to the house as well. He chuckled to himself as he remembered Sarah's firm instructions to be sure to look for her Post-it notes that would tell them where everything was to go. He continued to chuckle as he recalled her expression and body language: eyebrows drawn together, feet apart, and index finger wagging at them. It was difficult for Sarah to look firm and menacing in her attempt to be sure that the men would follow her instructions. Even she had laughed at herself.

It was great to have such terrific friends, Kevin thought, *I am so lucky that Matt and Sarah came into our lives before we'd gotten ourselves into real trouble with all the fear and the Feng Shui. There are so many people out there that spout religion, but so few that really practice it, really understand God, really have the courage to stand up against evil. It's so easy just to 'go along' and not make any waves.*

Kevin felt that Matt and Sarah were fearless when it came to their faith. They were never afraid to stand up for what was right. Kevin wanted to become more like them. He wanted to learn to trust God, to understand what God said to help them in life, and to develop the ability to act on those things. Kevin felt that he would make better decisions once he knew what God wanted. He was so proud of Mary, too. *It had taken guts to cold-turkey away from the Feng Shui stuff,* he thought. *It must have been really frightening to Mary . . . it was surely a leap of faith on her part. It was my sister's beautiful gift that seemed to trigger the change, but it was Matt and Sarah's understanding of God's word that taught us to recognize the dangers of Feng Shui. God sure does work in mysterious ways.*

> *Trust in Him at all times, you people; pour out your heart*
> *before him; God is a refuge for us.*
> *—Psalm 62:8*

Kevin knew that the men would pray before they began their chores today. They would also pray at lunch and then again in thanks when they were done. Kevin was still a little embarrassed to pray in front of anyone, but he was getting better at it. He had never before seen men pray so openly and so frequently, but he really loved that the men did this. To him, it took courage. It took a real man to believe, and then to stand up for what he believed and do so in public. Sarah and Matt and their family had become their role models, and Kevin was resolved to learn from them, to live his faith the way they did. He had come to realize that God doesn't like complacency.

Matt would probably ask Caleb to pray before they embarked on their moving venture since protocol seemed to be that the person that lives in the house they were in would either pray himself or ask the person he thought might have the most wisdom, best experience, or the highest-ranking clergy office to pray. Caleb, Sarah's older brother, was the oldest among them and a big bulky guy. Not fat, just big and strong and broad. He had hands like a bear and yet was as gentle a person as Kevin had ever met. He'd been surprised by the strength of Caleb's faith since Caleb didn't wear it on his sleeve for everyone to see. Kevin respected that and realized how similar in heart's attitude Caleb and Matt were. *Thank you, God, for bringing these guys into my life, for showing me their strength, for teaching me,* Kevin thought.

Kevin had also learned a lot about renovations from working with these men at Matt's house and now realized that he really enjoyed this kind of work. It was a great hobby and one that seemed to please the ladies. He grinned thinking of how the gals would cajole them to put up a shelf, or move a piece of furniture that was too heavy for them, and be so pleased if they accomplished the task in a relatively short time after it was requested. *Ahh,* he thought, *this is one of the secrets of the way to a woman's heart!*

Kevin had always known that God required the head of the household to take responsibility for the spiritual needs of his family. For years it had gnawed at him, but he'd put it aside because he really didn't know what to do. In the church he'd attended as a boy and then a young man, it was hardly ever mentioned and never explained. But since he began attending Matt and Sarah's church, it was discussed, or at least mentioned, nearly every service. He was learning what to do, and that felt really good. There were no more gray areas that made him indecisive and inactive. Now, he could talk to Mary about the Bible, about being a good parent to Rebecca, about caring for Elizabeth, about learning what God wants of them. Mary understood the blessing that came from this too and the incredible promise of an eternity as a part of the Bride of Christ. Having Mary understand and want it too made his job so much easier. Having friends to teach them, through their example and through their fellowship with one another, was also great. He wouldn't have been able to do it without their help.

Kevin wanted to make a friend of Rebecca, wanted her to come to love him, wanted to be a good father to her. He wanted to see her flourish in her faith too, maybe even joining them in their newfound faith. If this could all happen, his family life would be perfect, especially with the new baby coming. He wanted to be sure that Rebecca never felt that the new baby was more important in their lives than she was, and he knew he needed to pray and offer for that. But for now, he was content. He felt that they were on the right path and trying their best to learn.

Sometimes Kevin worried because he would feel such strong emotion during some of the services. So often what the ministers said struck a deep chord and an intense longing in his heart that he'd have to choke back the tears. Luckily he'd seen Matt choke up once or twice too, so at least he wasn't alone. Kevin was overwhelmed at times by a sense of thankfulness for what he'd found. Understanding why he was where he was, what his responsibilities were and what his goals were was actually liberating, not confining at all, and a wonderful relief! Kevin also knew beyond a shadow of a doubt, that bringing these special people into his life was a gift from God.

Kevin would also choke up when he saw Mary in a certain light, and his love for her would well up in his heart and seem to overflow. He'd always felt that way about her, but never spoke of it. But now, with these friends, he was free to express even these feelings. All the guys he'd be with today really loved their wives. None of them made crude jokes about other women, or flirted, or put their wives down. It was refreshing. It was fun too, when they'd all tease Matt telling him that with marriage he'd have to learn the four "gives" of a good relationship. "Give, Give in, Forgive, and . . . ahh . . . just Give up," they'd said to Matt, grinning from ear to ear.

But all in all, it was a joy to know men who put their wives before themselves. This was rare out in the real world. Again, it was liberating to be open and honest about loving someone. *Maybe it was a macho thing that most guys felt they couldn't admit to being really in love or wanting to give love and protect a woman or a child. Yet it was what God asked of husbands and fathers, because that is what Christ did for His bride . . . us. God asked a lot from the wives too, so it wasn't a one-way deal.*

They all had a busy day planned for today and would be sharing their accomplishments tonight over dinner. Elizabeth would be going out to the carriage house to take the measurements of the basic structure and note where the existing plumbing lines and windows were located. This would help them when they started to make plans to add walls and create an apartment for Elizabeth and Rebecca. Kevin wanted to cover all bases and make sure that it was comfortable. He wanted to arrange, as subtly as possible, for wheelchair-accessible entries into all the rooms and also to see if he could arrange for each bedroom to have its own temperature control. He'd seen some ambient lighting placed behind a slightly lowered crown molding that could act as a night-light when needed, and also be effective for mood lighting. He wanted to run the ambient lighting idea by Elizabeth. Most of all he wanted the place to please her and Rebecca.

Last night Kevin had looked through a manuscript that Matt and Sarah had dropped off for them to read. What he had read had surprised him and really moved his heart. He'd gone back and read two chapters more thoroughly. They were about Divine Proportion, and a "monkey swing" technique Grandma had devised that Kevin found fascinating. *When someone* really *studies God's words,* Kevin thought, *it's downright amazing to learn the immense scope of what He provides for us!*

Matt discovered the manuscript in the trunk they'd kept from Grandma's house and had just recently read it himself. He and Sarah felt that Kevin and Mary should read it and share it with Elizabeth so together they could make a better decision about what they wanted to do with the carriage house. They had also asked if Kevin would help Matt explain some of these concepts to the family in the next few weeks. Some of the concepts Grandma had discovered would require some study, but Kevin was fascinated by what he'd read and determined to put these ideas into action himself and to share them with the others.

But what if Elizabeth resisted, what if doing this would interfere with how she and Rebecca wanted things decorated? he wondered. *What do I do then?* He decided to ask Matt to pray with him for the right outcome. Mary also skimmed the manuscript and had been thrilled with it, so if Becca and Elizabeth would also agree, all would go well. Elizabeth was going to take measurements today, and suddenly Kevin wished he could have shown the manuscript to Elizabeth before she started with any plans. He really wanted this renovation to be done according to Grandma's manuscript. *Was this going to be a problem,* he wondered? *Would Elizabeth and Becca welcome our interest or consider it "interference"?* He'd have to be careful so he didn't get anyone upset and evoke any of the activities of those rotten spirits that loved to cause trouble.

One of the things that scared Kevin was something he'd recently learned about Satan. It was that he had all these helpers to do his bidding and attack people at their most vulnerable times and in their most vulnerable places. He'd also learned that Satan could use him to bring about these attacks. He wanted to understand this stuff better so he could do what was necessary to protect his family and to prevent Satan from using him to harm others.

When he'd looked some of this up in his concordance, he'd found that these spirits could even cause illness. He didn't like this. With Mary, Rebecca, Elizabeth, and the new baby in his care, he needed to understand how to protect them from these spirits. He wanted to learn more but felt it was something that he couldn't talk about unless it was to someone of faith who understood and believed that evil spirits could use us and also harm us so easily. Yet he knew this was all true, not only from what he'd recently learned, but also from a past experience that he remembered.

Kevin had met someone when they lived in Kentucky who was like a chameleon. He was as sweet as pie to people's faces but could lie like a rug. He'd cheat people whenever he could. He'd wrangle a price down until what he ended up with was an inferior job, then wouldn't even pay the contractor what he owed him for the job, claiming he had not done a good job. He was incredibly vindictive, always thinking of little ways to hurt anyone who tried to rebuke his actions. Few people knew his true character. But as Kevin got to know this man and saw what he did, the man finally understood that Kevin saw him as he really was and because of this, the man's eyes developed a strange glint when he looked at Kevin. Kevin felt a chill go down his spine when he looked into this man's eyes, as if he had looked into the worst evil, into the heart of a malevolent spirit. Ever since that experience, Kevin believed that evil could invade men and no one would necessarily know.

Kevin had also seen the beguiling nature of the evil because this man recruited others to do his dirty work and some of these others were so called "Christians." Kevin used the words "so-called" because he wondered how a true Christian could justify the cruel acts that this guy enticed them to commit against their own neighbors. It was scary to watch those who professed a strong faith in God yet could still justify terrible behavior toward their neighbors, their co-workers, or even their relatives, and never even once make apology or have remorse for those actions! And what was worse was that people like this seemed to prosper! But when he'd thought this, Kevin also recalled two of his Sunday school lessons. One described his initial feelings and the other told of the end result for people who harmed the children of God.

> *Truly God is good to Israel, to such as are pure in heart.*
> *But as for me, my feet had almost stumbled;*
> *my steps had nearly slipped. For I was envious of the*
> *boastful, when I saw the prosperity of the wicked.*
> —*Psalm 73:1-3*

> *Until I went into the sanctuary of God: then understood I their end.*
> *Surely thou didst set them in slippery places:*
> *thou castedest them down into destruction.*

How are they brought into desolation,
as in a moment they are utterly consumed with terrors.
As a dream when one awaketh: so, O Lord, when thou awakest,
thou shalt despise their image.

—*Psalm 74:17-20*

Now, having learned so much more about God's plan from Matt and Sarah and from listening to the sermons at church, Kevin realized that evil not only exists, but also actively searches for ways to harm the children of God. He now knew that Satan actually stalks the children of God in an effort to break them away from God, and that he can use people to bring that harm.

Kevin had also begun to learn about the protection God offers from these assaults, and he wanted every bit of the armour that God offered. He had started to make a list about Satan's abilities from what he'd read in the Bible, but when he mentioned this to Matt, Matt told him that he and Sarah already had made one from their own research for their journal, which they'd called *When God Took Grandma Home.* Matt offered to make Kevin a copy not only of the list of what Satan could do but also a second list of how to obtain God's protection. Matt told him then that if ever Kevin needed prayers, the whole family would gather together to pray with him and for him. Matt explained that they would ask God to bind the spirits that lived in Satan's agents so they could bring no harm to the children of God they attacked. Kevin planned to discuss this subject in depth with Matt when he and Matt began work on the carriage house.

Kevin was afraid of these spirits. He'd read one especially chilling verse in scripture that made him realize he didn't want to mess with these things without knowing how to be protected. The verse he remembered described how seven new spirits, worse than the first, would enter a person if his heart was not properly cleansed of the one spirit that had lived there, then the person would end up worse off than before.

Then he goes and takes with him seven other spirits more wicked
than himself, and they enter and dwell there,
and the last state of that man is worse
than the first. So shall it also be with this wicked generation.
—*Matthew 12:45*

Well, enough thinking for one day, Kevin thought, *I've finished dressing and shaving and now I'd better get to the kitchen. Mary's probably got our coffee ready so we can have a few minutes together before we both have to leave for our separate day's activities.* Kevin walked into the kitchen, and sure enough, Mary was waiting with their coffee. Mary always mixed a pure dark chocolate and a special cinnamon, *Cinnamonum verum,* into their coffee. This cinnamon was only grown in Ceylon and didn't contain the toxic component called *coumarin,* which he'd heard was in the *cassia* cinnamon grown in Indonesia. The combined aromas of coffee, chocolate, and cinnamon not only filled the room, but also made his mouth water. He looked at his watch and saw he had another fifteen minutes before he was scheduled to meet Matt. After giving Mary a big hug and loud kiss on the cheek, Kevin sat down next to Mary. As he looked at her, he couldn't help but think, *Gosh, I love this gal!*

Mary smiled at Kevin and asked if he was ready for the big day. He grinned and said, "Sure I am, but it's you I'm worried about. Do you think the dress will still fit seeing as you are growing that little football right around your waistline?" "Oh, Kevin," she exclaimed, "I thought you liked my big tummy, now you've made me feel FAT!" Kevin grinned and in his most seductive voice replied, "Ahh yes, my sweet, I cherish every ounce around your tummy, and even every hair on your head, I do, I do, I do, and I am sure that no one but me and my attentive eyes will notice that you have put on that one little ounce!" Mary burst out laughing and told him that she was actually proud of her waistline; that she felt being pregnant was a gift from God!

"The dressmaker told me that she had made allowances for 'future growth,' so the fit of the gown shouldn't be a problem, and Sarah thinks it's wonderful that they will have photos of the new baby even before it's born. And, Kevin, isn't it wonderful that Rebecca, the most beautiful flower girl in any wedding ever, will also be in the wedding photos with us and the new baby?"

Kevin smiled at Mary and reached over to touch her stomach. He spoke to his 'son' saying, "You be good to Mommy today, care for her, don't give her any trouble, and come home and report to me later tonight!" "Oh, Kevin," Mary said, "You still think it's a boy?" Kevin just grinned for a moment then reassured Mary by telling her that it didn't matter, he'd be thrilled with a boy, or a girl, or both, or two of each, or two of one and one of another, or . . ." Mary pretended to hit him on his arm to let him know how silly he was. But secretly she was so pleased.

Kevin got up from the table to get Kevin and Mary's vitamins. Sarah and Matt took a very complete vitamin powder mixture and added to this some powdered ascorbic acid. They mixed these powders with water and took the recommended dosage three times a day explaining that the liquid was better absorbed by the system than a tablet would be. Matt and Sarah told Mary and Kevin how well it worked for them, so Mary asked her doctor if it would be okay for her to take and showed him a list of the ingredients. He'd okayed them but wanted Kevin to take them too, so he'd stay healthy. Kevin now mixed their powders with an ounce of açaì juice, and brought their glasses to the table. They drank it down and simultaneously said, "I feel better already." They laughed that they'd both tried to be funny at the same time, in the same way, and even with the same words.

"Oh, Mary, can we lend Elizabeth Grandma's manuscript before she gets too far into her own plans?" Kevin asked, suddenly remembering what he'd wanted to tell Mary. "I was thinking that if Elizabeth knew about the suggestions for a godly home that Grandma put together in the manuscript she wrote, Elizabeth would probably try to follow them." Kevin sighed happily when Mary replied, "Sure, honey, that's a great idea, but I'm one step ahead of you! I made copies of some of the pages in the manuscript and planned to tuck a copy of two of the lists in with the graph paper I am giving Elizabeth. I'll let her know it came from Grandma's manuscript and that she can read it when she finds the time."

Kevin replied, "You are such a gem, Mary, my precious, no wonder I love you, you read my mind and anticipate my every whim!" Then Kevin went on to add, "Mary, aren't you curious about the phone call Matt received, who the secret caller was, and what the surprise is for Sarah? I don't recall her ever mentioning a long-lost friend or relative, do you?"

"I don't know either, Kevin, but knowing Matt it must be pretty hard to hold something back from Sarah. He loves her so much and probably shares everything with her, so I bet it wasn't easy for him to make that promise, especially knowing that the stress of the wedding is already a lot to deal with."

Kevin said, "I'll have to tease him about that today when we are with the guys. You know, stuff like 'Ahh, holding out on your wife, ehh, Matt?'"

"Kevin, you wouldn't dare! That's mean, you know he'd never do that."

"Ohh, Mary, guys are different, they don't get hurt feelings, they don't get mad at some teasing, they're not sensitive like the gals, and maybe he'll even tell us guys the secret. He knows we wouldn't tell Sarah, or . . . you!"

"Now Kevin, are you implying that us women can't keep a secret and you men can?" "Never . . . . . would I ever tease you like that?" Kevin replied grinning, raising his eyebrows and pretending to twirl a mustache.

"I don't think Matt will tell anyone, Kevin, Matt is really a straight arrow. I think that if he said he would keep it a secret, he will keep it a secret from everyone."

"Yeah, you're probably right," Kevin replied, "because if the cat got out of the bag from some one else, even by accident, Matt would feel bad about it. Yes, you're right, he probably won't say one thing about the caller or the surprise. But that doesn't mean I won't tease him today!"

"Well, I'd better run." Kissing Mary goodbye, he added, "See you about 4:30!" and headed toward the door.

Happy with Mary's response and with the way his day had started, Kevin danced a jig on his way across the street to meet with Matt, Caleb, Joshua, and Jim, feeling that it was sure to be a special day for everyone.

Kevin had prayed with Mary before she left the bedroom to make their coffee. He had asked God to protect them today and bless their efforts with what was best for all of them. He felt good about that. It wasn't something they'd done in the past, and so they sometimes still forgot, especially when they were in a hurry. But Mary had put a note on the inside of the door, and it read, "Did you remember to pray?" This worked well and was helping them get into a regular pattern of praying before they left the house.

As Kevin started up the walk toward Matt's door, Josh pulled up in his sports car and parked. Matt opened the front door at the same time, yelling, "It's about time, guys, let's get this show on the road. Come on in for coffee and donuts, and Caleb will pray!"

Mary sat for a few minutes after Kevin left and then went to the laundry room to throw the wet clothes from the washer into the dryer so they would dry. She wanted to fold them and put them away before she had to leave. As she worked, she too thought of the man that she and Kevin had known in Kentucky. She too wondered how they could protect their family from the cruelty of people like him. So nice on the outside, even fooling his wife, yet so vindictive and cruel on the inside. Mary had been amazed at how smooth he could act. He'd looked right at Mary as he told lie after lie knowing Mary, like Kevin, knew the truth of the matter. He frightened Mary. Mary felt sorry for his wife, wondering if she also saw or had even been the victim of his attitude of evil and the vindictiveness of his spirit.

For we do not wrestle against flesh and blood,
but against principalities, against powers, against the rulers
of the darkness of this age, against spiritual
hosts of wickedness in the heavenly places.
—*Ephesians 6:12*

Mary didn't know that the same thought had crossed Kevin's mind earlier; but like Kevin, she was determined that she would learn more about the armour of God, about Satan, about principalities and powers that worked for evil here on earth, and about the promises God made to protect against them. Suddenly she felt a twinge of her old fear, but as she left the laundry room, Mary yelled, "NO!" to put thoughts of fear from her head. She was determined not to think bad things while she carried the baby. She wanted the best for her family, and with God's help, she'd get it! She knew now that she could control her thoughts and not allow those spirits in! She began to think of the carriage house and hoped that Elizabeth would want it to be done according to Grandma's suggestions so they'd all share in that blessing too!

Then Mary went to their office and from their desk retrieved a pad of graph paper that Elizabeth could use to create the floor plan of the carriage house. She also found a mechanical pencil with a good eraser on the end for Elizabeth to use. Next she went into the garage to Kevin's tool chest and found a large retractable tape measure. Mary thought that perhaps a small straight edge ruler to use with the graph paper might also come in handy and went back to the desk. *There,* she thought, *that should do it.* But then Mary remembered a magazine she'd recently read that had a template for furniture pieces on the back cover. *Elizabeth could cut these out and move them around on the floor plan to find a good arrangement for the furniture,* Mary thought and went into the family room to find the magazine. Mary went back to the office again to find some tracing paper just in case Elizabeth might need this too. She saw a nice little portfolio that also had a tie at its center to keep the contents together. She brought everything she had gathered into the kitchen and sat at the table to place everything into the portfolio to make it all neat, concise, and easy for Elizabeth to carry. Mary also tucked two of the lists from Grandma's manuscript into the portfolio, but before she did, she read both of them again:

STEP 5: WHAT DECISIONS WE NEED TO MAKE

1) We need to think about a place to have morning prayer with the entire family
2) We need a place to hold evening prayer with the entire family
3) We need a place for Bible study with the entire family
4) We need a place to hold family discussions
5) We need to consider where we can hold larger fellowships
6) We need a place to honor requests for special interventions of prayer
7) We need to determine where to share experiences of faith
8) We need to provide for prayer and short reading sessions with small children before they go to sleep
9) We need to decide where we will hold family projects/game time
10) We need to consider the comfort of the young and the elderly
11) We need to consider where we will have private prayer or small discussions
12) We need an area where discussions can be a lesson and a teaching opportunity

STEP 6: WHAT WE WILL NEED TO PROVIDE

1) Provide enough seating for family and friends, considering fellowships where many might gather
2) Provide comfortable seating areas as well as short-term pull up seats for fellowships

3) Provide seating spaced in such a way that family members can see and hear one another easily, giving special consideration to elders who might not see or hear well

4) Provide seating conducive to smaller children and remove distractions

5) Provide firmer, higher chairs with arms for the elderly

6) Provide lighting fixtures that allow good light for reading the Bible

7) Provide softer lighting that is conducive to quiet-time conversation

8) Provide the potential for private discussions, for one-on-one prayer; let family members know this is available

9) Provide a specific place for Bibles, concordances, and other spiritual material

10) Plan specific areas for daily family prayer, especially when rushing out in the morning

11) Provide areas for family games

As Mary finished her quick review of these lists, she thought of Elizabeth and how much goodness Elizabeth had already instilled in Rebecca's heart. *Oh,* Mary thought, *how I love Elizabeth. She thought only of Rebecca and me, to bring us together, in spite of her own personal concerns. She is just about the most unselfish person I know, and so very brave to move here like this, away from everything familiar to her.* Mary prayed silently, *Dear Lord, please let me envelop Elizabeth with love and make her happy. Let me never give her cause for concern. She is so alone except for Rebecca and us. Please let us foresee Elizabeth's needs for her new home and give her that joy.*

With that thought still in Mary's mind, Elizabeth walked into the kitchen and gave Mary a hug. "Big day for you today, huh?" she said. Mary told her that Kevin had teased her about fitting into the gown and about the dressmaker's caution of allowing plenty of extra material in anticipation of Mary's future "growth" before the wedding. "Even if the dressmaker has to let the gown out again today, she'll probably just do running stitches so she can let it out again before the wedding if it's needed," Mary said. "She left a lot of extra material 'in case you're having twins,' she said." Elizabeth grinned at Mary and replied, "I think you look great and even with a little more waistline . . . will look even better!

"Do you want another cup of coffee?" Elizabeth asked. Mary replied, "No, one cup a day is best for me, but I'd like to sit with you for a minute and show you what I've put together for you. Then I have to get ready to meet Sarah; she'll be driving today. The gals are going to have breakfast together at the diner before going to the dressmakers. Are you sure you don't want to join us?"

Elizabeth told Mary that she'd love a day of quiet and that she wanted to measure the carriage house and finish making the lasagna for tonight. She also told Mary that Rebecca was almost ready and would be out shortly. Mary waited until Elizabeth brought her coffee to the table before she began to open the portfolio and show her what she'd gathered for Elizabeth to use. She explained that she'd made copies of some of the suggestions in Grandma's "decorating" manuscript that Sarah and Matt had recently found and had tucked two of them in with the graph and tracing paper, along with a furniture template. "That's perfect!" Elizabeth exclaimed, "Thanks so much for getting it all together, and for the lists and template. I hadn't thought of a template, and I figured I might have to run to the store for the graph paper. I'm anxious to read Grandma's—"

Before Elizabeth could finish her sentence, Rebecca burst into the room, loudly exclaiming, "Ohhhh, pancakes and bacon, pancakes and bacon and *syrup*. Ohhh, I can't wait to get to the diner! Didja know they have *boysenberry* syrup?" Mary and Elizabeth smiled, so happy to see Rebecca's enthusiasm. They knew that a lot of changes were coming her way, some good, some heartbreaking, and they wanted so badly for her to be happy. "Yep," Mary said, "pancakes and bacon and boysenberry syrup . . . here we come!" and got up to hug Rebecca, then said, "I'm going to take some clothes out of the dryer and then refresh my makeup. I'll be ready in a few minutes, okay?"

Elizabeth walked over to Rebecca, put her arm around her shoulders, and told her she loved her. Then she reminded Rebecca to be good, and to be patient while everyone tried on the gowns for the fitting. She also reminded her to be sure that the shoes she bought fit well and were not too tight because her feet were still growing. "Ohh, Maaaaa, I will. Don't worry. It will be fun to be with everyone and listen to all their chatter. They tease each other, and they are always so happy. And it will be funny to watch the dressmaker again with Mary if she has to let the gown out one more time! Won't you come with us?"

"No, honey, but thanks for asking. I want to finish the lasagna for tonight. Don't forget, there will be twelve of us for dinner and that's a lot of lasagna! It should be lots of fun to be together. I want the food to be ready, so I can pay *rapt* attention to what is being said! I also want to measure the carriage house so we can begin the exciting job of planning our new home . . . and the perfect bedroom suite for you! I will also rest a little so I'll be rarin' to go tonight!"

"Ohhh, Ma, I am so excited about having a new room and decorating it in a more grown-up way, and it's really cool that we will all be living so close to each other, you, me, Mary, Kevin, Matt and Sarah. That will be great! But, Mom, please do rest, I love you so much and want you to stay healthy."

"I love you too, honey, and I will rest, I promise," Elizabeth replied.

"I guess I'll be back about 4:30, Mom, . . . maybe *very* fat from pancakes, bacon, boy . . . sen . . . berry syrup, *and . . . a big scrumptious lunch too*!"

"Now, wait a minute, honey, don't forget that there's also rich delicious lasagna and hot Italian bread tonight," Elizabeth teased. "Ohhh, Ma!" countered the slender little Becca.

Mary came back into the kitchen looking wonderful, her bright red lipstick complementing her gleaming coal black hair, her usual poncho, lightweight linen for the summer, hiding her pregnancy so well. After hugging Elizabeth, Mary said, "Hold down the fort for us, Elizabeth, and now don't work too hard and make sure you rest and relax a little! We'll see you later this afternoon." Then to Rebecca, "Let's go, sweetie"! And off they went. Suddenly the house was quiet.

Elizabeth walked to the window to watch them as they strolled hand in hand across the street. They looked so good together, and had a noticeable rapport, which made Elizabeth breathe a great sigh of relief. It would have been terrible if Elizabeth could not have found Mary and worse yet if Mary had turned out to be someone Elizabeth would have worried about in terms of Rebecca's future. *Thank you, God,* she thought, *for bringing us together. Help me to get through this.*

> *But He knows the way that I take;*
> *when He has tested me,*
> *I shall come forth as gold.*
>
> —*Job 23:10*

Chapter Five

DEBBIE, JOSHUA'S FIANCÉ

*But, beloved, we are confident of better things concerning
you, yes, things that accompany salvation, though we speak in
this manner. For God is not unjust to forget your work
and labor of love which you have shown toward His name,
in that you have ministered to the saints and do minister. And we
desire that each one of you show the same diligence
to the full assurance of hope until the end that you do not become
sluggish, but imitate those who through faith and
patience inherit the promise.*

—Hebrews 6:9-12

"Imitate those who through faith and patience inherit the promise,"
Debbie read from the open Bible on her lap. *Hummph,* she thought.
*That's what I wanted to do, but I've blown it. I've tried to imitate them, but
my own impatience and stupid mistakes have really messed it up. I am so
tired of trying so hard and getting nowhere.* Debbie closed the Bible and
began to cry as if her heart were breaking. *I can't keep doing this,* she
thought, *I can't try any harder than I've been trying. If it keeps going like
this, I will die from the stress.*

Debbie would give anything not to go for the dressmaker's fitting
today. She was so worried that she'd make yet another stupid mistake
somewhere along the line. All the others seemed to do everything

so perfectly, with so much patience. But she was too impulsive, inclined to move much too quickly, too often making mistakes in the process.

She longed to be more like them. She hadn't been raised with anyone who she really could say was a good role model for her. That was not to say that everyone around her had been bad, they weren't. It was just that those around her hadn't known these things she was now learning. This is why she hadn't learned as a child how to do certain things correctly, or do it the way God wanted it done. Her parents had never had any good role models in their own lives. Their parents, her grandparents, hadn't known the things that she was just discovering either, so how could anyone really fault her parents? It wasn't as if they knew and ignored it or threw it away. They just lived a totally different lifestyle, not bad, but not good, either.

Debbie didn't remember ever seeing a Bible, open or closed, in her home or in any of her relative's houses. They'd only gone to church on Easter and Christmas, and that was to what Debbie now termed a "feel good" church because it taught that the members only had to accept Jesus Christ as their Savior and they would be saved. Period. They didn't have to do anything else. They didn't have to try to stop swearing, temper the cruelty in their so-called teasing, worry about getting drunk, or losing a paycheck through gambling. There was never anything taught about overcoming, about learning then doing what God asked, about striving to become more Christlike in their nature so they could become a worthy bride for Christ. They were not taught any of that. But because of that, they simply never considered that perhaps God wanted them to change some of these habits. They went to church for the festivities and the music. They never tithed, never prayed that Debbie knew about, never sent their children to Sunday school or spoke about God at home. They didn't feel that Debbie needed church, or a college education, that it wasn't necessary to learn how to set a table properly, or even dress more appropriately.

They thought Debbie had her head in the clouds when she spoke of these things and finally they adamantly refused to discuss Debbie's "farfetched" ideas. Yet they were decent, hardworking, bill-paying people, who loved Debbie and each other, and in return Debbie loved them. But she always commiserated over the fact that they felt that for all of them life was fine just as it was. They were complacent. No matter what Debbie said, they remained complacent; comfortable in the way they'd always done things. Finally she gave up trying to explain.

Even as a child, Debbie had wanted to improve herself. She wanted a better life and was determined to work for it. In high school, she always worked hard to become an exceptional student so she could go to college on a scholarship. She knew that she would have to earn the money for college herself, she'd have to get a scholarship and also have a job while in college. But she wanted to do this. She wanted a college education.

Debbie had never been willing to be complacent about life, didn't even like to be around people who didn't look for ways to make things just a little bit better somehow, who didn't desire to "grow." She hated swearing, drunkenness, gambling, and crude remarks, and she loved calm and peace and goodness. She wanted a husband and children someday, but wanted a husband who would share the standards of behavior that she could feel were right for them; and more than anything, she wanted them both to teach these things to their children.

She longed for kindness to one another, not only in deeds, but also in words, everyday words spoken to one another, with no cruelty or crassness hidden in the guise of "teasing." These desires of her heart became an overwhelming drive in her that gave her the energy and the determination to forge ahead. She had to learn how she could make this happen in her life, but she knew she would succeed.

Because she couldn't find what she longed for at home, because she lived in the midst of the things she hated and had no one to talk to about her aspirations and her concerns, she never learned to trust others enough to share her hopes for the future. But she had persevered and had gotten good grades, so good in fact that she'd won the full scholarship to college she had longed for. That had been the best day of her life. She was filled with anticipation and she couldn't wait to leave. She had worked all summer sewing a new wardrobe for herself so she would "fit in" at college. She had lined up a part-time job on campus through the guidance counselor who had answered a myriad of questions, questions that Debbie felt would prepare her for her new life. She even began to listen for how she pronounced certain words, trying to detect and then change any bad habits. She was only seventeen years old at the time, but she hoped as only the young and brave can hope, that great changes awaited her.

Debbie met Joshua at college and was very impressed with him from day one. When he'd invited her to his church, she was surprised, but she agreed to go with him and really enjoyed it. Suddenly, listening to the minister, she recognized what was missing in her life . . . and in the life of her parents. *What I'm learning at church is like having a personal role model to teach me right from wrong*, Debbie thought. She wanted to learn it all. She wanted to fulfill every admonition and recommendation she heard. She wanted the peace and joy, the understanding that she could sense in these people.

Then, when it was time for her to meet Josh's family, she was impressed a second time. That clinched her growing realization that Josh's ways were the ways she would seek for her own life. It was through Josh and some of their friends at college that Debbie began to trust and to share her thoughts with others. It was a wonderful experience to finally have her thoughts understood and appreciated, even duplicated! She was no longer alone.

Then, as she and Josh spent more and more time together, she fell in love. She was doubly happy because she knew not only that she had a good man, but also that she couldn't ask for a better family than

Josh's family to marry into. As she had gotten to know them, she saw that while they had their human side, they also helped each other stay on the straight and narrow. They were there for each other, not sometimes, but always. Debbie also saw that there was never any hidden cruelty in the way they teased one another. No little jabs that could hurt. To Debbie, this was a real family, with real love for one another. She now realized that this is what she had always longed for, what her soul had been missing. It was, simply . . . kindness, love.

Evidently Josh had fallen in love too, because he had proposed to her last October. She could hardly believe it. She said yes so quickly that Josh hadn't needed to finish the dissertation he had prepared about how much he loved her and why they should get married! They had barely started their last year of college at the time, so they planned to wait until they had graduated and obtained jobs before marrying. Now, they had just graduated and had time to discuss their future and make their plans.

Josh was very demanding. He was a perfectionist. And he had a temper. But she was a people pleaser with a heart so big that she could forgive his every dictate. She could do this by deciding that he was trying to teach her to be like his sister Sarah and sister-in-law Ann, the only other women in his life. That was okay because that was what she wanted for herself as well, because she really looked up to them, and because she knew she had a lot to learn.

She'd already learned so much. She'd picked up many decorating ideas from looking at the way Sarah decorated her apartment, she'd seen Matt's sister Barbara make detailed to-do lists to be efficient. She'd also watched Caleb's wife, Ann, when she made salad dressing, and when she made spaghetti sauce, and when she set the table, so she could learn these things too. No cans to open for that woman! But Debbie loved every minute of it. She saw a great elegance in their behavior and saw their camaraderie, their love, and respect for one another. She desperately wanted to become a part of it and to feel that sense of integrity and community.

When she'd heard Caleb, Josh's brother, speak about his faith, she was impressed with his quiet strength and the force of his commitment. She wanted to learn more, so she listened carefully at church trying to get a better understanding of God and His ways. She'd even written down one of the verses she heard the minister use so she'd be sure to follow that instruction.

> *Beware that thou forget not the Lord thy*
> *God in not keeping His commandments and*
> *His judgments and His statutes.*
> *—Deuteronomy 8:11*

She was determined to live the right kind of life, and that verse pulled no punches, especially in its use of the word "beware". Recently, though, it seemed as if the harder she tried, the more demanding Josh became. She always could forget the occasional hurtful statements because he was soon kind and loving again and sorry for the harsh way he had spoken. But now, the hurt she felt from his more frequent remarks made her feel increasingly insecure and began to slowly, insidiously erode her self-esteem. Her loss of confidence was causing her to withdraw and not communicate in as lively a fashion as she once had.

This change in Debbie first disturbed, then angered Josh. One of the things he'd always loved about her was her zany spontaneity and bubbly personality. He was beginning to question whether the changes in her were a "punishment" to him, or perhaps a stubborn act of defiance, not seeing that the changes were really the reaction to a deep-seated pain. He didn't realize that for Debbie, there was a need to distance herself from the cruel words that reminded her of what she had lived with at home, and was now hearing from him.

Debbie began to develop an ever-growing fear that she would never be able to measure up to Josh's demands. Debbie didn't yet realize it, but Josh was beginning to do the very things that she had been running away from.

Debbie didn't want to go with the women today. She wished she could think of an excuse not to go. She had been feeling so insecure lately because she had not told them something she should have told them earlier. She was afraid that now they'd put two and two together and realize what she had done, what mistakes she'd made. They had discovered the mistakes, but so far no one knew who had messed up. She knew that they would figure it out soon enough, probably at breakfast. When they did, she didn't want to be there to face them. How could she have been so incredibly stupid and careless? She hadn't meant for it to happen. It was an accident. And she had tried to fix it. Now, she also realized that by not telling them right away, she had compounded her mistake.

Debbie was torn between telling them the truth now and waiting until later to see if her part in the problem would go unnoticed. She reasoned that because they all went to church and heard the same things she did, they would have to forgive her. They shouldn't be angry over an innocent mistake. But what if she was wrong?

But, she reasoned, *I will probably have to go today. After all, I am in the bridal party and I do need the gown fitted, and I want to be included in their circle. It's just that I'm afraid that they will be very angry with me if they learn the truth, and then will spurn me, dismiss me. That would hurt so much. If only I knew that they would teach me, help me, forgive me, I wouldn't be so darn afraid to tell them when I messed up. Then I wouldn't be so darn nervous. Then I wouldn't make so many stupid mistakes.*

Debbie didn't mind the work of making changes in her life; to her that part was both fun and very productive. It was the stress and fear that got her down and seemed to make her stumble. It was worrying that those she cared so much about would spurn her if they knew she'd made a mistake.

She had been pleased to make changes because she wanted to improve herself. Debbie recalled that early in their relationship Josh hadn't noticed how messy her apartment was the first time he visited her; at least he never said anything. Then when she'd visited his place and seen its neatness, even every can in the pantry was turned in the same direction, she was horrified and embarrassed by her own place. But she'd just gone home and fixed her apartment. It took two days of hard work, working at night, but it was well worth it, and now all the items in her pantry faced the same direction too.

After visiting Sarah's apartment, she'd been inspired to go to the thrift shop and find living room end tables that were more of a match to the other things she had. The apartment did look better now. But lately, Josh never noticed the changes she made so painstakingly. He would still pick on the small things. One day it was the direction that the toilet tissue came off the roll; another day it was the dust on a bottle of wine she'd had for a long time, and then it was how she would squeeze the toothpaste tube from the middle. She didn't mind being told these things. What was so hurtful was the *way* he told her, the sarcasm, the so-called teasing, and the fact that he said it in front of other people. Yet he never complimented her when she made changes for the better. He never even seemed to notice. Still she tried hard, but the more she tried, the more nervous and inhibited and withdrawn from him she became.

Eventually Josh noticed. Finally worried about the change in her once bubbly personality, he began to ask her what was wrong, but she was afraid that if she told him he'd be angry. He hated to be told anything could be his fault. Knowing this, knowing he'd turn it around on her when she tried to explain, she couldn't really make her point. Her words would come out in a jumble, and she would just make him even angrier. So she learned to remain silent, hoping things would soon improve, soon go back to the way they were earlier. After all, it hadn't always been this way between them; it had only been happening over the last few months.

Debbie felt that she related best to Matt's sister, Barbara, because Barbara always made time for her, went out of her way to include her in conversation. Somehow Debbie got the distinct impression that Barbara seemed to understand the things that Debbie had left unsaid. She seemed to emit a sort of empathy for Debbie, especially when Josh said hurtful things about her in front of everyone. Sometimes Barbara even chided Josh for doing it.

Barbara wasn't related to Josh, but being Matt's sister, she had gotten to know him at the many family get-togethers. Debbie had been wondering if maybe she should talk to Barbara about what she was going through with Josh and about the mistakes she'd made on the wedding arrangements. But just recently, when she'd met Elizabeth, Debbie had the feeling that Elizabeth had been able to peek into her heart and see her anguish. Elizabeth had taken her hand, squeezed it, and said, "You are very precious in the sight of God, Debbie, and precious to me too." Maybe Elizabeth would be the one who could help her.

Debbie felt that her heart was breaking, but no one seemed to notice. What could she do? How could she fix this mess she had brought upon herself? How could she fix what was wrong between her and Josh too? *I had no malice or ill intent in my heart . . . didn't that count for something? I've got to do something, I can't just go on like this,* Debbie thought, *I'll ruin the wedding, ruin my relationship with everyone. I've got to do something now before it's too late. Otherwise, I'll be devastated that I didn't try to fix my mistakes and my relationship with Josh.*

Suddenly, Debbie had an idea. Earlier, she had excused herself from meeting the women at the diner for breakfast. She had made arrangements to meet them directly at the dressmaker's then spend the rest of the day with them. She knew that Elizabeth would not be going. She asked herself, *Should I phone Elizabeth now and ask her advice? Should I drive there?* She quickly answered her own questions. *I can't go to Elizabeth's because Josh would recognize my car if he was delivering furniture to Matt's house.* Having narrowed her choice to phoning Elizabeth, impulsive once again, she picked up the phone to call Mary's house, hoping to reach Elizabeth.

When she spoke with Elizabeth, Debbie blurted out the news that Josh had broken their engagement last night and had stormed off angry. Once these words were out, she started to cry. It wasn't until she could compose herself that she could continue and tell Elizabeth how hard she was trying with Josh. Elizabeth listened carefully then said all the right things to calm Debbie down and make her less fearful. Elizabeth told her that she would always make time for her whenever she was feeling blue and needed a shoulder to cry on.

After reassuring her that God would be with her, Elizabeth told her to imagine it was Sarah who was in her position today as she interacted with the women, and then behave exactly as she believed Sarah would behave. She explained to Debbie that Sarah would interact with warmth and dignity, with quiet and reserve, and with faith that God would see her through everything, someway, sometime. This was amazing advice to Debbie. She loved acting and could do a good job of it. *Hey, if I could become anything someone wanted me to be, I must be a good actress,* Debbie thought. *I can do this. I really want to do this. Today, I will be just like Sarah would be if she were in my shoes!*

Elizabeth told her that to win Josh back, she must act as if it was okay with her that Josh had broken the engagement, but that she also needed to be patient and keep praying. "Dignity," Elizabeth said. "Let the ball stay in Josh's court for a while. I'm sure he will come back to you, but don't jump into a reengagement too quickly. Stand up to him, fight for your standards. Tell him that first you should see your minister for counseling, both privately and together, so you can learn to communicate properly about those things that are wrong between you, and then move to fix them."

"Remember," Elizabeth said, "with God all things are possible. If you both love each other, and I believe you do, God will bring into your life the way to mend this situation properly. But you must be patient and trust God to work it out. Give God time to do this. Believe me, Debbie, until you *both* really want to fix what is causing the problem, neither of you will be able to make things work out. And this can come only if you acknowledge what the problems are."

Debbie began to feel better and sensed deep inside her heart that everything Elizabeth said was right. She was determined to follow Elizabeth's advice to the letter. "Dignity," she repeated. "Responsive, but not ready to commit until things are worked out." And again she repeated the same phrase so she would not forget it. Then Elizabeth prayed with her over the phone asking God to help them.

Debbie thanked Elizabeth profusely, over and over again for listening, for advising her, for praying with her, and for believing in her. Elizabeth told her that she was only a phone call away whenever Debbie needed her and again assured her that she was precious in the sight of God and that Elizabeth and everyone else thought the world of her.

Relieved and encouraged by Elizabeth's kindness, Debbie opened up even more and haltingly confessed to her what she had not yet admitted to the others. The mix-up with the fabric, tablecloth, and chair styles had been her fault. After listening to Debbie's explanation, Elizabeth told her that she would have to tell them, and soon. She told Debbie that Barbara had already fixed some of the mistakes and the rest would be corrected today. Elizabeth said that they would forgive her, but warned her that a delay in telling them could damage their trust in her. She said that Debbie would have to tell them and explain that she would never withhold such a thing again. She told Debbie to pray about it before she left the house today and ask God to open just the right moment and the right setting for her to explain. "It may not be today," Elizabeth said, "but God will let you know when the timing is right, and it will happen before the wedding."

Elizabeth read Debbie God's words from the gospel of Matthew and told her to write down the chapter and verse, copy the words, and keep them with her all the time.

> *Ask, and it will be given to you seek, and you will find;*
> *knock, and it will be opened to you.*
>
> —*Matthew 7:7*

When Debbie hung up the phone after talking with Elizabeth, she thought deeply about what Elizabeth had just said. Elizabeth told her to bring her troubles to God, mistakes and all, then go today, as planned, to meet the women at the dressmaker's. Elizabeth promised her that if she were truly sincere, God would provide her with an answer, open the way to tell the truth, and direct her life to what it should be. Debbie felt a peace come over her as Elizabeth prayed with her over the phone and her hope was restored and once again, Debbie knew that God's way was the way she wanted to live her life.

Debbie decided to hang on to Elizabeth's words and trust her wisdom. She found the verse Elizabeth had read to her, wrote it down right away, and put it in her wallet as Elizabeth had instructed. Then she dried her eyes and began to get ready to meet the women at the dressmaker's. She was surprised when she realized that her fear was gone, and she was now looking forward to spending the day with her friends.

Debbie was parking her car near the dressmaker's shop when she saw the other women walk into the building. *Good,* she thought, *I won't be the first, but I won't be late either.* Relieved, she parked her car, and saying over and over to herself the word "dignity," she walked to the door. Without being aware of it herself, Debbie looked wonderful. She had showered, washed her hair, and blown it dry into its simple Dutch boy style. She dressed in black slacks and a silky cream-colored blouse with wide poet sleeves and wore a small, thin, black-and-white polka-dot scarf around her neck. She was only twenty-one years old, so she still looked just as fresh and pretty as a rosebud. Debbie also didn't realize that she had nothing to fear from the women. All of the women really liked her because they could see how hard she tried to put Josh first, how much she wanted to please them all, and how she had tried to fit in and become an integral part of the family. The women had also noticed that lately Josh seemed too nit-picky for his own good. They felt that Debbie would be a good influence on him. They didn't know that Josh was on the verge of a big mistake in turning away from Debbie.

Everything went well. The gowns fit well, except for Mary's, so the women went out of their way to let Mary know that everyone felt that all pregnant women were beautiful and having a baby was truly a gift from God. Since all the women were gathered together in a large private fitting room, Sarah decided they should have some fun while they waited their turns to be fitted. She suggested that each would take a turn running to a bin filled with cloth pretending it was a crib from which a baby beckoned them and then perform a different pantomime relating to the care of a baby. The other women were to guess what chore that was. Sarah began by pretending to be feeding the baby a bottle of milk. Rebecca jumped up after Sarah and pretended to perform a diaper change. Others acted out a bath, a cuddle, a walk in the park, a visit to the doctor's office, and Mary, not to be outdone, did an imitation of Kevin holding the baby for the first time. The pantomime of visiting the doctor's office, and of Kevin with the baby were the hardest ones to guess. Even the dressmaker had joined in one of the charades.

Still laughing and commenting about how immensely they were enjoying "ladies' day out," they left the dressmaker's to embark on their trip to the shoe store. Here, too, they had the greatest fun. Rebecca put on the most outlandishly high heels and tried to walk like a model. All the women roared when Sarah wondered if sneakers would work with her wedding gown. Barbara chose gaudy gold thongs with brightly colored sequins and beads and told everyone that these would be perfect for such a stuffy wedding and walked with her nose held high in the air.

Finally, getting serious, they all decided on a shoe that was simple in style and easily dyed to match the gowns. Barbara suggested making little bows for the shoes out of the same fabric that would be used for the sashes on their gowns, so even the shoes would look custom made. She explained that by simply using a small clip to attach the bows, they could be removed for future wear. Everyone thought it was an amazing idea.

The next stop was the florist. Within minutes they'd chosen the flowers and the colors, and Barbara matched the ribbons the florist would use to the sashes and dresses. Perfect. Since they were still suffering the effects of such a large breakfast, they wanted to wait a while for lunch. "Yeah," Rebecca said, "Pancakes, bacon, and *boysenberry*!" They all laughed and groaned, held their tummies, and in unison yelled, "*Salad* for lunch!" Because they had finished at the florist quickly, to stall for time, they decided to run to the caterer before lunch. They had to check on the chairs and the color of the tablecloths since there had been a mix-up in the order.

The chair problem was easily solved as well. What seemed like no time at all, they located the proper chair and copied the number by which to identify it. Then they asked the salesperson to remove the improper number on the invoice and replace it with the one that matched the number on the chairs they had just selected. They obtained a copy of the invoice so there would be no problems later on, making sure it also noted the right color for the tablecloths. Now, excited by the prospect of descending on the restaurant for lunch, the women left, arm in arm, chattering away about what they might order.

Once they were seated and each had received a menu, they saw how extensive the selection was. It took them all what seemed to be an eternity to discuss the options and make their final choices. It took much longer than it had taken at the florist or caterer, maybe more than both combined. They were all happy to be together, and their giddy conversation and laughter showed it. None of them were anxious to finish lunch and go home.

After they had finally ordered, Mary broached the subject of Sarah's mystery surprise, asking if she had a clue as to what the surprise could be. Ann, sensing Sarah's discomfort with the subject, decided to lighten the moment by suggesting that everyone make a game of it and make up the most outlandish surprise that could be imagined. Sarah smiled at Ann in thanks, and the game was on without anyone noticing what had actually transpired.

Sweet little Rebecca suggested that Matt had bought Sarah a huge yacht complete with a swimming platform. "Great idea," Sarah exclaimed, "and it will come with stylish captain's hats for each of us to wear!"

Barbara said, "No, that's not Matt's style . . . it's a brand-new Lincoln Town Car with Sarah's name in gold along its side!"

Debbie added, "Well, I think it's a gift certificate at the dressmakers for an entire new wardrobe so Sarah will always look right in style and elegant wherever Matt takes her!"

Mary thought that Sarah would receive a magnificent necklace, earring and bracelet set, probably in fourteen- or eighteen-karat gold. "The set will be crammed full of exquisite precious stones, perhaps diamonds and emeralds, or maybe rubies or aquamarines, or maybe all of the aforementioned! Oh, and it would also have a matching brooch, too," Mary added. Then she held her hands up and tilted her head as if showing off and modeling the most expensive jewelry. The women laughed at Mary's posturing, enjoying her "hoity-toity" pantomime.

Ann said, "How about a master gardener, hired for one year to do anything Sarah wants in the garden; fountains, walkways, retaining walls, flowers, trees, and even a tiny little greenhouse!" All the women groaned with yearning, knowing that this was every woman's dream!

Now that all the women had contributed their ideas, Sarah finished up the game, saying, "Well, I don't know why you are so sure it's a gift, but if I had to choose one of your suggestions, it would be Ann's . . . I love the idea of a gardener to do everything I'd want in the landscaping. I wouldn't have to be on Matt's back all the time for help. Wow!"

Ann, knowing it was time to change the subject, asked everyone what the latest plans regarding the carriage house were. Rebecca began to talk about how excited she was to be able to design a bedroom for herself. "I want a really grown-up room this time," she said.

"Elizabeth is measuring the space today so she can begin to make plans." Mary told everyone. "I gave her some lists that Sarah had from Grandma to provide her with some ideas about where to start. But Rebecca is to have carte blanche where her own room is concerned."

Sarah asked Rebecca what her favorite colors were and Rebecca adamantly replied, "*Not* pink again!" Debbie asked her what colors she was thinking of, and Rebecca said that because she didn't want to make a mistake in her choice of colors, she wanted to ask the women if they would make some suggestions.

Debbie suggested a soft, very soft, yellow with white woodwork. She said, "Maybe a white chair rail too. White crown molding and a white wooden valance over the windows would be a good backdrop for whatever else you would want in the room." Barbara added that she agreed completely. Because yellow was sunny, that color would be cheerful and bright and would fit in beautifully in the woodsy setting with all the green leaves and brown bark of the trees.

Sarah suggested that Rebecca consider one antique piece in the room, maybe an armoire, or perhaps a secretary desk, because this would definitely give the room a "grown-up" flavor. Caleb's wife, Ann, suggested a love seat or bench to make the room inviting to a visiting friend by providing some comfortable seating. To this, Mary added, "If the room is big enough, the love seat could also open into another bed for stay-overs." Rebecca squealed with delight, saying, "Wait, wait. Let me write this all down, I love it, I love it, I love it *all*!"

Debbie felt so good. Not only Rebecca but also everyone else had liked her ideas. She'd been able to participate without feeling too frightened, and just like Elizabeth had said, everything was working out. *Ohh, if only Josh would come around,* she thought, *if only he would miss me and realize that he loved me!* For the moment she felt herself sinking toward depression and self-pity, but she now knew how to stop it. Quickly, once again in her mind, she repeated Elizabeth's instruction to her: *"Dignity, warm yet reserved!"*

Then Rebecca grabbed her hand and said, "Thank you, Aunt Debbie, thank you, everyone," and she was fine again. She would trust, and she would be patient. And Rebecca had called her *Aunt* Debbie! That had felt so good.

Debbie had begun to release her stress and look to the women who had now become her role models, and her friends. She knew she did not want to lose them even if she lost Josh. Debbie began to grow from that day forward in faith, and in patience. Little did she know that God was already working on what He wanted to bring into her life.

> *Have you suffered so many things in vain-if indeed it was*
> *in vain? Therefore He who supplies the Spirit to*
> *you and works miracles among you, does he do it by*
> *the works of the law, or by the hearing of faith?*
> —*Galatians 3:5*

Suddenly Josh appeared at their table, asking the women, "What are you doing here, I thought you were all going to the dressmaker's, then going home for the big fellowship tonight?" Sarah took the offensive from her kid brother and asked right back, "What are *you* doing here, I thought all the fellows were moving furniture?"

Caught off balance, Josh forgot his question and answered Sarah's, reminding her that this restaurant was also famous for their subs. He had been sent on a special mission to bring the troops their lunch.

He told the women that he would be bringing sandwiches to Matt's apartment where all the men were to meet for lunch. When they finished lunch, they'd move on to the storage unit to pick up Grandma's furniture.

"Well, gotta go," Josh said, and Debbie again felt her heart sink. He hadn't said a word to her. But as Josh moved away from the table, he turned, winked at Debbie, and said, "You look great today, Deb." Debbie, remembering Elizabeth's words, quietly said, "Thank you, Josh."

Josh seemed surprised that she hadn't gushed her usual 'Ohh thanks, ohh thank yous' but had turned back to her conversation with Rebecca. "See you tonight," Josh said to no one in particular and walked to the take-out counter in the far corner of the restaurant to pick up the subs for the hungry troops.

Debbie continued her animated conversation with Rebecca about her room and asked Mary when the renovation would start. She never looked toward Josh. While he waited to order, Josh couldn't help sneaking a peek at Debbie, thinking how nice she looked, how poised she was . . . and how well she fit in with everyone. Maybe he had made a mistake in breaking it off. *Well*, he thought, *I can always fix it tonight.*

The women had noticed that nothing at all had gone on between Josh and Deb when he came to the table. Josh hadn't kissed Deb on the cheek, hadn't even acknowledged her until he was leaving! *That's not how you treat your future wife*, they all thought. While they said nothing aloud, they all were thinking similar thoughts. *Good girl, Deb, you handled that perfectly. He's a little too cocky, a little too sure of himself. He needs someone who will stand up to him, and then he'll be fine!*

Barbara couldn't help herself. When she caught Debbie's eye, she gave her a big smile and an enthusiastic thumbs-up. The other women, seeing it, smiled in approval without saying a word. *They noticed,* Deb thought. *They saw it, and they approved of me, they are rooting for me!* Her heart soared, and she hoped she would never disappoint them. Seeing the relief and joy run across Debbie's face, the women engaged her in conversation and tried to make her feel good by letting her know how much they liked her. Only Rebecca did not understand what had happened. Debbie now knew that the wheels of God turn slowly, but surely! Things would be different for her from now on, thanks to Elizabeth and God.

Chapter Six

JOSHUA

As Josh looked at Debbie from across the room, he couldn't get over how composed she was and how good she looked. She was the best looker at the table! In fact, she was the best looker in the restaurant. But she'd almost ignored him. He couldn't believe it! Thinking back, he realized she'd barely said two words to him, then she very politely ignored him. *What the heck happened? She didn't seem the least bit upset over the fact that I broke our engagement. She even smiled at me! What am I missing here? Didn't I make it clear that I was breaking our engagement? Well . . . yeah, I sure did.* In fact, thinking back, he would hate to have his sister or brother hear that conversation because he realized that he had been a real cad.

But Deb wasn't upset. Had I pushed her too far this time? Did she decide to move on? Did she have someone else? That thought made his blood boil and his stomach lurch. *But I'll be doggone if I will do all that give, give in, give-up stuff. Not me. I mean, gee whiz,* he thought, *I know what the Bible says about husbands, Caleb has drummed it into me long enough. Maybe after I'm married I can do some of that stuff. Right now, well I've gotta be the man here, the boss.*

"Sir, sir, I'd like your order please." Josh heard this voice as if it came from far away because his mind was elsewhere. It wasn't until the clerk repeated his request that Josh finally heard him. "What, what did you say?" Josh stammered. "Oh, my order, well yeah, well . . . ," and suddenly Josh forgot the order. He had to dig into his jeans pocket and hope the list was there. "Two roast beef subs with everything, two meatball subs with extra cheese, and one Italian, hold the onions. Also, five packages of chips and five large Cokes. To go," Josh read, his mind still half on Debbie.

Josh turned to take another look at the women, but they'd left. The table was empty. Josh would have to wait until tonight to find out what happened. *Oh well, I'll survive,* he thought, *no big deal.* But without realizing it, Josh was scowling. His stomach seemed a little weird for some reason. *Maybe I'm coming down with a cold.*

When Josh arrived back at Matt's apartment, the men were famished and after Caleb said grace, they dove into the food right away. They sat on the floor, having already loaded most of the furniture into the two trucks while they waited for Josh to return. After they wolfed down the subs, they sat with Cokes and chips in hand and began to talk, wondering how the women were doing on their rounds of dresses, shoes, and flowers. Josh never said a word to the men about seeing them. Then the conversation moved to the fellowship they'd all attend tonight, and how they all looked forward to the lasagna. "Yeah, but be warned." Kevin said, "Mary has planned that we will all earn our supper by first helping to make the salad! Togetherness, you know." "Well, as long as we can sip some of that sweet fruit flavored zinfandel while we are doing it," Caleb remarked. Suddenly Josh erupted into the conversation, saying, "Why do you guys take orders all the time? I tell you I wouldn't!"

"What's gotten into you, Josh? Making a salad together is a form of fellowship. We'll talk, and laugh, and tell jokes, and we'll all be together. What's wrong with that?" Kevin asked.

"You're all a bunch of wimps," Josh said angrily, then jumped to his feet and walked to the bathroom.

"What's gotten into him?" Matt asked, then answered himself, "He must have had a fight with Deb." "And lost!" added Caleb with a laugh. "He's got a lot to learn. He's still wet behind the ears. But he's got a good gal there. He's very blessed with Debbie, but he doesn't seem to realize it. I sure hope he doesn't blow it."

After taking turns in the one bathroom, they cleaned up the remains of lunch. Caleb, Josh, and Jim then headed to the storage unit. Kevin and Matt stayed to sweep the apartment, vacuum the carpet, and wipe down the kitchen and bathroom. When they had finished, they brought the keys to the landlord and headed over to the storage unit to help the others with the last of the items that had belonged to Grandma and had been stored until Matt and Sarah bought their first home. *Sarah will be thrilled to be surrounded by these precious items from Grandma's house,* Matt reflected.

Caleb, Jim and Josh had already loaded their truck with Grandma's furniture, so there were just a few boxes left to be placed onto Matt's truck. When they completed loading everything they left for Matt's house and in no time, had placed everything where Sarah's Post-it notes directed. Soon they were off to their respective homes for a quick rest and to shower and change for the fellowship at Mary and Kevin's later that afternoon.

When the men arrived at 5:30, they were greeted by the wonderful aroma of garlic and meat sauce emanating from the four pans of lasagna cooking in the oven. Everyone was freshly rested and showered. The men were dressed in clean jeans and sport shirts, the women in slacks and blouses. Except for Elizabeth! Elizabeth never wore slacks. Tonight she was in a nice crisply ironed dress. She looked rested from the nap she had squeezed in after making the lasagnas and then working a few hours on the carriage-house plans.

Becca had told Elizabeth all about the day she'd had and how everyone had made suggestions for decorating her room. She also told Elizabeth how they'd all done pantomimes about babies to make Mary less uncomfortable when the dressmaker had to let Mary's dress out . . . again! Elizabeth was happy and relieved to see that Rebecca was still excited by the day's events and that she'd fit right in with everyone, feeling comfortable with her newly extended family. Rebecca never told Elizabeth about Josh and Debbie because she hadn't understood what had happened.

Josh arrived a little while after everyone else, and for him, he was quite well dressed. He'd squeezed a haircut in between the time he'd left Matt's house and now. He thought he looked great and he was right. His eyes scanned the room for Debbie. Barbara and Elizabeth, who'd both been watching him from the moment he came in the door, and had noticed his new haircut, smiled to themselves.

Debbie looked absolutely wonderful. She'd pulled one side of her hair back and fastened it with a large colorful barrette that matched the red in her flowing blouse. She had on a pair of dark blue jeans, sleek, fitted, long and narrow, and wore a dainty pair of red ballerina shoes. She never looked up when Josh came in, staying busy at the stove stirring the extra sauce the men would probably want on the lasagna.

Josh waited a while, then walked up behind Debbie to say hello. Debbie turned, smiled, and cheerfully replied, "Hi, Josh, how are you?" Then taking a head of lettuce from Barbara, she moved from the stove to the island to deliver it to Caleb for shredding. Barbara, who had been watching Josh and had moved to help Debbie at exactly the right moment, was pleased at how skillfully Deb had moved from Josh to Caleb. She'd made it look so natural.

Elizabeth quickly stepped in and engaged Debbie in conversation at the island. Josh was left standing at the stove, suddenly holding the spoon with which to stir the sauce, not even knowing who had placed it in his hands. Again, he was dumbfounded by Debbie's action. Usually she chose to cling by his side, but tonight she seemed cool to him, maybe even cold.

Barbara gave Elizabeth a secret thumbs-up. Elizabeth smiled, knowing exactly what Barbara was up to, delighted that she now had another ally to help Debbie. *If Debbie and Josh were not meant to be a couple, so be it,* thought Elizabeth, *but I want Debbie to come through the breakup unscathed, and remain a friend to the family.* Barbara was thinking, *I want Josh to realize that he may lose something precious if he doesn't learn to be a little gentler, a little less macho.*

The doorbell rang, and Kevin ran to answer it. He found their friend John, a retired deacon of the church, at the door with his grandson Jayden. When John realized that Kevin had company, he apologized and turned to leave saying that they'd just wanted to invite Kevin, Mary, and Rebecca to the youth concert the next weekend. He handed Kevin a flyer that indicated the time, date, and location of the concert. Kevin insisted that John and Jayden come in to join their fellowship, and after much persuasion, they finally did.

When John was introduced to Elizabeth, he asked her if she had attended a health seminar at the library last week. She told him that she had, but looked puzzled by the question. John explained that he remembered Elizabeth, because she was the one new face there. Elizabeth did not remember John because he was only one of the many faces new to her. But with this interest in common, they began an animated discussion of what they'd learned at the seminar.

Rebecca and Jayden paired up because of their age, but because of their age they were shy with one another at first. Jayden was trying desperately to think of things to say. But in time they both relaxed. Rebecca excitedly told him about the carriage house she and Elizabeth would be fixing up and soon moving into. Jayden had envisioned a tiny cottage in the backyard, so when Rebecca took him out to show him the carriage house he was surprised by its size. "Cool," he said, "this will be like living in the woods and having all the privacy you'd want!"

When they returned to the main house, everyone was busy making the salad and bantering back and forth. When one of the women mentioned seeing Josh at the restaurant earlier, Caleb shouted across the room to Josh asking him why he never mentioned seeing the women when he got back with their subs. Josh, embarrassed, didn't answer, but Elizabeth and Barbara glanced at each other meaningfully, realizing that meeting the women, seeing Debbie, must have meant something to Josh. *Good sign*, they both thought.

When the salad was done, everyone but Mary and Ann began selecting their seats for eating. Mary and Ann finished cleaning up the kitchen from the salad making. Sarah began a game that the family often played, wanting to encourage John, Jayden and Rebecca to join in. "I have a few questions prepared, and whoever answers first gets to choose the largest cupcake with the most icing. I'll ask the question, then if no one guesses the correct answer right away, I'll give you hint number 1, and if no one answers then, I'll give hint number 2. I may also have hint number 3. You'll get three points if you answer the question right away, two points if you need the first hint, and one point if you've needed one or both remaining hints. Kevin will keep score." Sarah began by reading the first question on her list.

BIBLE QUIZ

1. Who was the first known (named) carpenter to be given specific measurements for something he was to build?
   a. Hint number 1: It was to be made of gopherwood.
   b. Hint number 2: It was to be three hundred cubits long.

2. What was the first item to be built with beautiful and specific decorations on it?
   a. Hint number 1: It was to have two angels atop.
   b. Hint number 2: The angels were to be of hammered gold.

3. Who was the first recorded designer/architect who gave his builder specific details for both the inside and outside of a structure?
   a. Hint number 1: He told him to make the entryway ten cubits long.
   b. Hint number 2: He told him to carve angels and palm trees on the walls.
   c. Hint number 3: He told him to decorate the interior with precious stones for beauty.

4. Who was the first recorded man asked by God to pay strict attention to the decorative details of a building?
   a. Hint number 1: He was to make wreaths of chainwork for the top of the pillars.
   b. Hint number 2: He was to carve one hundred pomegranates of wood.
   c. Hint number 3: He was to put the pomegranates on the chainwork.

5. The Bible speaks of curtains. What fabric were they and what was the color of the loops?
   a. Hint number 1: The fabric was woven from something grown in the fields.
   b. Hint number 2: The dye came from the indigo plant.

ANSWERS TO THE BIBLE QUIZ

1. Noah in building the Ark
2. The Ark of the Covenant
3. God, regarding Solomon's Temple
4. King Solomon when building the Temple
5. The fabric was finely woven linen and the loops were blue

John won. He had the most points because for most of his answers, he didn't require the hints. No one guessed the last answer so Sarah read it. She'd also read any hints that had not been used before the correct answer was given. Everyone loved the quizzes that Sarah came up with. They were fun. They got everyone laughing and in a playful spirit.

They were happy too, that a "newcomer" to their circle had won and that John had seemed to enjoy it so much. Caleb called out to Sarah saying that his favorite question of all time had been the one that asked who was the hairiest man in the Bible. "I know that one from Sunday school," said Jayden, "Esau!" Everyone applauded Jayden and John was proud that Jayden remembered what he'd learned in Sunday school.

"Elizabeth," John asked, "could you bring this quiz to our next health seminar and conduct the quiz for us? It would be a nice break from the sometimes heavy information we give out, and it might get more people interested in the Bible!" Elizabeth was delighted and said that not only would she be glad to do that but that she would look forward to it. Matt told John that sometimes they interjected some silly riddles and gave him an example. "What do you call a minister who lives in Germany?" When Matt saw that John looked perplexed and Jayden didn't seem to know, Matt answered his own question saying, "A German shepherd." John burst out laughing and agreed that sometimes it was great fun to be silly, and added that it might be a good idea to interject something light like that into the quiz for the seminar!

The next game they played was similar to the game Grandma had always played with Matt's brother. Either Grandma or Matt's brother would call out the name of an illness or problem, and the other would call out a remedy. They would alternate calling out remedies until one could not think of another remedy and would then lose the game. In this game, however, someone would rattle off a short Bible verse pertaining to a particular subject and the others had to stay on that subject. Caleb was going to start.

"Let's try to remember something we've read or heard that pertains to the relationship between husbands and wives. Even if you say it wrong, but get the gist of the verse, you get the point," Caleb said. "Okay, I'll start. God says to love your wife as yourself and wives, respect your husband!"

> *Nevertheless let each one of you in particular*
> *so love his own wife as himself, and let the wife*
> *see that she respects her husband.*
> —*Ephesians 5:33*

Matt remembered something about God saying man should not live alone but couldn't remember how the rest of the verse went. John quickly found it in the Bible that Mary had placed on the island and handed it to Matt:

> *And the Lord God said, It is not good that the man should be alone;*
> *I will make him an help meet for him.*
> —*Genesis 2:18*

Kevin remembered the one that said that men should not get angry quickly:

> *A wrathful man stirs up strife,*
> *but he who is slow to anger allays contention.*
> —*Proverbs 15:18*

Kevin ran for his desktop and opened to his computer's concordance as Sarah remembered the admonition to be kind and tenderhearted to one another:

> *And be kind to one another,*
> *tenderhearted, forgiving one another, even as*
> *God in Christ forgave you.*
> —*Ephesians 4:32*

Josh surprised himself by remembering one about how herbs for dinner could be better than meat if there was love with the herbs.

In just a few minutes Kevin found it, and Josh, very satisfied with himself, read:

> Better is a dinner of herbs where love is,
> than a fatted calf with hatred.
>
> —*Proverbs 15:17*

Elizabeth remembered one her husband had used a lot:

> There are many plans in a
> man's heart, nevertheless the Lord's
> counsel—that will stand.
>
> —*Proverbs 19:21*

Caleb ended the game with one he said was for all of them:

> But be doers of the word, and not hearers only,
> deceiving yourselves.
>
> —*James 1:22*

They all enjoyed the game, surprised that they had known so many verses that could pertain to the subject, and determined to keep learning. They loved games like this because not only were they fun, but they were also a good way to learn scripture.

Trying to be funny, Caleb called out to Matt to ask him what this big secret was that he'd heard about, and suddenly Matt felt terrible to have to keep this wonderful surprise from Caleb of all people. Caleb, Matt knew, would never breathe a word about the caller or the surprise; in fact he'd support and promote it!

But Matt had given his word, so he turned to answer Caleb quietly with the hope that his words would make Caleb get the message and drop the subject. He was hoping no one else would be listening to him. "Caleb, you can't imagine how much I want to tell everyone. But

I really need you, all of you, to look at this from my point of view. I was told something that I didn't really need to know. I was asked to keep it a secret, even asked to give my word that I would keep it a secret. It's simply a surprise for Sarah. So as much as I want to tell you, and everyone else, I want all of you to respect the fact that I can't tell you. Trust me, it will be okay in the end, and it will be a surprise for you too, one you will like." Matt's words caused a sudden silence in the room which made him realize that everyone had been listening to him after all.

There was no doubt in anyone's mind that Matt had spoken from the heart with total honesty. Everyone recognized that they would be asking him to compromise his integrity and hurting him by continuing to press on with their questions. Each one made the personal decision to try not to mention it to him again and Mary, to lighten the moment and take everyone's mind from what had just been said thought she'd better call the group to dinner.

"Time to eat," Mary announced, urging everyone toward the buffet line, and the conversation turned to the food at hand.

As Josh sat alone on the fireplace hearth eating his lasagna, Caleb joined him asking, "What's wrong little brother?" At first, Josh just grunted then when pressed again told Caleb that nothing was wrong. Caleb quietly stayed by Josh's side and soon, in the quiet companionship, Josh began to open up to him. "Why do you always talk about the weak role that God seems to want men to play?" he asked. Caleb, understanding Josh's ego was involved here, gently explained, "God gave men the toughest role, the one that only a man of strength could achieve."

"How's that?" asked Josh. "Well," Caleb said, "Christ laid down his life for us, for His church, for the children of God. In return, God asks that we become Christlike in our nature, that is to say that we lay aside our ego, perfect ourselves by killing our old nature. Believe me, this is tough to do. It takes a real man to do it, Josh. God also asks that we place others, friends, family and other children of God, ahead of ourselves not only to see that they are happy, but most of all to be an example to them so they begin to love us and develop a bond with us. Then they will listen when we teach, when we admonish, or if we have to tell them they need to make changes in their lives.

"If we don't have their respect, we'll never be able to help them grow as God wants them to. We can't demand what we want and have it last. They have to want to change. That might mean forgiving someone lots of mistakes, but it is our only way of obtaining their love, and their trust for the future. It's easy to cut someone dead, to drop them cold, to throw a harsh 'macho' word at them, but it's tough to earn respect by being fair, and kind, and forgiving.

"God tells us that because we make mistakes ourselves, we can never demand someone do for us out of our righteousness. But when we've earned their respect, they will want to follow our lead, give us their trust, and listen to what we teach. This is even more important to accomplish if you are a minister or a husband and have been given a responsibility by God. It's the toughest yet the most rewarding thing I've ever tried to do.

"Josh, you need to lead, not demand, you need to earn the respect you may already be due but have not yet shown you deserve. Be a real man. Get yourself in order first and then turn the other cheek. Love without conditions and give help wherever you can, especially to another child of God. This starts at home, after that it can fan out to family, congregation, and neighbors. Josh, I don't want to see you get married until you understand these things, but I'd sure hate to see you lose Debbie. She's really wonderful and so willing to follow the right guy. Forgive, and give, and you will be blessed. Trust me."

Josh was silent for a minute, then said, "Caleb, I love you, and respect what you have built within this family so much. I wish I could be like you. It's true that my own self-righteousness does make me look down on those who, in my own mind, have failed me in some way even when they've been good otherwise. It probably is my ego, but how am I supposed to change? I'd feel like a wimp. I'd feel like I was giving in on everything."

"Start with Sarah and me. Then move on to Debbie. We are the ones who love you and have the guts to tell you when you are wrong and we'd respect you enough never to do it in public. I know a minister for whom I lost all respect. He was so wrapped up in himself that he could not understand that sometimes things happen because of a comedy of errors or one stupid impulsive move that someone wishes they could take back. He was too quick to judge and simply decided, without question or explanation to cut me out. And he did so erroneously and destroyed the trust I had in him. How can someone like that minister to our souls? Therefore we have to ask ourselves, 'How we can minister to the needs of a wife or innocent little children who depend on us if we are like him?' It's hard, and I mess up all the time, but Ann loves me and supports me in my faith. She forgives me when I mess up. Sarah also loves me and forgives me when I make a mistake with her. But they also tell me when I'm wrong."

Josh replied, "Caleb, that's what's so frustrating to me, you always seem perfect. I can't even begin to live up to that."

Caleb quickly cut back in, "I'm far from perfect, and often get discouraged, but again you don't always see my faults because Ann and Sarah, everyone for that matter, covers me in my mistakes, never brings them up in front of anyone else. That encourages me to do better, so I don't disappoint them, and it also causes me to love them so much that I could burst. The main thing I want to accomplish is to gain your trust and keep it. I know that if I can maintain someone's trust, they will forgive my mistakes more easily."

"But, little brother, I can see that something's happened between you and Debbie, and I gotta tell you, buddy, it's you who has to make it right. Right or wrong, like it or not, God has charged you with that responsibility if you plan to marry her. Look at a minister. God has charged him with looking after His sheep. If he steps on their toes and cuts them, he has only hurt himself and taken away his own crown. As husbands we are just like ministers, we are the priests of our household. God has charged us to make sure everyone under our care, under our roof, are right on target with their faith. But why would they listen to us, if we're jerks, if they can no longer trust us?"

"You know, if you open up to Debbie and tell her that you're having trouble and need her help with this, I'll bet she'll be shoulder to shoulder with you. Sooner than you think, you'll be doing it yourself . . . and you'll be the better man for it."

Josh turned to Caleb with tears in his eyes, "Darn it, Caleb, I sure hope I am up for it, I hate to have you think less of me, but I don't know if I can do it. I guess it's true that I do trust you and that's why I'm having a hard time *not* making the corrections you are asking of me."

Caleb smiled gently at Josh and said, "Pray, offer, tithe, surround yourself with men who will talk about it, this will strengthen you and this, I promise you, will work. And Josh, from it will come the greatest peace, and the greatest joy. Nothing that life throws at you will harm you or those you love. When you trust God, you also learn to trust yourself. Think about it, buddy."

Caleb got up from the hearth to refill his plate and let Josh mull over what he'd said. He sighed with relief that he'd finally said what he should have said long ago. *Maybe, though, this is God's timing for saying it. Maybe now Josh is ready to take it all in. Please, God,* he thought, *help Josh do this.*

Josh, left to his own thoughts, acknowledged that ever since he and Debbie became engaged, he'd been grumpy and picky and edgy. He understood way down deep what Caleb was asking of him.

Debbie didn't understand it yet, but Josh knew that if he married, he would feel that he had to become more like Caleb. He honestly didn't think he was up to it yet. It meant a lot of sacrifice, and he was resentful of having to do that, especially when it hurt his ego. *I guess that's why I've been so rotten to Debbie lately. Maybe I'm not ready. Maybe I'm scared of the responsibility. Maybe I'm subconsciously trying to push her away because I don't think I can do this correctly.*

Josh's thoughts ran wild as he sat on the hearth finishing his dinner. He felt confused, tired, and angry all at once. These disconcerting thoughts made him angry with Debbie. If it hadn't been for her, he wouldn't be going through this right now. He knew that he couldn't be happily married and still be the way he was; he'd feel too guilty. But if he stayed the way he was, he might lose Debbie. He didn't want to lose her. It was a catch 22 that made him even more angry.

As he continued to think, Josh realized that his mother and grandmother had laid a very strong foundation in his heart and Caleb had been the role model for what Josh knew he should become. This is what he was really struggling with. He had to decide which way to go. He wasn't the type to be a fence sitter. This was a decision that he had to make before he got married. Debbie was not the problem. He was! He knew that now.

If my mom and Grandma, and my Sunday school teachers and youth leaders, hadn't been such strong examples to me when I was a child, where would I be today? Josh thought. *Maybe, I'd be in the bar, drinking, gambling, swearing, fighting, carousing, maybe even on drugs. I guess Caleb is right, they did what was right for me, and if I don't do it for my own family, who will? Will I be less of a man and leave that to my wife to do? If I did, I'd eventually resent it and then would my marriage fail because of it? Or should I never marry and have a family because I refuse to do it?*

Chapter Seven

REBECCA

There were two Rebeccas; the fourteen-year-old, only child, who'd been sheltered most of her life, and the young woman wise beyond her years from being steeped in the wisdom and strengths of her elders. One was still a little girl, alone, afraid, wanting to cling to her mother. The other was now a young woman, independent, developing new aspirations, surrounded by new role models.

Rebecca didn't like the way she felt. She could cry one day from missing her father, being afraid for her mother, and wanting to withdraw from all these new people. Yet the next day she could rejoice, completely forgetting her troubles, anticipating being with her new family, and happily participating in their conversations.

She hated the guilt that her ambivalence brought her. She was sometimes overwhelmed with a feeling that demanded she stay by her mother's side to show her love and loyalty, yet at other times she so easily succumbed to the joy and chatter of this exciting new family. Then, it seemed, she was willing to be apart from her mother to be with them. *How can I know what's right and what's wrong?* she thought. *My mother would tell me to be with them because she is so loving, giving, and unselfish, but I feel this sense of duty to spend every minute with her. Sometimes I hate the others because they are the cause of my disloyalty . . .*

even though I know that's a ridiculous assertion. Wouldn't Dad want me to take his place with Mom, and help her through all this heartache? How am I going to find out what I'm supposed to do, to think? Why do I feel so unsure, so guilty?

Rebecca's thoughts went back to her father and the many wonderful conversations she and Mom had had with him. *Everything he said was like an interesting story about life and hardship handled with joy and faith. When he was here, everything seemed orderly, life was predictable and safe, and the path to walk was clearly laid out.* Then she remembered the questions that had haunted her from the time he died. *Oh, why did he have to die? Why did God have to take him and leave Mom to face everything alone?* But now, thanks to Sarah and the journal she and Matt had written about life after death, she felt somewhat reassured, although the ache of missing her father was still there.

Just last week, Sarah had loaned Rebecca the journal she and Matt had written about Grandma's death and about their struggle over the death of Matt's brother. They'd titled their journal *When God Took Grandma Home.* It had brought incredible comfort to Rebecca, and she had shared it with Elizabeth as Sarah had recommended. It was one of the most interesting things she had ever read, and for the first time in her life she felt that she truly understood God's plan for those who die. It helped comfort anyone experiencing grief to understand that there was indeed a plan and a place and a reason. But nevertheless, Rebecca hated death, hated the pain it brought, hated her terrible fear of losing her mother.

She picked up the poem she'd written for her father so long ago and read it again, trying to gain some insight about how to think, what to do. Her words about the intense pressure and heat needed to refine gold, and the part about God never giving us more than we could carry and always bringing us through, comforted her. This made her thankful that she had kept the poem, thankful that her dad told her to hang on to those words. *But still,* she thought, *it doesn't answer my question about Mom. I can't help but feel that I should be with her every minute. Oh God, please make my mom better, make her happy; please help me to help her.*

Suddenly Rebecca made a decision. *I will be perfect. I will stay by Mom's side. I will go to church with her without a single complaint and listen carefully to what is said. I will make my bed every day, do my own wash, and learn to iron. I will always be perfectly polite to everyone, but never let them think that they can take the place of my Mom. I'll even study the Bible. Maybe, if I do all these things, God will make Mom better.*

If Sarah had known the thoughts that Rebecca had, she would have recognized that Rebecca was in the "bargaining" phase of grief. But Sarah didn't know, so Rebecca had to move through her grief without any help. Except for God's. In Rebecca's mind, a pact between her and God had now come into being. If He didn't do His part, she'd never go to church again, and it would be His fault. *God wanted everyone to be saved,* she reasoned, *so He wouldn't do that to her, wouldn't want her not to go to church ever again, especially if she kept her part of the bargain.*

Because this plan seemed to be exactly what she needed, she put aside the knowledge that she might not be doing the right thing by trying to coerce God into a deal. Her heart told her, from what she read in Sarah and Matt's journal, that she was supposed to trust God to have done in the past and do in the future what is exactly right. But, unbeknownst to Rebecca, purging these thoughts was part of the "denial" phase of grief. To seal this new pact she had made with God by an action, Rebecca left her room and went into the kitchen to make a cup of tea with which to surprise her Mom. Rebecca felt good again, somehow relieved by having a purpose, a plan, relieved that she made a deal with God despite what the journal said.

When the tea was ready, Rebecca carried it into the living room where her mother sat with the Bible in her lap, and after handing

Elizabeth the cup of tea Rebecca sat at her feet with her hand on her mother's knee. "Well," Elizabeth asked, "to what do I owe this wonderful, sweet, kind gesture?" "Nothing special, Mom, only a little something to tell you you're terrific," Rebecca replied. Elizabeth smiled at her and with her free hand stroked her daughter's head thinking how truly blessed she was to have her.

"What are you reading, Mom? Rebecca asked. "Why don't you read it to me, and tell me what everything means?" *There*, she thought, *I hope God sees that I'm keeping my bargain.*

Elizabeth was pleased by what Rebecca said, but she also wondered what thoughts were going on in this little teenager's head to bring about these actions. *But*, she thought, *I'm not going to look a gift horse in the mouth; I'm going to savor every minute of her thoughtfulness!*

"Well . . . . ," Elizabeth said, "I've been kind of fascinated by some passages I've been reading where God is giving instructions to Solomon for building the temple. I was particularly taken with the verses that address the adornment of the interior of the temple. I guess it caught my interest because we are going to be designing the interior of the carriage house. It's reassuring to know how much God enjoys a lovely environment, and how particular He was about the temple's décor. Listen to this, Becca:"

He made wreaths of chainwork, as in the inner sanctuary and put them on top of the pillars; and he made one hundred pomegranates, and put them on the wreaths of chainwork.

—2 Chronicles 3:16

And he made the veil of blue, purple, crimson, and fine linen, and wove cherubim into it.

—2 Chronicles 3:14

*Their knobs and their branches shall be
of one piece; all of it shall be one piece of
hammered pure gold.*

—*Exodus 25:36*

"I think it's so fascinating to know that God takes such an interest in design and in proportion. I learned some of this from a manuscript that Sarah's grandmother wrote. Grandma points out that scripture tells us that God ordered very specific sizes for the various structures He wanted built. The Bible is so magnificent. Whatever you need can be found there . . . even about decorating!" Elizabeth exclaimed. "We'll have such fun together making our choices and designing our space, and you'll have the added bonus of helping design the art studio!"

"Well, Mom," Rebecca replied, "I don't think I'll be spending much time painting, I'd rather spend time with you. But yeah, we will have fun together as we design our space and choose colors and stuff. Maybe just the two of us can do it and get to spend a lot of time together."

Elizabeth wondered what was behind Rebecca's statement about not spending any time painting but spending a lot of time together. Suddenly, thinking of her words, "I'd rather spend time with you" and "spend a lot of time together," Elizabeth knew! Becca was worried about her, Becca was frightened! Touched to the core by Rebecca's concern, but ever thinking of others, Elizabeth realized she would have to figure out how to solve this really serious situation. She would need to figure out what would be in Rebecca's best interest and how to calm her fears.

Rebecca carried her mother's empty tea cup to the kitchen, rinsed it, and placed it in the dishwasher feeling very proud of herself for doing what was right, for being thoughtful, for living up to the bargain she'd made with God! Then she went back to the living room and, again hoping to please Elizabeth, began to ask questions about how a person knows what they should place in a room, other than the things like a bed and dresser that denote the basic function of the room.

Elizabeth, now fully understanding Rebecca's motives, decided to answer her question briefly then move the conversation to Becca's wants and needs for her own bedroom. "Well, honey, I guess you do start with the function of the room and meet those basic needs. Then perhaps you would develop a wish list of other items you might like, determine how much space you have to accommodate those extras, and go from there. You mentioned that at lunch yesterday you'd loved the idea of yellow walls and a love seat that converted into a bed. What else?"

"Mom, it was so great, so many ideas were presented, and I really liked them all, but I don't know how to put them together so I would end up with a room like you'd see in a magazine, yet comfortable and useable. They mentioned a chair rail, whatever that is, and crown molding . . . and . . . and a wood valance. And then, after I did all this stuff and got all the furniture in, how will I know how to choose the bedspread and drapes and other stuff that have to match?"

"Whoa, slow down, honey, that's a lot of questions all at once. Here's what I know about decorating: crown molding is the wood strip that goes around the top of the room between the ceiling and the walls. A chair rail is a flat molding that goes around the walls of the room about table height from the floor. It is very useful because it allows you to paint the wall two different colors or wallpaper one part. It was originally used to prevent the hard wood backs of the chairs from damaging the softer plaster of the walls.

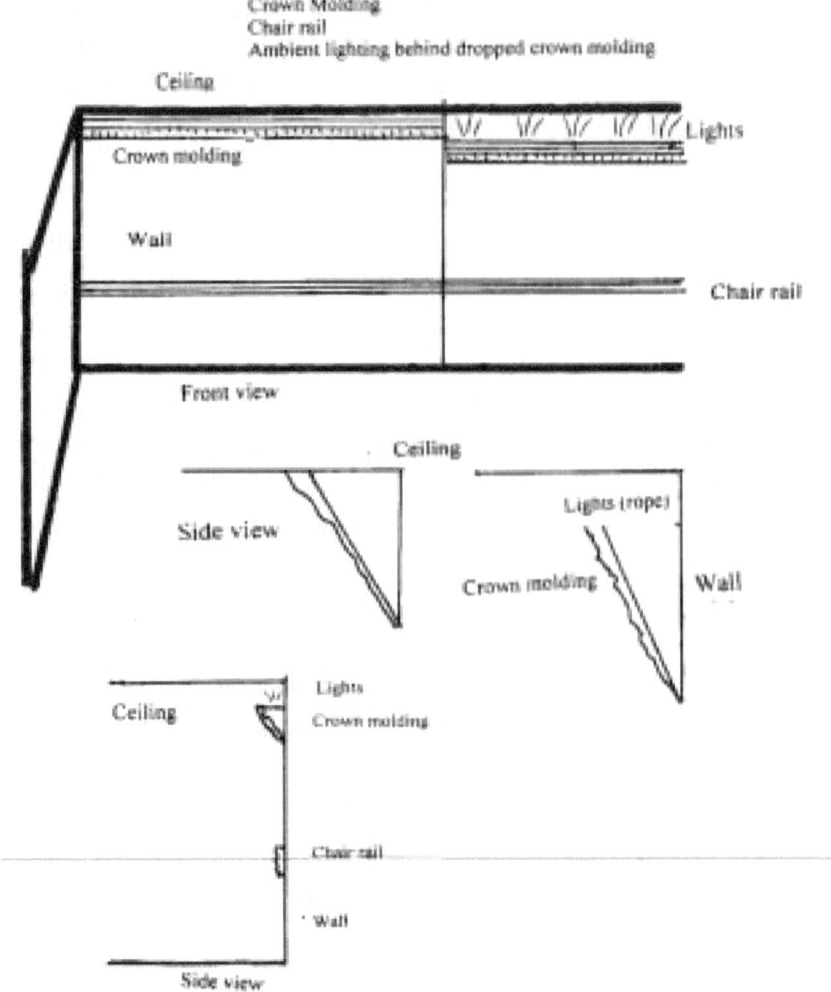

Crown Molding
Chair rail
Ambient lighting behind dropped crown molding

Ceiling

Crown molding

Wall

Lights

Chair rail

Front view

Ceiling

Side view

Lights (rope)

Crown molding

Wall

Ceiling

Lights

Crown molding

Chair rail

Wall

Side view

"A wood valance is usually a sort of three-sided box that is secured above the windows to hide the curtain rods. When these three elements match the other moldings like baseboard, door and window trim, and even the doors themselves, this creates an architectural interest. This can be more interesting than having everything non-contrasting. Remember how Matt and Sarah did this in their house? They created all those wood elements in the house that matched each other, then painted the walls a complementary color so the house was already beautiful and interesting even before they put their furniture into it. Does that make sense to you? Here, let me make a little sketch for you."

"Ma, I love Sarah's house, and I do love all that wood, but I think because ours is in the woods, ours shouldn't be dark wood like Sarah's. And maybe I'm not really the formal type."

"Honey, yours could all be white. A semigloss white, which has a nice sheen, is beautiful, makes it's own architectural statement, and is chic, yet can be informal based on what style furniture you use. Sometimes we don't know what we like or how to verbalize what our vision is. In this case, 'a picture is worth a thousand words.' Design magazines have pictures of settings that you might like. With these, we can get a feel for those things you do like, your 'hopes and dreams and wishes.' Remember that it is also possible to combine different elements and different styles."

"We should make a list of what our needs might be. I was thinking for instance, since you love to read, that you might want to consider a built-in bookcase of wood, painted to match the moldings you mentioned. It could have storage in the bottom with doors, and open shelves on the top. It would become a beautiful architectural element, but also be very functional."

"I love that idea, Mom."

"Honey one other thing, if the word of God and our desire to fulfill that word are more important to us than the possessions we accumulate, we can feel safe in accumulating and using those possessions. But if they do become our focus or identity in life, we may be called to relinquish them, as the young man in the Bible was asked to do. We have to be watchful that the 'things' we have or want are never more important than seeking God's word, learning what He asks of us, and actually striving to do those things. Let's look up that verse about the young man; I think I remember that it's in the gospel of Matthew."

Jesus said to him, "If you want to be perfect,
go, sell what you have and give it to the poor, and you
will have treasure in heaven; and
come and follow me."

—Matthew 19:21

"Christ had to say this because He could see that the young man was too attached to his possessions. Only when we can give them up, can we keep them. Remember what God asked of Abraham?"

"That he kill his son?" Rebecca asked.

"Yes, it was a test to prove that Abraham, despite loving his son with all his heart, loved and trusted God more. Abraham had longed for a son for many, many years and when God finally gave him the son, but not until Abraham was very old, Abraham truly cherished him. Then God tested Abraham, knowing Isaac was most important to him. Because Abraham was willing to give his son Isaac to God despite the pain this would cause him, and because his trust in God was so perfect, God could let Abraham keep him."

"Boy, I hope I'm never tested that hard," said Rebecca. Suddenly Rebecca wondered if she was supposed to tell God she would allow Him to take her mother from her, and this thought frightened her. So she quickly changed the subject and said, "Mom, tell me more about what the Bible says about decorating."

"Well, honey, while Noah was the first carpenter we meet in the Bible, surely King Solomon was the interior designer of the Bible. King Solomon used woods, gems, metals, and other materials from many lands and cultures, in building the temple. But it was King David, Solomon's father, who developed the plans for the temple through inspiration from God. King David also amassed many of the materials for the temple that Solomon was to build. David had wanted, with all his heart, to erect the temple in honor of God whom he loved so much, but David's sin was too great. David was disappointed when God told him that because of his sins, he could not erect the temple. But God loved David and told him that the plans he had inspired in David for constructing the temple would be carried out nevertheless and that David's son Solomon would build the temple. Thus, David began to amass those things he thought would contribute to making the temple beautiful. Let's look up those verses in the Bible so we can read how David felt."

> *"All this," said David, "the Lord made me understand*
> *in writing, by His hand upon me, all the works of these plans."*
> *And David said to his son Solomon, "Be strong and of*
> *good courage, and do it; do not fear nor be dismayed, for the*
> *Lord God—my God—will be with you. He will not leave*
> *you nor forsake you, until you have finished all the work for*
> *the service of the house of the Lord."*
> —*1 Chronicles 28:19, 20*

"King David gathered around him all the priests, the leaders, and the craftsmen that he had hand chosen to help Solomon in building the Temple. He then told them of all the materials that he had gathered for the temple."

> *Furthermore King David said to all the assembly:*
> *"My son Solomon, whom alone God has chosen, is young*
> *and inexperienced; and the work is great, because*
> *the temple is not for man but for the Lord God."*
> —*1 Chronicles 29:1*

> *Now for the house of my God I have prepared*
> *with all my might: gold for things to be made of gold,*
> *silver for things to be made of silver, bronze for*
> *things to be made of bronze, iron for things to be made*
> *of iron, wood for things to be made of wood,*
> *onyx stones, stones to be set, glistening stones of*
> *various colors, all kinds of precious stones,*
> *and marble slabs in abundance.*
> —*1 Chronicles 29:2*

"As you read the details regarding the building of the temple, you will be amazed at God's interest and direction in every area of construction from plans to carvings, from columns to curtains. Do you have any questions about anything I just told you?"

"No, Mom, but I do have to admit that all the things you've just shown me have really interested me. The Bible doesn't seem so dull right now. That was really cool. Maybe we could do this every day until I learn what you want me to learn."

Up until this last sentence, Elizabeth had felt content, but here again was a little clue that something was bothering Rebecca. Elizabeth needed to find out exactly what that was. She needed to make sure Rebecca would be alright.

"Honey, that would be great, I'd like that. Maybe we could also occasionally invite someone else to join us as we read the Bible, what do you think? This way we'd be sharing the word, helping each other learn, and participating in fellowship with other believers as God wants us to do."

Elizabeth wanted Rebecca to establish other relationships, close ones, so that if anything happened, Rebecca wouldn't be alone. She would have others to lean on. Elizabeth wanted them to be people who had a strong faith in God and would continue to nurture Rebecca's faith.

Rebecca had a flash of insight. She had always felt that her mother cherished the time they spent in discussion together, but now she suddenly realized that her mother, always thinking of Rebecca's best interests, also wanted her to get close to other people. So even though Rebecca wanted this time alone with her mother, she agreed with what her mother had just said. After all, she'd made a pact with God. She was bound and determined to keep her end of it.

"Okay Mom, that sounds great, but how about every now and then it's just us?" When Elizabeth smiled in agreement, Rebecca continued, asking, "Who do you think we should ask to join us?" "Let's ask just a few people, maybe Debbie, John, and Jayden, what do you think?" Elizabeth replied. Rebecca agreed. She really liked Debbie, and they were only a little over six years apart in age! John knew a lot about the Bible and would be good company for her Mom. As for Jayden, well, he'd be okay because he was so quiet anyway.

Elizabeth suddenly jumped up, ran to a book she had left on the other table, and from it pulled a poem she'd kept from an old magazine. "Honey, I want you to read this . . . it sort of speaks to our great project of building and decorating the carriage house. Can you type it up on your computer, and make some copies so we can give one to Mary and Kevin, Sarah and Matt, and anyone else who would like a copy?"

Rebecca took the slip of paper and began to read:

Precious Seeds

Despite the chaos in the world, our hearts are filled with peace,
as we're gently, gently sheltered, and all our stresses cease.
We gather at the end of day at home, our place of rest,
the earthly home God's given, one His love has blessed.

We've built our little Bethany through God's amazing love,
being doers of His word, thus gaining gifts from God above.
But it wasn't at the onset, before His word we sought,
we understood the battle for our soul that Satan fought.

We did not place our life and soul into God's hand so kind.
We'd only known the word of God with our imperfect mind
until we finally realized we could do nothing on our own,
and let the precious seeds of His wondrous words be sown.

—Helen Gumienny Glowacki

"That's really beautiful, Mom, the others will like it too. I'll type it up now, if you'll lie down for a little while, deal?" Elizabeth agreed, happy with the time they'd just spent together.

Before Elizabeth could get up from her chair, Rebecca remembered something she'd wanted to tell her mother. Almost forgetting she'd wanted her mother to lie down, Rebecca said, "Oh, Mom, I just want to show you something first, I'd forgotten about it until now and talking about God's designing made me think of it. I did a short one-page report in school just a while ago that explained how color was made in those times. Let me get it and show you." And Rebecca ran into her room to retrieve the report she'd written.

HOW COLORS ORIGINATED

It is interesting to note how color was originally produced. In earlier times, color was a precious commodity, available only to those who could purchase the various dyes from caravans traveling through their area selling herbs and spices from other regions. It was through trial and error that the people of earlier times found various materials that could be used for dying fabrics. In Biblical times, most of these materials came from plants, some from shells, some from insects, and others from the bark of various trees. For example:

1) Purple came from the Murex shellfish caught off the Phoenician Coast.
2) Blue came from the indigo plant.
3) Red was obtained from the madder plant and a scale insect, kermes.
4) Yellow came from boiled plants such as almond leaves.
5) Olive greens also came from certain plants.

6) Pomegranate bark produced black.
7) Other barks and nutshells produced shades of browns and tans.
8) Yellow overdyed with indigo produced a deep green.

Traders and merchants sought the materials that would make the dyes that produced the various colors. When the materials needed for making the color were rare, the color became more valuable. With an ever-increasing demand for the dyes, a vocation evolved that provided an income to those who could find these materials and make the dyes. And the art of color was born.

"Isn't that cool to know, Ma? I found the information in a book from the library." Elizabeth was pleased and suggested that Rebecca show her paper to the other women when they got together again.

As Rebecca walked her mother to her room, she asked, "Mom, do you have any idea what the big surprise could be for Sarah that everyone is talking about?"

"No, honey, I haven't a clue. We really don't know anyone outside of those at last night's party, so it's hard to even venture a guess."

"But, Mom, maybe it doesn't have anything to do with a person, maybe the caller was a salesperson, and maybe it's like a piece of jewelry or something that Matt ordered for Sarah to give her on their wedding day."

"Perhaps you're right, Becca. That's very possible. But then again, if that were so, why would Matt have said that he was asked by someone else to keep the secret?"

"Oh yeah, I forgot about that part, Mom. Maybe someone else is going to give them both some kind of a special gift."

"That theory does fit well with everything Matt has said. Well, we'll just have to wait and see. I guess we'll know pretty soon."

"Okay, Mom, I want you to rest now."

Rebecca kissed her mother's cheek before she left, then went into her room to begin typing up the poem. *My mom is such a special person, God just couldn't,* couldn't *take her away! If He does I'll* never *go to church again!*

Chapter Eight

JOHN

When John arrived at Kevin's house last night to deliver the flyer for the Youth Concert, he never expected to end up attending such a wonderful gathering. He'd been delighted to be asked to stay. He was even more delighted to find Elizabeth there. He'd first seen her at the health seminar, but had not been able to have a conversation with her when the meeting was over. She had seemed such a down-to-earth, no-nonsense person. From her questions and comments, he could see right away that she had a strong faith in God and a very big heart.

He was still thinking about her when he arrived home from that meeting. She had left early while he was busy with the guest speaker. He knew her name was Elizabeth, he had seen her nametag. But he hadn't asked her where she lived, if she would be attending the next seminar, even her last name. Without this information, he had no way of contacting her. The next seminar wouldn't be until next month, and he couldn't even be sure that she would be there. He'd liked her. He wondered what her interest was, why she'd attended the seminar. He'd seen that she took a lot of notes and wondered what information she was seeking. He hoped he'd get to see her again . . . and this time he would ask her last name and where she lived.

John's wife had died about ten years ago after a long illness. Since then, John volunteered his help at some of the local hospitals, clinics, and health seminars, and actively sought to learn about new techniques and medicines, especially the natural medicines that could help in many different illnesses. During this quest, John made a close and dear friend of a naturopathic physician and became an ardent supporter of the benefits of good nutrition and the use of vitamins and other supplements to enhance good nutrition.

His wife had died from Lou Gehrig's disease, also known as ALS or amyotrophic lateral sclerosis. It was a terrible disease, cruel, insidious, fatal in two to ten years after being detected. Its symptoms were the progressive death of the nerve cells that control the muscles. Muscles cramp or twitch, limbs lose strength, feet and ankles become weak, swallowing, speaking, and breathing become difficult, and great fatigue exists. Finally, unable to swallow, death comes to its victims who are paralyzed but still fully cognizant and able to think, see, hear, smell, taste, and touch perfectly.

As John recited this information in his mind, he could hear his own residual bitterness, surprised that after all these years he hadn't gotten over that. This disease had killed his wife, and he hated it with every fiber of his being.

It had been very difficult for John to watch his wife's slow decline; he'd felt helpless. Then he'd gone through a period of anger, first at the disease, then at God for allowing it. Finally, months after she died, he accepted her death as God's will. But he still asked God to show him why he had needed that experience, why he had been the one to remain living, and most of all, why his wife had to suffer through such a terrible, slow death. It wasn't fair to her. *It wasn't fair!* So he searched and finally demanded answers from God, telling Him he would accept everything if only He would explain why it had to be the way it was. John felt that there had to be some specific reason, something he was supposed to do or know from this, but he didn't know what it was. He ended up just volunteering to help where he could, but still asked God, every day, why his questions hadn't been answered.

John also kept busy with church work. He was a great evangelist, an easy testifier of the gospel. He had excellent communication skills, an ability to understand people, and a genuine interest in their well-being. He didn't have his own ego to fight so forgave easily and listened well. He also had learned a great deal about and from the Bible. He had been a deacon in the church, but had given up his office to spend more time with his family.

His daughter, a single mom, needed him now that she was divorced and raising her son alone. His grandson Jayden needed him to be his male role model. John kept after Jayden about his school grades and about attending church and the church's youth activities. It had paid off! Jayden now went to church because he wanted to. That was a true blessing!

He and Jayden often got into debates about what passages in the Bible applied to today's world, to modern day circumstances. It was great fun and a wonderful learning tool for Jayden. Even Jayden admitted to being impressed as he saw he could apply scripture written thousands of years ago to a need he had today.

John was almost bald. He had a fringe of hair around the perimeter of his head and kept it trimmed short, hating the look of men who let the one side grow really long to comb up and over the bald head. *Ridiculous,* he'd think, *don't they see how it looks from the side, how fake it is, how easy to spot, how the wind sometimes picks it up in one plastered piece, and it hovers there like a spear? How vain, and how dumb not to know you look better bald!* Then he stopped himself, thinking: *You know, John, you're saying this, making this cruel judgment, and yet you wore your own hair that way for a long time . . . maybe that's why you're so judgmental of others who do it. If Jayden hadn't told you how bad you looked, you'd still be doing that comb-over today! Better cool it before you get into trouble with the Lord.*

Jayden was the apple of his eye. John had worried when Jayden's father turned to drugs and dragged the family into a financial hole. A divorce finally had to take place. He'd counseled his daughter. He'd told her that

God did not want her to be unequally yoked. John had even typed up that special verse from the Bible so she could refer to it when she was feeling badly or was overwhelmed by the fear of being completely on her own.

Do not be unequally yoked together with unbelievers.
For what fellowship has righteousness with lawlessness?
And what communion has light with darkness?
And what accord has Christ with Belial?
Or what part has a believer with an unbeliever?
And what agreement has the temple of God with idols?
For you are the temple of the living God.
As God has said: "I will dwell in them and walk among them.
I will be their God, and they shall be my people."
Therefore "Come out from among them and be separate, says the Lord.
Do not touch what is unclean, and I will receive you.
I will be a Father to you, and you shall be my sons and daughters,"
says the Lord Almighty.

—*2 Corinthians 6:14-18*

John loved that scripture; it had helped so many people struggling with the decision to leave someone who chose not to come to the Lord, but to continue to do things associated with evil. He had talked himself blue in the face trying to help his son-in-law, but had finally given up when he made promise after promise and then did what he wanted the minute John left him. He was one of the most selfish men John had ever met. He lied without remorse, knowing full well that what he was saying was a lie. He set a terrible example for Jayden and didn't even care! What was worse, he not only would not encourage Jayden to go to church, but in fact often stood in the way by asking to see him when Jayden should be in church or at a youth function. John had even sent him two Bible verses about his responsibility to Jayden's spiritual life to try to reach him, but it was like talking to a wall.

Train up a child in the way he should go,
and when he is old he will not depart from it.

—*Proverbs 22:6*

You shall teach them to your children,
speaking of them when you sit
in your house, when you walk by the way,
when you lie down, and when you rise up.
—Deuteronomy 11:19

When John learned that Jayden's father wasn't even paying the paltry child support the court had ordered him to pay, he made the decision to put all his time and effort into being there for his daughter and grandson. His daughter worked hard to keep a home for Jayden and to earn enough for his needs. She was usually exhausted when she got home from work. John's heart went out to her. But he was also proud of her, of her love for God, and of her efforts to lay that love into Jayden's heart. John wanted to make sure he did everything in his power to help them keep God's word and understand that God was with them even through this difficult struggle.

John took early retirement, which the company made well worth his while. This way, he could be around for Jayden, help his daughter, and see that Jayden's extra curricular activities were productive ones. He had taken the place of the after-school babysitter and saved his daughter that expense. His daughter was so appreciative, so loving, and Jayden was receptive to the direction he'd wanted to provide, so John felt rewarded for his efforts.

He'd found a couple of passages in the Bible that would help his daughter remember that this situation would someday pass and that she shouldn't be afraid of the future. He'd typed these up in italics and put them in a little frame for her bedside table so she could read them every night. He made a second copy for her wallet.

To everything there is a season, a time for every purpose
under heaven. A time to be born, and a time to die; a time to plant,
and a time to pluck what is planted.
—Ecclesiastes 3:1, 2

Do not be afraid of sudden terror,
nor of trouble from the wicked when it comes;
for the Lord will be your confidence,
and will keep your foot from being caught.
                    —*Proverbs 4:20, 21, 22*

But John also kept himself busy with other activities as well, church of course, and also his hobby of learning more about alternative medicine. That's where he'd first seen Elizabeth. She had attended a health seminar, and he'd noticed by her questions that her mind worked like his. He was happy to meet and finally talk to her at Mary and Kevin's house last night. When he and Jayden were getting ready to leave he had found the courage to ask Elizabeth for her telephone number. He was thrilled to learn that she planned to move here permanently.

John had no interest in remarrying at his age. When he told Elizabeth he'd like them to be friends, she had understood him perfectly, proving again that he had been right to think they operated on the same wavelength. She'd understood clearly that he wasn't chasing her, or flirting with her, but truly wanted just to be friends. Elizabeth was pleased by this request, for she too needed a friend, not a boyfriend, just a friend, especially one who could share her faith and understand what it was like to be an older parent. She'd liked him and Jayden too and respected his efforts to serve his family and the community. Before he left last night, he gave Elizabeth his phone number and got hers too. He hoped to see her again.

When Mary and Kevin told Elizabeth that they would be meeting their banker on Thursday afternoon to apply for the loan for the carriage house renovation and then meeting with the architect to make arrangements for him to view the property, Elizabeth asked them if they would mind if she invited some friends over. She told them she wanted to invite Debbie, John, and Jayden to join her and Rebecca for a Bible study in their family room during the time Mary and Kevin would be gone. They readily and gladly agreed. Elizabeth then phoned

John to ask him if he would like to get together for a Bible study, telling him that Rebecca would be there and Jayden was also most welcome. John agreed to come and told Elizabeth that if she would make a pot of her now famous blackberry tea, he would bring some very scrumptious finger foods such as cookies, petite fours, and fresh strawberries. *How thoughtful*, she said to herself after she'd hung up.

Now, she wondered, *what shall we study?* Elizabeth found that she learned best when she chose a subject, located the subject in the concordance, copied down the indicated references, and then looked up and read these verses. She learned better when she searched a single subject and had cross-references to help her fully understand what God wanted her to know. *If only I could come up with a subject that would really interest all of them. It won't be easy because we are spanning three generations!*

As Elizabeth pondered this problem, she made a mental list of subjects, thinking *husbands and wives would be good for Debbie, but not so interesting for Jayden and Rebecca. Heaven might be too intangible and too broad to start with since Debbie is new to this. Hell and death might also be too overwhelming for now. The Ten Commandments the kids have already studied. So it's either the Holy Spirit or Satan. The Holy Spirit may also be a little hard to understand for Debbie since she's just starting out. So let's study Satan. This way we'll all be kept on the lookout!*

Elizabeth walked to Rebecca's room where she was working on her computer, and asked her about the topic. Becca said that she really liked the idea of studying about Satan and gave Elizabeth a thumbs-up. Elizabeth went to the concordance and began copying down whatever chapter and verse references seemed appropriate. When the list was long enough, she rewrote it and made five copies so they'd each have one to work with. *Maybe I'll also copy one of the scriptures in full so they'll have a head start and then develop a game plan for the rest.*

She called John to make sure this subject was one he'd approve of since Jayden would be coming. She was pleased that John thought it was an excellent subject and that he had commented enthusiastically when Elizabeth explained her method of Bible study. "Great idea," he said.

Elizabeth's list ended up citing Satan's worst attributes:

SATAN is (a)

1) Liar. John 8:44: "When he speaks a lie, he speaks from his own resources, for he is a liar and the father of it."
2) Sly, cunning. Genesis 3:1: "Now the serpent was more cunning than any beast of the field which the Lord God had made."
3) Murderer. John 8:44: "He was a murderer from the beginning, and does not stand in the truth, because there is no truth in him."
4) Deceiver. Genesis 3:13: "The serpent deceived me, and I ate." Also Revelation 12:9: "Satan, who deceives the whole world."
5) Tempter. Matthew 4:1, 3: "Then Jesus was led up by the Spirit into the wilderness to be tempted by the devil." "Now when the tempter came to Him, he said . . ."
6) Can move men to do his bidding. 1 Chronicles 21:1
7) Can walk back and forth on the earth. Job 1:7
8) Can cause illness. Job 2:7
9) Can take God's word from men's hearts. Mark 4:15
10) Can enter man. John 13:27
11) Can blind the minds of them which believe not. 2 Corinthians 4:4
12) Can transform himself. 2 Corinthians 11:14
13) Can send messengers to hurt man. 2 Corinthians 12:7
14) Can hinder people. 1 Thessalonians 2:18
15) Can produce signs and has powers. 2 Thessalonians 2:9

The previous verse (2 Thessalonians 2:9) said, "The coming of the lawless one is according to the working of Satan, with all power, signs, and lying wonders." Elizabeth wanted to tell the group that this verse explained that Satan is capable of producing signs, which can support a belief in certain practices, symbols, or people. She also decided to mention that to safeguard us from being misled in this manner, God warns us not to embrace the practices of astrology, divining, numerology, and other occult practices and that 2 Corinthians 4:4 warned that Satan can "blind the minds of them which believe not." She also noted that the signs Satan produces take advantage of this blindness to mislead us.

When everyone arrived on Thursday, they all expressed their excitement about what they would learn. John suggested that they also take a quick look at some verses that explained or supported the fact that Satan was right here on earth, right now, looking to harm us. Elizabeth asked John to discuss his thoughts first; then she'd follow with her thoughts, as this seemed the most appropriate way of explaining Satan's power. John passed out copies of the verses he'd selected.

"Through scripture," John explained, "God tells us that Satan and his angels have power. We are told that one-third of the angels that were in heaven accompanied Satan when he was cast out of heaven. Therefore Satan has a large workforce to do his bidding. They all work diligently to harm man and try to prevent their loyalty to God. This is why we are warned to take measures to stop these spirits from gaining a foothold in our lives."

How you are fallen from heaven, O Lucifer, son of the morning!
How you are cut down to the ground, You who weakened the nations!
For you have said in your heart: 'I will ascend into heaven,
I will exalt my throne above the stars of God; I will also sit on the mount
of the congregation on the farthest sides of the north; I will
ascend above the heights of the clouds, I will be like the Most High.'
Yet you shall be brought down to Sheol,
to the lowest depths of the pit.
—Isaiah 14:12-15

So the great dragon was cast out, that serpent of old, called
the Devil and Satan, who deceives the whole world;
he was cast to the earth, and his angels were cast out with him.
—Revelation 12:9

"In the verses I just gave you, God tells us that the root of all our problems is Satan, but that God will bring Satan down at the end. Interestingly, we are also told that it is Satan who weakened the nations, implying that his influence is what has caused the fall and perversions of what started out well."

To everyone's joy, Debbie had also brought a verse. Hers was about Job's struggle with Satan and how God gave Satan permission to strike him. She said that this had impressed her during a service she listened to at church, and she'd written it down.

> *But now stretch out Your hand and touch*
> *all that he has, and he will surely curse You to*
> *Your face. And the Lord said to Satan, Behold, all*
> *that he has is in your power; only do not lay*
> *a hand on his person.*
> *—Job 1:11, 12*

> *So went Satan forth from the presence of the Lord,*
> *and smote Job with sore boils from the sole of his foot unto his crown.*
> *—Job 2:7*

John spoke up, saying, "Yes, that last verse even demonstrates how Satan can affect our health. Sadly, in other areas of scripture we see how evil prospers here on this earth and how, as a result of Satan's power, we can fall prey to his wiles. When we read of the time when Satan tempted Christ we even learn that Satan can reward those who follow him. This is why those who follow Satan often prosper, although their prosperity may be very short-lived."

Jayden and Rebecca also made comments and contributed to the discussion. When they noticed the time, they all remarked that their two hours of study and their conversation made a most interesting and productive time together, but had passed too quickly. Then they began to devour John's wonderful finger foods. John and Debbie had developed a great rapport, and this pleased Elizabeth. She hoped that she could somehow use John's help to mend the relationship between Josh and Debbie.

As they ate, John asked, "Does anyone know what the surprise is that Caleb asked Matt about the other night?" There was silence for a moment while everyone considered, but then Debbie replied that she had no idea what the surprise could be. She felt that Matt had seemed quite adamant that no one should know and added, "No one will ask Matt again, because they want to respect his wishes."

Rebecca replied, "Mom and I talked about it yesterday and thought that maybe it's a gift that someone is giving to them both and Matt knows about it, but it is to be a surprise to Sarah. We thought that maybe the caller was either the salesperson or the one giving the gift."

John nodded his head slowly, and said, "That could be it. It seems to fit in with everything that we already know. But what gift could it be that would cause it to be such a huge secret and also seem to make Matt uncomfortable?"

Jayden piped in with "Maybe it's a really big screen TV and cost more than Sarah wanted Matt to spend?"

"Nah," Rebecca said, "that's not important enough to have made Matt sound so upset at having to keep it secret from Sarah."

Elizabeth agreed with Rebecca, saying "It does have to be pretty important for Matt to have spoken as he did at the party and for him to keep something from Sarah. I don't really think it's that kind of gift. If it is a gift, it would have to be something very, very personal to Sarah."

"Well," Debbie said, "We better follow what Matt asked of us and not be so curious so we don't get them upset so close to the wedding day."

Everyone agreed with Debbie's advice and they turned to polish off the rest of the goodies that John had brought. Then, they began their goodbyes, planning another study next week at John's house. As they stood, John prayed with them to close the meeting, quoting:

What will be the end of those who do
not obey the gospel of God?

—*1 Peter 4:17*

Debbie left the house first, and Rebecca and Jayden walked her to her car. When they were gone, John commented to Elizabeth, "Debbie seems like such a loving young woman and earnest in her desire to learn, to change her life for the best, but she seems to want to please everyone. That puts a strain on her. I also noticed the other night that Josh seemed to ignore her, didn't really talk to her, yet kept watching her. Is everything okay between them?"

Elizabeth told him in confidence that Josh had broken his engagement to Debbie only a few days before and was too stubborn to patch it up or to seek counseling for them both. "But I'm sure he loves her, it's as plain as the nose on your face," John replied.

"Yes, we all feel that way, and Debbie loves him . . . maybe too much!" Elizabeth noted. Then she added, "I overheard Caleb talking to Josh. He too seems to want to reach Josh and teach him about what God asks of a husband, so he too must realize something's going on. In fact, even Barbara, Matt's sister, knows. I could tell by her reaction to my moves to help Debbie pull off the aloof but dignified bit we women must sometimes employ with you men." Elizabeth batted her eyelashes at John in an imitation of a woman trying her wiles on a man and laughed thinking how silly she must look.

John laughed, too, enjoying Elizabeth's antics and her statement and said that he wanted to help, that between them all they'd whip Josh into shape. Elizabeth was pleased. She had yet another co-conspirator. This might be fun! Elizabeth rubbed her hands together in anticipation of a great adventure with John, Caleb, and Barbara, the result being a happy reunion for Debbie and Josh. John read her thoughts and smiling from ear to ear said, "Yeah, we can do this!" and left to join Jayden and get him home to his mom in time for them to help prepare dinner. John was happy to have found a friend like Elizabeth and sent a quick prayer to God to let Him know that he was thankful.

Chapter Nine

JAYDEN

There had been days when Jayden wanted to grab his father and shake him . . . make him see what he'd done to his family . . . make him change. But by now, years after the divorce, he'd just about given up on his father ever being normal, ever being what he should, ever being what Jayden prayed for. What was so disconcerting and difficult to understand was how much he still loved his father. He should really hate him for what he did to everyone, but he couldn't. He felt sorry for him, even while he was so angry with him.

His mother had probably suffered the most. She had to do the work of two parents. She worried about money, but she didn't want to have to take money from Grandpa. She always tried to make sure Jayden did well in school and learned in church. She wanted him to participate in extracurricular activities so he'd never look back feeling he'd been cheated of his childhood. She felt it was bad enough not to have the right kind of dad, the right kind of role model.

Sometimes he'd hear his mother crying, alone in her room, and he didn't know what to do. That's when he'd hate his father the most. But he knew he wasn't supposed to hate. And really, he didn't; it probably was just anger, an anger so strong that it felt like hate. Jayden didn't understand yet that he was also angry because he didn't have the power to change anything, not his father, not his mother's difficulties, not his grandfather's worries. Some of his anger went inward because nothing he could do would make a difference.

Jayden's hope was that God would somehow fix everything. And to show he would be thankful for that, he wanted to do what God asked now. He wasn't being forced to follow God; he'd actually made up his own mind last year. This was why getting his emotions in check was important to him . . . so he'd know he was okay with God. He went to church regularly and he went because he wanted to; he liked it, liked what he heard and learned. He had a lot of respect for the people who cared so much about him; the youth leaders, the ministers, the Sunday school teachers. They were great role models.

Jayden also prayed without fail every morning and every night, and whenever he could remember he also prayed when he ate or left the house. He tithed from his allowance, paid close attention to the services, and believed them, so he thought he was okay. The only times it was hard was when he was thrown in with kids who wanted to do things he felt he shouldn't. That was why he liked the youth group at church. Usually those kids were . . . well . . . fairly well behaved anyway, and so much easier to be around because they all knew way down deep they were on the same path and might remain friends not only for life, but also for eternity!

He was glad to have met Rebecca, and really glad that they had gotten together for the Bible study. When he first met her the night of the party, he thought she was stuck-up because she didn't talk to him very much. But now he realized that she'd been shy. They both liked each other now, and he hoped that Becca would come to some of the youth group get-togethers with him. She didn't have a father either. And they'd both been, and probably still were, angry with God to a certain extent about that.

Jayden didn't quite understand the relationship between Mary and Kevin and Becca and her mother, but he knew that in some way Becca was related to Mary. He'd asked Rebecca if they could get together just to hang out, and she'd said yes. He was going over to her house this afternoon, but he didn't want her to think it was a boy-girl thing, he really didn't like girls that way yet, it was just that he thought that since Becca didn't have a father and was religious like he was, they'd be able to talk about some stuff that he couldn't talk about to anyone but his grandfather. He hated to bother his grandfather so much. His grandfather was struggling with trying to help his mom and him enough as it was. Grandpa had been so devastated and disappointed in his father's drug and alcohol use and still worried so much about his mom.

Jayden thought his grandfather was perfect, and he wanted to be like him someday. He liked the way he laughed and conversed so easily, knew so much about stuff, especially the Bible and served God with every ounce of his strength. Jayden wasn't sure he could live up to that, but he hoped he could.

They'd had a blast at the Bible study because Satan was a cool subject, and even he had learned a lot. Scary. He had something else to tell Becca about Satan when he saw her. He was planning to ride his bike over to Becca's today, so he went into the kitchen to write a note for his mom in case she came home before he did. That was one thing she wouldn't let him off the hook for. She wanted to know where he was all the time. It was okay but sometimes made him feel like she didn't think he was grown up yet.

As soon as he rang the doorbell at Mary's house, he got nervous wondering if he and Becca would have enough to talk about. Suddenly he hoped that Elizabeth would be around and that his grandfather would show up, so they could talk if he and Becca didn't have enough to say. But no such luck, Elizabeth was taking a nap. Becca said that she planned for them to sit in the garden overlooking the carriage house and eat snacks that Elizabeth had prepared earlier. They walked into the kitchen to get the tray filled with lemonade and lemon cookies.

He took the heavy tray from her hands and said gallantly, "Lead the way!" then he followed her into the yard.

When they were seated, and the cookies and lemonade placed in front of each of them, Becca said, "Wasn't that neat about Satan? It's scary to think he can fool us, even enter us and live in us. It's awful! I was worried about that, so later that day my mom told me about the protection God offers us, and it wasn't so bad then. I just hope I do have protection from those terrible spirits!"

"Well, if you think that's bad, wait until you hear this one," Jayden said. Rebecca looked at him with wide eyes wondering what it could be and asked, "What?" Jayden asked her if she'd ever gone out trick-or-treating, and she said, "Well, yeah, of course, haven't you?" Jayden replied, "No, never. It's too dangerous." "Why?" Becca countered.

Jayden began in a silly, deep, and quavering voice to tell Becca that "during the dark ages, about two thousand years ago in Ireland, England, and Northern France, the Celts, known as cruel and barbaric warriors who worshipped many gods, held a heathen festival that was filled with superstition and occult ceremony in honor of the Celtic god, the lord of death, Samhain."

Then, seeing Becca's eyes widen and not wanting to frighten her, Jayden continued in his natural voice, and went on to say, "The Druids, who were the more educated and priestly group within the Celtic people, taught that terrible curses and punishments would befall those who did not participate in the ceremonies honoring Samhain."

"Seriously, Becca, this is the truth, and I guess I shouldn't have tried to be funny by trying to make my voice sound like a ghost or something, because this is something *dangerous* that we need to know about, so listen up.

"These people believed that the worlds of the dead and of the living became one on the night of Samhain, October 31. Samhain, the lord of death, allegedly gathered the condemned and evil souls from eternity and allowed some of them to return to earth and associate with the living. The festival of Samhain was marked by the visitation of ghosts and mischievous spirits. While many writings say that cruel human sacrifices were offered, historical writings seem to indicate that animal sacrifices were made. But from the dying sacrifice, the Celtic priests would make predictions about the future." "How gruesome," Rebecca said.

"While the festival of Samhain was the origin of Halloween, (All Hallows' Evening)," Jayden continued, "the influence of these occult beliefs and practices, persisted through the subsequent centuries. In AD 43 two Roman festivals joined this one. One was Feralia, which commemorated the passing of the dead, and the other honored the Roman goddess Pomona."

"In 835 AD, in an effort to convert this heathen custom into a spiritual celebration, Pope Gregory IV decreed November 1 as All Saints' Day when departed souls would be prayed for. These three festivals were joined together and celebrated with bonfires, parades, and costumes."

"Over the years some satanic groups considered Halloween the time when Satan could be called upon to exert his influence in various matters, and an event called Irish Mischief Night, when fairies, elves, the traveling dead, and wicked supernatural spirits were thought to roam, also mixed with these other events. These festivities combined into what we today consider Halloween. When we look at the costumes of ghosts, witches, ghouls, skeletons, and bloody masks, fingers, and clothing, we can see that Halloween trivializes and mocks the souls who have died but whom God still longs to save. God would never want us, His children, Christ's Bride, to join celebrations that had their origins in such activities. They are in overt opposition to His love and his future plans for those who have already died and wait for His Son. The Bible tells us not to imitate what is evil." Then Jayden, from memory, quoted two verses from the Bible:

Beloved, do not imitate what is evil.

—3 John 11

Therefore be imitators of God as dear children . . .
. . . and have no fellowship with the unfruitful works of darkness,
but rather expose them.

—Ephesians 5:1, 11

"You have to admit," Jayden continued, "some of the costumes, with blood dripping from mouths and bloody fingernails, and the ghosts and witches and dead people, couldn't possibly be pleasing to God. We wouldn't dare wear those costumes to church, would we? Or would we dare to wear them to the wedding feast with Christ? So why would we try to wear them behind His back? And do those who claim that this is a time when people honor the dead really think we can do this by wearing these terrible costumes?"

"Wow," Becca said, "I never heard this before. This is really bad. I wasn't ready to believe you at first, I mean about Halloween being bad. But as I think of it, I guess I'd be awfully afraid to dress up like that if I thought about what God might feel about it. Knowing this, I'd feel that I might be displeasing God. Even if I wore an okay costume, just being around the other kind of costumes would give me the heebie-jeebies. I'd know that they depict that Samhain ceremony and couldn't possibly be pleasing to God."

"I want to tell my mother about this, I don't think she knows either. In fact, I know she doesn't know, otherwise I'd never have been allowed out for Halloween. It also hit home when you said that we are not supposed to imitate evil stuff. My mother is going to be upset that she missed this one. I can't wait to tell her."

"Yeah, well, I learned this in Sunday school a long time ago," Jayden replied. "And remember, just the other day we learned in our Bible study that Satan is pretty sneaky, can blind us, fool us, make us complacent, and that he will do anything to prevent us from being a part of the Bride of Christ. Maybe he uses this celebration to hurt the Holy Spirit in us and somehow open us to evil spirits."

"Oh, Jayden, that thought is so scary that even if I wasn't sure Halloween was so bad, I'd never let my kids be even potentially open to that! Jayden, do you just stay home on Halloween?" Rebecca asked. "No, not usually," Jayden replied. "We go to the church or to one of the minister's houses, or even one of the homes of someone from the congregation for a fellowship. Sometimes we make a campfire and sit around toasting hot dogs and marshmallows and sometimes we play games. Usually we have a lot of people coming, like from our Sunday school group and from the youth group. We hang out . . . but we don't answer the door to give out candy, or look at the costumes. Anyway, we are usually in the back yard, or in the church, so we don't even think about the people ringing doorbells. Actually, the other kids in the neighborhood realize that if the lights aren't on, you don't usually give out stuff. Or if they know this is what you believe, they stop coming to the house at all. Some of the kids from my neighborhood are really scared to go out now that I've told them why I don't, but they are so fixed on getting free candy that they do it anyway. I guess they figure it's worth the risk. It's not to me. But hopefully they feel guilty about dressing up in the really bad costumes for Halloween because they know why we don't go out and maybe some day they'll quit doing it."

"But we have fun without going out on Halloween to 'trick-or-treat,' and since we have plenty of good food and fellowship with one another, we don't miss a thing, in fact we feel as if we have given something to God because we followed His words . . . and we don't ever have to worry about razor blades in apples or poison in candy." Rebecca laughed, but then began to ponder what she had just learned. They were both quiet for a few minutes while they munched on their cookies and sipped their lemonade, lost in their own thoughts.

Then Rebecca asked Jayden, "Do I have to ask forgiveness for doing that in the past? Does my mother?" Jayden didn't know and said that he'd ask his grandfather. Then he commented that he felt it couldn't hurt to ask forgiveness anyway. "What should we be doing to protect ourselves against Satan?" Rebecca asked. "What if we saw him making someone we love, or even just a stranger, or a neighbor, do something bad?"

Jayden explained that children of God had many things they could and should do, and many things that they shouldn't do. "It's always good to try to help someone and to share what we have learned," Jayden said. "But sometimes, when others have proven that they will continue along a bad path, it's best to run from them. I think the Bible says to "flee."

Go get your Bible and let's see if we can find something, do you have a concordance?" Rebecca ran into the house to get what Jayden asked for. This subject was so interesting, but it also scared her. She knew that she wanted to find out what to do to protect herself and her mom . . . and everyone she loved for that matter.

When Rebecca returned, Jayden went first to the concordance to look up the word "flee" and selected a verse from Timothy.

> *But thou, O man of God,*
> *flee these things; and follow after righteousness,*
> *godliness, faith, love, patience, meekness.*
> *—1 Timothy 6:11*

Then he went to the book of Acts where he remembered he'd find the scripture he really liked about wolves devouring us. He explained that this was a warning from God about the very things they'd just talked about.

> *For I know this, that after my departure savage*
> *wolves will come in among you, not sparing the flock.*
> *Also from among yourselves men will rise up,*

speaking perverse things, to draw away the
disciples after themselves.
Therefore watch.

—*Acts 20:29-31*

Then he looked up the armour information he wanted to show Rebecca.

Therefore take up the whole armor of God,
that you may be able to withstand in the evil day,
and having done all, to stand.

—*Ephesians 6:13*

The night is far spent, the day is at hand.
Therefore let us cast off the works of darkness,
and let us put on the armor of light.

—*Romans 13:12*

Put on the whole armor of God, that you may be able
to stand against the wiles of the devil.

—*Ephesians 6:11*

Jayden needed the concordance to find the other scripture that had convinced him that there were only two real choices that anyone could make, and that was to obey God and be blessed, or not to obey God and be cursed. He found it in the concordance under the word "curse" then looked it up in the Bible and read it to Rebecca.

Behold I set before you today a blessing and a curse:
the blessing, if you obey the commandments of the Lord your God
which I command you today; and the curse,
if you do not obey the commandments of the Lord your God,
but turn aside from the way which I command you today,
to go after other gods which you have not known.

—*Deuteronomy 11:26, 27, 28*

"Hmm," said Rebecca, "that lays it out quite strongly, doesn't it. I never liked Bible study before, but the way we've been doing it, it's really interesting. I've a lot to learn, I think."

Jayden felt this was a perfect time to ask the question that had been bothering him. "Becca, can I ask what your relationship to Mary is? I'm confused. I mean, you're gonna move here for good and stuff, and unless they need the rent money, I don't see any connection, since I think you've just met."

"Yes, my mom and I just met Kevin and Mary a short while ago. My mom, Elizabeth, is my adoptive mother, but Mary is my real mother, my blood mother," Rebecca said quietly and slowly. "To me, Elizabeth is, and always will be, my mother, and I am so worried that all this is going to hurt her . . . and . . . and . . . she's very ill." And Rebecca began to cry.

Jayden didn't know what to do. Then he tried to comfort her by saying, "Don't worry, Becca, God has a reason for everything and a solution too. You are so good and sweet, and you love Him so much, and want to study His word, so He won't let you down. Please don't cry." When Rebecca continued to cry, Jayden went on talking for lack of knowing what else to do. "Becca, my dad is a drug addict, and I live with my mother who is alone except for me and grandpa, and sometimes I'm really upset too. We have to pray and trust God. I know it's hard, but we have to. Thanks for telling me, though, about your mom, I mean. I kinda thought we had a lot in common. It's different really, but it's the same too."

Rebecca looked at Jayden, and saw pain in his eyes, and thought, *We do have a lot in common, we are both worried about people we love, and unable to do anything about it.* Suddenly she knew that she and Jayden would soon become best friends, and she was pleased. She took Jayden's hand and squeezed it, and said, "Thanks, Jayden, I'm so thankful to have someone to talk to . . . I'm okay now."

They went back into the house, Jayden carrying the tray of now empty dishes and glasses, and Rebecca carrying the Bible and the concordance. They met Elizabeth in the kitchen. "Have you two been reading the Bible and looking up some verses?" asked Elizabeth when she saw the books. "Yeah, Mom, it was fun," replied Rebecca, "and have I got a lot to tell you about Halloween. I'm *never* going out for Halloween again! You're gonna *flip* when you hear this, Ma!"

It was good to see Rebecca animated once again. Elizabeth was so impressed with them for apparently conducting their own Bible study that she wanted to call John as soon as she could to tell him.

As Rebecca repeated what Jayden had told her about Halloween, and with Jayden filling in the parts Rebecca couldn't remember, Elizabeth became sick with apprehension. *Why hadn't she known this?* she wondered. *Why didn't their church or minister teach this to them? How can God ever forgive her for subjecting Rebecca to those ugly evil spirits all these years? Could any of those spirits have gotten a hold on either of them because of this? I must call John as soon as possible and ask him about this. Does Mary know this?* Elizabeth reached over to draw Rebecca to her side, wanting to protect her, worried about the mistakes she'd made as a mother and not known she was making. *Please, God, don't let Rebecca suffer from something I've done wrong,* she prayed.

Soon thereafter, Jayden was on his way home from Becca's, bicycling as fast as he could, enjoying the wind rushing through his hair from the speed of his pedaling. He had been worried that they would not have enough to talk about but he had been wrong. He had a great time today. He felt good that he'd been able to teach Rebecca some of the stuff he knew, especially about Halloween. Briefly the thought crossed his mind that maybe he got an extra jewel in his crown today for testifying, because wasn't that what he'd done? *I used to think of testifying as ringing doorbells, spouting admonitions, and getting doors slammed in your face, but now I see that it can be just normal conversation and interest . . . although, I guess you have to know God's words to do it.*

Jayden was fifteen, and still growing. He was already about five eleven, and slender but not skinny. He had brown eyes. Maybe that was why he liked Rebecca's ethereal blue eyes. *I guess opposites attract!* he thought. His hair was very curly and light brown in color, and he wore it to the bottom of his ears. A curly tendril always fell onto his forehead. He wore clear plastic braces on his teeth, embarrassed by them because most kids were done with that stuff by now. But he'd resisted getting braces. He didn't give in right away; waiting a year because he knew his mother would have to pay for them. His father hadn't even been working at the time and could barely manage keeping up with the rent for his own apartment, so he didn't help.

His father had started life out so well . . . a good education, a big executive job, making big bucks, driving a fancy car, buying a great house, but then came the drugs, "recreational" at first, then more addictive. And that was the end of him. He lost it all. He lost everything of importance. And his brain was such that he didn't even seem to discern between what was right and what was wrong anymore. It seemed to Jayden that once the spiritual fell in importance, other influences gained in strength. Then it was just a matter of time before it was too late to break free of those spirits.

Jayden would never touch even a drop of alcohol let alone a joint or anything even stronger. *No way,* he thought, *never! I've seen firsthand what they can do to your life. You might think you are in control of it at first, but you really aren't. It's just another ploy of Satan, a way to hook you, make you think you are okay until it is too late. That stuff is a guaranteed path to destruction, physically, emotionally, and financially. Yeah, spiritually too.*

Jayden thought of his mother and how strong she was to go through all this and still plug away. He thought of his grandfather and how he always tried to be there for them, how he was always teaching them about God, and encouraging them to trust Him. Jayden never wanted to be a burden to his mom or grandfather. He was determined to work hard, get an education, and eventually be a help to them.

He knew his jeans were a tad bit too short because of a new growth spurt, but he never asked for anything because he knew the financial struggle they all had. Today, because he'd wanted to impress Rebecca, he'd worn the bright red polo and new white sneakers that his grandfather bought him last week. And as these thoughts ran through his head, he remembered the college fund his mom had started for him when he was a baby and to this day was saving for him. She'd grabbed that before his father could spend it on drugs. This took some of the pressure off his mom because she would have taken ten jobs if necessary to get him through college.

Already at an early age Jayden had planned to do well in school so he could go to a good college, get a good degree, and be able to look after his mom whenever she needed any money. His grades had always been good because he'd recognized long ago the need for studying and of course, because his grandfather always helped him when he didn't understand something.

Suddenly the thought occurred to him that he would like his Mom to meet Rebecca's family because they would be so good for her, and maybe she could find some friends there. Grandpa was already in their circle of love; so was he, so why not his mom? He smiled with the thought that he'd talk this over with his grandfather and that between them they could make it happen.

Jayden had gained enormous respect for his mom as he watched how she handled the divorce, her job, her tight financial situation, and even how she handled him. He wanted the best for her, and he knew that he would be happy if she met someone who would make her happy.

Jayden thought about the way Matt had handled that "secret surprise for Sarah" stuff and wished his mom could have someone who would care that much for her. He wanted her to have a close relationship with other people who acted, believed, and strove so hard to be better. She deserved to marry again, to have someone, especially after he left the house to go to college. He wanted her to have someone that others respected too, like they did Matt and Caleb. Those guys had a certain presence. They were soft spoken, but somehow when they said something, others listened and trusted them.

I'm really glad that Grandpa decided to hand-deliver some of the concert flyers the other night. It brought us to Mary and Kevin's house and now into the hearts of all these really super people. I want my mom to share in this too.

Then he remembered that he wanted to ask Kevin and Matt if they'd let him help them renovate the carriage house. It would be really cool to spend time with them, and he wanted to learn that kind of stuff so he could have a really nice house someday himself, and a really super family to put in it!

Suddenly Jayden was home, surprised that the trip seemed so short! He saw Grandpa's car next to Mom's car in the driveway, and figured that dinner was probably almost ready. Coming to a stop so abruptly that his bike skidded sideways, Jayden hopped off the bike and walked it toward the backyard. He lifted the bike up the steps and onto the porch where he usually kept it, then, pushed the back door open yelling, "Hey, Mom, I'm home!"

Chapter Ten

THE MONKEY SWING

It was Saturday night, and the whole group was at Kevin and Mary's house again. Matt and Sarah, Elizabeth and Rebecca, Caleb and Ann, Josh and Debbie, and John and Jayden. Barbara and her husband Jim were due to arrive any minute. This would bring their numbers up to fourteen, the same as their last get-together.

They were all talking about either the wedding, now only a week away, or the carriage house and the renovation that was just now entering the planning stage. Some were teasing Matt and Sarah, asking if they would either postpone the big wedding or cut their honeymoon short to come home and help with the renovation. Kevin was spouting some weird stuff about decorating through mathematical formulas and monkey swings for proportion and balance, but no one was taking him seriously. It seemed too complex. Mary was trying to tell everyone that Grandma had discovered how to decorate a home according to God's directions.

Everyone was having their own conversation on one or the other of these subjects, so the house buzzed with the noise of twelve voices all going at once. Rebecca was enthralled by the fact that Kevin had made copies of her drawings for her room in the carriage house for everyone to assess . . . but she was a little nervous about the possibility that her ideas weren't good enough. She had taken the measurements of her room from the preliminary drawings her mom had made of the proposed floor plan for the bedroom area of the carriage house. The other rooms were still a work in progress.

When Barbara and Jim arrived, the chatter in the room was even worse. Now there were fourteen voices all going at once, all trying to fill Barbara and Jim in on what they'd said. The words "construction," "renovation," "permits" "kitchen cabinets," "skylights," and "Grandma's decorating manual" could be heard. Suddenly the room went silent as Kevin yelled at the top of his voice, "QUIET EVERYONE!"

When the room was quiet, and he had everyone's attention, Kevin continued by saying, "Before anyone makes even *one* decision, or makes up their mind about any of the things we've been talking about in regard to the carriage house, I want you to ponder something that I think is really important. Once you understand it, we can attempt to apply it to Rebecca's room drawings and Elizabeth's floor plan. Okay?"

"Well," replied Caleb, "tell us what's so important . . . Come on, what's taking you so long!" Kevin began by explaining, "Matt and Sarah found a manuscript in one of the trunks that had come from Grandma's house. It was a trunk that had belonged to Grandma. The manuscript, written by Grandma, particularly intrigued them because it seemed to be about decorating and how to make a project successful. They were so impressed by what they read that they brought the journal to us."

Kevin continued, "When we'd read it, we copied some of the most important pages to give to Elizabeth so she could apply the principals to her floor plan." "What are the rest of us," Josh called out, teasing Kevin, "chopped liver that we don't get to read it?"

Kevin laughed and replied, "That's why you're here. We want to share these ideas with everyone and challenge you to provide some opinions about how we should approach our project. After all, if Matt and Sarah are going to leave this project for the very selfish reason of getting married and going on a honeymoon, we'll have to handle everything ourselves." Kevin joked.

Matt jumped in front of Kevin, fists made, knees bent, and danced around Kevin looking fierce, and pretending to jab at him, just like he had seen Grandma, or Sarah for that matter, do many times in jest. Kevin took his cue and put up his fists. They began circling each other, unable to keep the silly grins off their faces. "Get him, Matt," yelled Sarah as the rest of the group formed a circle around them, "Don't let anyone try to con you out of our honeymoon . . . we're going, and that's that!" When Mary joined Kevin with her fists up, circling Matt and trying hard not to laugh, Sarah joined in too, saying, "Hey, let's keep the odds even!"

Big Caleb joined Kevin and put his fists up too, saying, "Hey, Kevin, I'm on your side . . . we'll get this whole project done before Matt even gets back from lolly-goggling around some fancy hotel." Caleb too looked silly circling, dancing on his toes, arms to his chin, fists made, grinning, like the rest of them.

But before the group got too rowdy, Mary, always the sweet pacifier, left the circle and went to stand on the kitchen stool. She hit an empty pot with a large wooden mixing spoon three times to get everyone's attention. Then she said, "Okay, everyone, we've got a lot of tough ideas to figure out tonight. First we're gonna have a glass of fruit-flavored zinfandel, then we're gonna eat, and after that we're gonna figure this out. In fact, instead of seeing who is the bigger man through a fisticuff demonstration like we've just had, let's find that better man . . . or woman through . . . *math*! But first, let's eat!"

Kevin, knowing the game was over, joined Mary and, still being silly, got on his knees in front of her and pleaded, "Mary love, please, can't I at least try to explain the monkey swing and the math thing while we're eating, please, honey?" Of course Mary relented, asking everyone to get their food from the island and then find seats where they could both eat and listen to Kevin. "Keep it brief, Kevin," she admonished, knowing it might be especially difficult to explain the math thing.

Once everyone had filled their plate, they settled themselves where they would be comfortable. As quickly as he could, Kevin wolfed down a huge Italian sausage with German sauerkraut on a piece of French bread and then began to address everyone. "Who knows what a monkey swing is?" he asked.

"I do!" Jayden answered. "It's a swing that kids use in the yard. It hangs from the tree by one rope, not two like other swings, and the rope goes through the center of the seat, not the sides like other swings. It's hard to balance on them though."

"That was a great explanation, Jayden. Does everyone understand what a monkey swing is now?" Only John said he'd never seen one, so Kevin described it again in a little more detail. "Okay, like Jayden said, it's a single rope hanging from a tree that goes through the center of a wooden platform and is tied underneath so the platform is attached to the rope and can be used as a sort of saddle or seat. The child sits on the platform with legs straddling the rope and holds onto the single rope with both hands."

"This swing requires a more concentrated effort to maintain balance than does the traditional swing. It requires that the child balance his weight evenly on the platform so he will not lean to one side, tilt, and fall. The child is required to balance his body from front to back, and from side to side at the same time, while the traditional swing requires only front to back balance. If the child isn't balanced, he needs all his strength to hang on to the rope, rather than having his body help him. His body weight actually hinders him if it isn't perfectly balanced on the platform."

Mary asked Kevin if she could interrupt for a minute, and he graciously complied, bowing her into the space he'd occupied, grinning too! "Just to clarify why Kevin is telling you all this, Elizabeth is working on a floor plan for the carriage house, and has already figured out the proper measurements for the bedrooms and to us they look great! Last week Matt and Sarah brought us a decorating manuscript that Grandma wrote, and in it Grandma explained how the swing with the single rope through the center, the monkey swing, is an excellent tool to help us design and decorate our homes."

"Like the explanation Kevin gave, that you have to balance your body evenly around the monkey swing or you may fall off, a room needs to be balanced by properly distributing the 'weight' of its architectural elements and its furnishings. Without this balance, the room will seem to 'lean' to one side. Like the child falling off the swing, furnishings will feel as if they will 'fall off' the room's floor. Balance all around makes the floor feel level and gives us a sense of safety. This keeps our psyche happy! Does that make sense?"

After everyone murmured their assent, Sarah added, "Grandma said that balance is the most important aspect of good design because by being pleasing to the eye, it creates a sense of harmony. Grandma said that because everything in the room will affect balance, we must carefully consider 'everything' in the room, not only the furniture, but also everything else such as the architecture, accessories, style, size, colors, and textures."

"Grandma used the phrase 'Balance affects everything, everything affects balance.' She emphasized that proper balance produces a pleasing sensation in us and said that it's best not to make a mistake in the early stages of decorating, especially in constructing walls and room sizes, because it is harder to fix later than earlier. But then Grandma went on to explain that balance doesn't mean, as we might now think, that distributing 'weight' equally is what we need to do. Balance does not refer to a pound for pound distribution, but rather to the illusion or 'feeling' of balance throughout the whole space or area. This is in order to achieve the sense of a level base with no perceivable tilt to the room."

"Thus, a heavy weight or large-size item in one part of a room can be balanced by either a corresponding weight or size, or the illusion of corresponding weight or size, in an opposing part of the room. The balancing item could be a piece of furniture, but it could also be a 'heavier' color paint, or wallpaper."

Kevin added, "Grandma noted that when we achieve this balance from one end to the other and from floor to ceiling, we create a sense of harmony. Because the concept or illusion of weight is so important in achieving balance, she gave examples to understand what she meant. She said that red is a 'heavier' color than light blue and that dark wood creates the feeling that it 'weighs' more than lighter colored wood. Similarly, a dark enclosed console seems much 'heavier' than an open shelved white wicker piece, and heavy velvet draperies would not be a proper choice with a 'lighter' small print cotton valance. Also, a small delicate porcelain sculpture would not be in proper proportion to a large bronze, nor would a delicate 3" x 5" oil painting in a filigree gold frame look balanced when hung with a large unframed bold colored abstract painting. These examples are referring not so much to the weight in pounds of these objects, but more to the disparity in size, delicateness, color, texture, and other attributes."

"Look at our fireplace: the massive wall to wall stones with the heavy wood mantle above would never work with a white rattan décor of lace and ruffles, because the 'weight' of the rattan will not be enough to offset the apparent 'weight' of the stone and mantle. However, with careful thought to balance, through the use of the 'weight' of color, the brown rattans might work as opposed to the white rattans if rattan was your preference."

Sarah interjected that from what she'd read, the determination of proper balance must not be about furniture alone, but start with the 'weight' of existing, or added, architectural elements. "And believe it nor not, decorating does not have any rules other than the rule of achieving proper proportion and balance in all things . . . the keywords being 'in all things.'"

"This seems mind boggling," Barbara said. "No, no," Mary answered. "Now that we are aware of the fact that balance produces harmony, and harmony produces pleasure and well-being, all we need is to ask, 'How can I know I've attained proper balance? How can I tell whether one piece of furniture 'weighs' more than another in terms of interior design balance? How can I know what needs to be balanced or offset by something else? How can I create illusions to counterbalance an imbalanced area?' If we can answer these questions, we will know how to end up with a pleasing room with good interior design."

Sarah added, "If we visualize that this room is a monkey swing, and pretend to place the architectural elements of the room onto the platform of the swing, we can see if we'd think we could or could not balance the swing. If the swing is not balanced, the perceived weight of these architectural features will need to be balanced by whatever else we place into the room."

"Therefore, we must first note carefully all the architectural elements such as a fireplace, bookshelves, built in cupboards, steps, columns, doors, windows, arches, niches, moldings, planters, and other unique characteristics of the room. This gives us the first step toward our project and will help us make decisions about the placement of other items within the room, probably the things we want to make the room function the way we want. I mean, now, we'd be able to see whether a drop leaf secretary desk would work better in the room than a pedestal desk . . . if we knew we wanted a desk in the room we were working on, that is."

Everyone had finished eating, except for those considering a second helping. They began to talk with one another, questioning this unique concept while recognizing its value. Mary suggested they "take fifteen minutes" to talk amongst them selves, freshen up, or refill their plates before Matt attempted to discuss the math part. While some refilled their plates and sat again to listen, others continued to discuss the concept of the monkey swing.

Caleb and Jim were talking, and Caleb said: "Let me try this out on you to see if I understand it correctly. Visualize walking into a living room in a model home. The living room is unfurnished, but you note a large fireplace on one wall flanked by two large windows. On the adjacent wall are built in bookcases, built to cover the entire wall. The entry into this room is in the corner opposite the corner joining the fireplace wall and the bookcase wall. The other two walls coming toward the entryway are empty of any doors or windows. I guess if we were sensitive to weight balance, then from the entryway there may be a sensation of tilt toward the opposite corner, causing us to brace our feet to offset the 'feeling' of a tilting floor. I guess you would gain more sensitivity in this area as you learn more about the monkey swing techniques, and thus what to look for."

Jim replied, "Sounds pretty good to me, Caleb. Now let me ask you a question. Imagine that you've walked into a friend's home for the first time. She has the same home you just described with the fireplace and bookshelves, but has flanked the fireplace with two wing chairs with small tables beside them. She's placed a couch in the center of the room facing the fireplace, and added a cocktail table to the front of the couch. There is also an oriental rug under the cocktail table area. She's added a sofa table behind the couch. Standing at the sofa table, the furnishings truly make a beautiful and well-balanced picture. However, as you move back to the entryway of the room, if you look at the entire floor as the seat of the monkey swing, you'd sense the tremendous weight at the other end of the room. You would 'feel' that the floor is tilted toward the fireplace and that you will be walking 'downhill' toward the sofa table. If you like this arrangement for its comfortable setting, yet you know its wrong, does it have to be changed?"

Caleb thought for a moment, then added, "No, maybe not, because if this feeling of weight and tilt on the fireplace end of the room, now with all the furniture added as well, can be offset by creating the illusion of weight near the entryway of the room, this furniture arrangement could stay." Jim, after thinking about it for a moment asked, "Like what?" And Caleb said, "Well, what if large round columns were added to the entryway to the room, and maybe wider dark stained moldings, maybe an artificial tree too." "Yeah, I guess you're right," Jim conceded, "that addition makes this 'floor balance' concept okay then. To sum it up then, you can do what you want, then make the necessary adjustments to make the balance part work for you"

The women were enthralled by the fact that the men were getting into decorating! They listened to the side conversations of the men and grinned at one another. Barbara leaned over to Mary and whispered "Thanks for getting this conversation started . . . it's neat!" Sarah said, "Hey, if we could get this concept down pat, maybe we'd always have an excuse to buy new furniture!" And Jayden, wanting to join in, and overhearing Sarah, retorted, laughing, "Oh no, hey, guys, listen, the women are teaching Rebecca all the wrong stuff!"

Suddenly Sarah spoke up saying, "Oh incidentally, while we are on the subject of monkey swings, I do want to warn all of you about something. You all know that I know that Matt said there is a surprise in store for me. Well, if the surprise is that you are all going to buy me a monkey swing, all I can say is 'better not.' I will not hang one in my house, even if you think it will save me from making a lot of decorating blunders! However, I will consider hanging one in the backyard . . . provided each of you show me that you can swing properly on it."

"On the other hand, maybe we should all get a monkey swing. Rebecca and Elizabeth can use it to plan the carriage house, Caleb and Ann could use one to help them with that addition they've been thinking about. One would help Barbara convince Jim to spend their money for the new furniture she's been hinting about. Kevin and Mary need one so they can balance the baby's room and the baby can learn to use it for a plaything. Since Debbie and Josh are young enough, they can use it as a swing! How's that?"

"Okay, okay, we get the point. You've ruined our surprise for you, Sarah. Now that we can't give you a monkey swing, we'll just have to think of something else to give you," Mary joked. "But now, it's time to get back to work."

Josh had been sitting too quietly, so Caleb asked him, "Why so quiet, Josh?" Josh grumbled, "Since when do we guys get to call the shots in decorating anyway?" But Matt said, "Well, if we take an interest, and we learn that the one important fact in dealing with women is to know that you must never start a sentence off with the word 'no.' Just say, 'Hmmm, good point, honey, but . . .' Then we'd have a say!" "Yeah," Kevin replied, "it's not what we say, it's always how we say it!" And Sarah said, "Well, it is important for all of us to know how to talk to one another! When we hear 'no' this and 'no' that, it is discouraging, but if we heard 'Okay, we'll consider your request' or 'Let's look into it and talk about that again,' we'd be okay!"

Caleb added, "Okay, guys, we have to admit that the 'Venus/Mars thing' does exist, and we do have to adjust the way we respond if we want to get *our* way, you know . . . 'psychology'!" He suddenly burst out laughing and his contagious laugh made everyone laugh. They all knew that they did have to think before they spoke to keep everything harmonious.

Debbie timidly added, "I used to be so impulsive. I am just now learning to think first, speak later! But you know, this math and monkey swing stuff makes so much sense that it's a good way for men and women to discuss the furnishing of a house because it takes the emotion out and puts in its place the need. If an area needs another piece of furniture to balance it, with this method even the guys would see that more furnishings were needed. We'd all have a mathematical reason, not an emotional one to help us make the decision to purchase something!"

"You're absolutely right, Debbie, that's a really good thought. Excellent! So let's get back to how we can figure out what we would have to do to get a room in proper balance, how we'd have that super conversation Debbie just mentioned," John said.

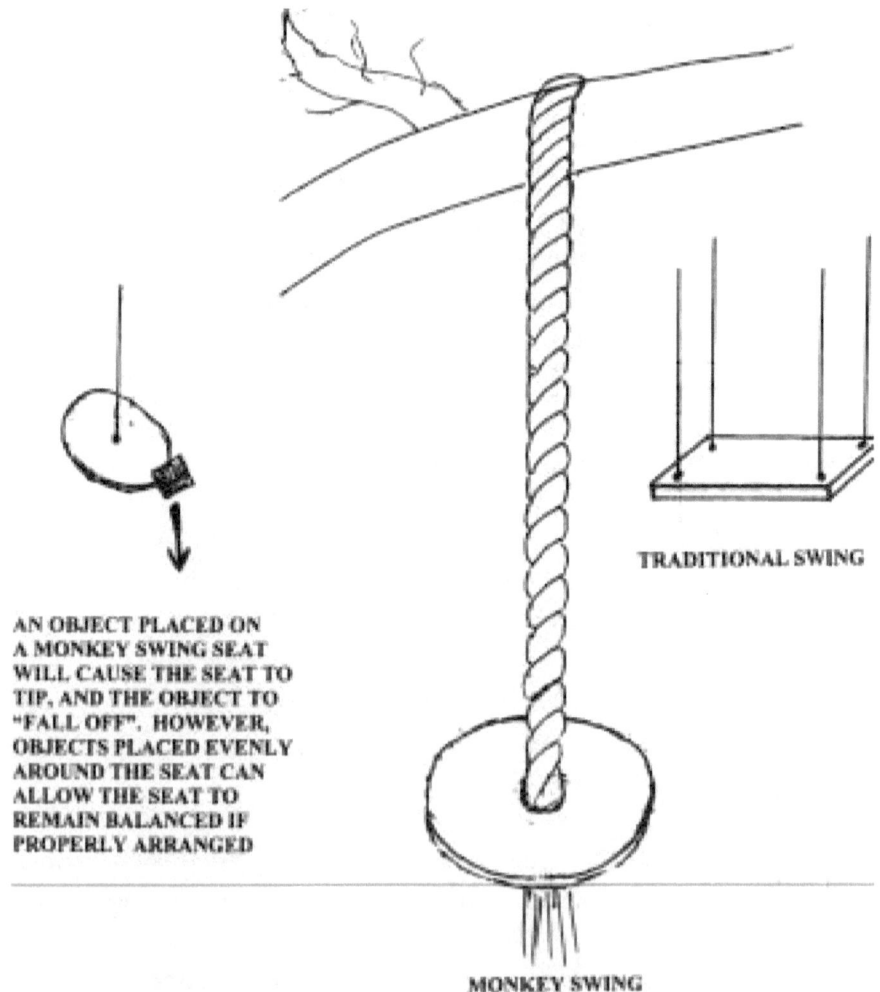

TRADITIONAL SWING

AN OBJECT PLACED ON A MONKEY SWING SEAT WILL CAUSE THE SEAT TO TIP, AND THE OBJECT TO "FALL OFF". HOWEVER, OBJECTS PLACED EVENLY AROUND THE SEAT CAN ALLOW THE SEAT TO REMAIN BALANCED IF PROPERLY ARRANGED

MONKEY SWING

"According to what's been said, we will need to think of the space as it stands with all its current and projected architectural features as if it has been placed on the monkey swing and try to determine whether or not it's balanced. All we need is a picture of a monkey swing, or better yet, let's make one."

"That's a cool idea," added Jayden who, along with Rebecca, had been listening to John. "Why not make one for the backyard . . . we could even place little objects on the seat of the swing to get a feel for how to create the balance we need. In fact . . ." Suddenly Jayden jumped up and grabbed the lid of Mary's pot. Mary, understanding what Jayden was about to do, grabbed some string from her kitchen drawer and handed it to Jayden.

Jayden tied the string tightly around the center of the handle of the pot, held the string at the other end, with the lid dangling at the tied end, and said "Voila! A monkey swing!" He passed it around the room so everyone could see how easily it tipped if a weight was put anywhere without an opposing weight to balance it. Everyone talked at once as they played with the lid.

After a few minutes, Mary again hit her now lidless pot with the wooden spoon and everyone turned to Matt, who had moved to the center of the room. "Okay, wait a minute, that's not all. It's a start, but we need your math abilities here now. The monkey-swing concept was easy compared to what we're gonna give you now! But this is so interesting that once we get it, we'll be able to use it with the monkey swing idea to do anything in decorating, maybe we can even hang out our shingle!"

Matt went on to explain, "According to Grandma, the ancient Greeks learned that the oval is more pleasing to the eye than the circle, and the rectangle more pleasing to the eye than the square. From this truth the Greeks wanted to determine what proportions of rectangles or ovals were the most pleasing. They determined that the most pleasing proportions were those that had ratios of 2 to 3, 3 to 5, or 5 to 8."

Many of the women groaned, and the men pretended to smirk and gloat over their perceived superior math abilities, but quickly decided they made a mistake in doing this as Rebecca jumped to her feet spouting math. The women had the last laugh as the men were forced to change their tune when Rebecca put them in their place, saving the day for the women by saying, "I've just been studying that!" "A ratio is how one part relates to another, a mathematical relationship between two numbers. The numbers here are sort of like the Fibonacci Numbers that are even found in nature! I remember that both the Greek ratio system and the Golden Ratio are connected to the Fibonacci Numbers, though Fibonacci came later."

"Fibonacci was a thirteenth century Italian mathematician who first used his series to describe how rabbits multiply. It was later found that the Fibonacci Numbers exist quite widely in nature. The outside formations of pineapples, pinecones, and sunflowers are just some examples. I can try to help you understand the relationship between the Greek ratios of 2 to 3, 3 to 5, and 5 to 8, and The Golden Ratio (0.618), by trying to explain the similar Fibonacci Numbers if you want me to." The women, so proud of Rebecca, a *woman* after all, said in unison, "Go for it, Rebecca, show these guys your stuff . . . we know what they're thinking . . . that *men* are better at math. Well, hey, guys, did any of you know about Fibonacci?"

So, encouraged and not as nervous anymore, Rebecca began by saying, "The Fibonacci Numbers are a mathematical series found by adding two consecutive numbers to obtain the next number in the series. Although there are two ways to start this series, they lead to the same place. Let's 'start' with one and two as the first two numbers. Adding these two together gives 3 for the next number. To move on to further numbers, we need only add the last two numbers we have. Here, two and three gives five, and continuing we add three and five to get eight. Thus, the first five Fibonacci Numbers are 1, 2, 3, 5, and 8. If we had started with zero and one instead, the series would come out 0, 1, 1, 2, 3, 5, 8 which is the same except for the 0, 1 in front."

Kevin came out of his office carrying his dry erase board and stand, along with a marker and an eraser. He placed it next to Rebecca, and without missing a beat, Rebecca picked up the marker and began to illustrate. "Beginning with the 2, we see that pairs of adjacent numbers correspond to the pleasing Greek ratios. Using the 2 and the 3 gives us the 2 to 3 ratio. Using the 3 and the 5 gives us the 3 to 5 ratio. Using the 5 and the 8 gives us the 5 to 8 ratio. Further combinations also correspond to favorable proportions, but we'd only need the first three to do this in decorating. Although, as this series is carried out further and further, the ratio between two successive numbers approaches closer and closer, math people say 'converges,' to the value 0.618 that corresponds to the Golden Ratio. So we see that using any one of these three mathematical expressions leads to the same pleasing room proportions.

"Leonardo da Vinci used the Golden Rule when he painted. In fact, he used it to plan the face of the Mona Lisa and the shape and dimension of her eyes before painting her. The mathematician Pythagoras and the builders of the pyramids used it as well. The spaces between columns in Greek architecture such as the Parthenon and even many graveyard crosses are some examples. Seashells, as well as sunflowers, pinecones, and pineapples are some examples found in nature. Thus, the Golden Ratio is often referred to as Divine Proportion."

"Now, I'm stuck and don't know how to use these to get room measurements, so I'll just turn the rest back to . . . ," and as she looked questioningly around the room, Matt jumped up. He wrote "12 x 18" on the board and said, "So, how do we learn what the ratio of our room is? To obtain the ratio of the room, measure the width and the length of the room. Convert these two measurements to feet, rounding off the inches. For example, your room measures 11'8" x 18'3". You would round off the inches to the nearest foot which would make the measurements 12' x 18', which I've written on the board. Looking at the two numbers, we'd find the highest common factor or divisor for both of these figures. For example, 2 and 3 and 6 are all numbers that will divide into both the 12 and the 18. But we are looking for the highest common factor or divisor, so we would choose the 6 to work with."

"Then we divide this common factor into the width figure, then into the length figure. If you have used the highest common factor, the ratio of the reduced width to the reduced length is the ratio reduced to its lowest form. For example, when we divide 6 into 12, the answer we obtain is 2. And when we divide 6 into 18, the answer we obtain is 3. Our results then are 2 and 3." Matt wrote these numbers on the board.

"So," he continued, "the results of our math matches up to one of the three desirable ratios of 2 to 3, 3 to 5, or 5 to 8. Our ratio, 2 to 3, is one of the desirable ratios, and this means that the room itself is already in good proportion.

"Remember, if you have not used the highest common factor or divisor, you will be able to divide again. For example, if you did not see that 6 was your highest divisor and you used 2 instead, your divisions of 2 into 12 and 2 into 18 would have resulted in 6 and 9. Looking for the possibility of yet another divisor, we could see that 3 will divide into both 6 and 9 resulting in 2 and 3, finally giving the same answer that we obtained by finding the highest divisor in the first round.

"Explained in a slightly different manner, a room which measured 12' x 20' would have a highest common factor of 4, and once divided by that 4, it would reduce to a ratio of 3 to 5. This means that a 12 x 20 room is also in the proper proportion. Here again, if you did not see that 4 was your highest divisor and if you used 2, your divisions of 2 into 12 and 2 into 20 would have resulted in 6 and 10. Looking for the possibility of yet another divisor, we could see that 2 will divide into both 6 and 10 resulting in 3 and 5. This is the same answer that we just obtained from the highest divisor.

"Both room measurements divided by their highest common denominator provided the final ratios 2 to 3 and 3 to 5, and each of these is one of the three ratios that represent good proportion. This means that both rooms need no changes or illusions and are ready to decorate. This is all we have to know."

John stood and said, "Well, that was a great explanation. There is one other way to address these ratios, so to be really complete, let me explain this method so you'll know them all. It's really almost the same thing, just another method. Rebecca mentioned it before. It's called the Golden Ratio or Mean and refers to the division of a line into two parts such that the ratio of the smaller part to the larger is the same as the ratio of the larger part to the original line. This ratio works out to be 0.618. Thus we see that the ratios of 2 to 3 (=0.667), 3 to 5 (=0.600), and 5 to 8 (=.625) are all very near the Golden Ratio value. We can see from these ratios of Fibonacci Numbers that they converge toward 0.618 just as Rebecca said.

"The Golden Ratio tells us that for a room one unit in length, the width should be 0.618. For rooms of other sizes, multiply the long wall (length) by 0.618 to obtain the "perfect" size of the short wall (width). For example, if the long wall of a room is 20 feet in length, we multiply this length by 0.618 to obtain the proper width of 12.36 feet, or 12 foot, 4 inches. Thus a 12 x 20 foot room would be very nearly in perfect proportion. This technique of using the Golden Ratio is useful in designing a new home, in redoing an existing home, or in modifying a structure such as the carriage house.

"Enough math, now? I agree. But do try to understand that these numbers are evidently the key to a successful design. With them you can determine whether or not the room you are about to decorate has existing problems of disproportion that must be corrected early in your design project. An improperly proportioned room can be balanced, but it will never look as good as one with better proportions. The balance is what provides a sense of harmony and tranquility, but it is really successful only in a well-shaped room. Both proportion and balance are necessary. I'm done!"

With that John bowed deeply, held his palms face up at waist level, and moved his fingers open and closed to let everyone know he expected applause. Then he bowed to Rebecca, ushering her to accept their continued applause. Grinning, and with great dignity, he went back to his seat. Rebecca, not to be outdone, stood and also bowed from the waist, and returned to her seat.

Then Caleb stood and said, "Remember too that according to the Bible, God himself laid down specific measurements for the ark that Noah built, also the Tabernacle, and its Ark of the Covenant, Solomon's Temple, and many other structures and items. In addition to God's instructions regarding size, and type of wood, God also specified the designs and materials to be applied as decorative items. In fact, it is estimated that, in today's dollars, the temple would cost from two to five billion dollars to build. The Temple stood for four hundred years.

"If God took such interest and care in the design and beauty of His plans for the Ark and the Temple, we can be sure He will look favorably on our desire and efforts to have a beautiful home, a Bethany in which to live, pray, and raise and teach our families, a place where His Holy Spirit will also abide. He will even help us with our struggle to learn the math of good proportion should we ask Him! So let's promise to do this every time we get together to work on any project!"

As the room became quiet, Rebecca yelled, "Let's have dessert!" Mary agreed with her and together the women began putting the leftovers away. The men gathered up all the used paper plates, napkins and plastic utensils, and placed these in the large trash bags Mary provided. Sarah loaded the glasses into the dishwasher, while Jayden wiped down the island so it would be ready for the next course. Ann began cutting the brownies into squares as Rebecca put out the iced cupcakes.

After Rebecca, Mary, and Elizabeth had put out clean plates and utensils, a bowl of cut-up fruit, a plate of cookies, and another of brownies, Kevin unceremoniously placed a half-gallon carton of Blackjack Cherry ice cream, along with a huge scooping spoon on the island. The women began to voice their worry about calories, but the men went right for the brownies and ice cream.

As the women stood together around the far end of the island, eating their forbidden desserts, Barbara said, "Suppose that we assume that a room is 10 feet wide by 20 feet long, and when we find its ratio, it does not meet the pleasing Greek ratio criteria. How are we supposed to fix it?"

Sarah explained, "Grandma said that one solution would be to 'visually' elongate the 10-foot wall by two feet. If we could do this, it would work because a 12 by 20 foot room does meet the criteria. We cannot lengthen these 10-foot walls physically, but Grandma says we can do it visually. We visually elongate the wall to achieve the "illusion" of additional length. As an example, a piece of furniture that is both long in length, and low in height can be placed on the wall to create the desired illusion. Other suggestions would be the use of a chair rail on only the two 10' walls, or using wallpaper or a faux paint creation with horizontal stripes on those walls."

"Conversely" Sarah continued, "instead of the room being 10 x 20 feet, what if the room was 13 x 20 feet? This would require that the two opposing 13' walls be visually "shortened." In this case, one might choose to place a tall narrow piece of furniture, such as an armoire or secretary desk, on the 13' walls in order to achieve the illusion of shortening them and thus creating proper proportion for the room. Similarly, vertical wallpaper, paint that provides tone on tone vertical stripes, or vertically placed moldings can be used. Even a tall tree will have the same effect. Thus, we see that there are many ways to solve the problem of disproportion once we have detected it. The trick is to detect it."

Barbara, who had listened very carefully to the entire discussion, summarized her thoughts. "This concept of harmony through good proportion with all the different names of the Greek ratio system, The Golden Mean, Divine Proportion, as well as being related to the Fibonacci Series may have us groaning with the idea of math, but once we understand the principles, I'm sure we will be able to decorate flawlessly. I can see now that it is 'balance and proportion' that is the all-encompassing rule for good design. I can see how they insure a sense of harmony in the design. In most cases, it matters not the style, the age of your furnishings, or even the fact that nothing 'matches,' as long as the items and their placement provide the right proportion and balance. Sarah, your grandmother was one smart cookie, I'd never viewed decorating in that light before and now it makes perfect sense to me. Thanks for sharing!"

Chapter Eleven

THE BEGINNING OF CHANGE

The wedding plans seemed under control, and Matt and Sarah's house was finished to the point they'd hoped for. After their adventure into the concepts of the monkey swing and the Greek ratio system, everyone's spare time seemed to be filled with talk of, and drawings for, either the carriage house or a project for their own homes. But underneath these joyous activities, a few storms were brewing, and change was underway.

Just this morning, Debbie had gone on her own to the minister to begin counseling. She had already decided, also on her own, not to pursue the reinstatement of her engagement to Josh. *That,* she thought, *I'll leave to God. And if God does bring us back together, Josh will have to make some changes and go to counseling himself. I have to make changes too, but I know I will do what I need to do to be sure that I am starting out my life the right way.*

The minister agreed that she should "let go and let God" and see what happened. They set a time next week to talk together again. Then tonight, after the decorating discussion, Debbie found the courage to tell the women that she was the one responsible for the mix-up at the dressmaker's and the caterers. Barbara and the other women were in the kitchen and the men had gone to the garage to look at a new lawn tractor that Kevin had purchased. Barbara was talking to Sarah asking her if she was okay about the big surprise that awaited her.

Sarah had replied, "At first, I was surprised by how strongly Matt reacted. I'd felt that it just didn't seem important enough for Matt to react as he did. For a while, I felt a little resentment that he would say absolutely nothing, not even a hint. But as I thought about it, I understood that Matt would not do anything . . . ever . . . to hurt me, so he must have good reason."

"I really wanted to know, and at first began to think up all sorts of things that it could be. I thought it might be some sort of gift, but when everyone seemed so curious and innocent in their questioning, I began to realize that if none of you had anything to do with it, it must be coming from Matt or from somewhere outside of our little group. My mind tried to figure it out, but then I suddenly felt that I really should allow Matt to have what he'd asked of me. I should just wait to see what it would be. I felt better then because I felt that it was the right thing to do. I was being asked to trust him and I do, so I am! So to answer your question, Barbara, yeah, *now* I'm okay with it, but it was a test in the beginning, I can tell you.

"But then again, since I'm human, . . . Hey, guys, any clues?" And Sarah laughed.

Everyone said at once, "No clues, we'll all just have to wait . . . along with you!" and joined her laughter.

That's when Debbie jumped in telling everyone that she had a confession to make and they all turned to her expectantly, waiting for her to speak. Debbie, with hands sweating from anxiety, started off by saying she was sorry and hoped they would forgive her. Everyone assured her that whatever it was, she could be sure they still loved her and that she was already forgiven.

Hesitantly, Debbie admitted that the opposite fabric choices for the gown sashes and tuxedo cummerbunds, the mix-up in chair styles, and the wrong tablecloth colors were all her fault. She explained that she had spilled coffee on the lists Barbara had made for her to bring to the dressmaker and the caterer. This caused the ink to run and make the words indecipherable. Debbie explained that when she tried to decipher the chair numbers, she evidently transposed some numbers, and at the dressmakers, she'd looked at the fabrics and selected from memory which fabric went on which item. She apologized for ruining the lists, for giving out the wrong information to the dressmaker and the caterer, and for not telling them what had happened as soon as she learned that there was an error.

Barbara assured her that the errors had all been corrected and no harm had been done. She told Debbie that they admired her courage in coming to them, adding that if she'd told them right away, it would have been fixed sooner. She also said, "Debbie, we all make mistakes, but as long as we own up to them, we can often fix whatever happened. We all realize that spilling the coffee could have happened to anyone and that we all need to forgive mistakes and spend our energy fixing those mistakes, not pointing our fingers." She then added that sometimes God allows Satan to trip us up when we become arrogant and start believing that we don't make mistakes! "Then we get a quick and very humbling lesson," she said.

The women felt badly that these mistakes had frightened Debbie and asked her to promise that in the future she would always come to them with this type, in fact any problem. Debbie was very appreciative of their support and explained that, because this had happened, she learned so much from their example and their kindness. She told them that she had just begun counseling that morning to learn to be less insecure, less impulsive, and hopefully make fewer mistakes. "While I love Josh with all my heart," she told the women, "I realize now that it would be wrong to get married if I am afraid to be honest and we can't work through problems like adults."

The women were proud of her for seeking help and trying to do the right thing, but they were worried about Josh because they didn't want him to lose her. After giving Debbie a big, sincere hug, they told her that they would all pray not only for her, but for Josh as well.

*Hearken now unto my voice, I will give thee counsel,
and God shall be with thee: Be thou for the people to God-ward,
that thou mayest bring the causes unto God.*
—*Exodus 18:19*

The gathering ended fairly early, about ten o'clock, as they usually did on Saturday nights. The Sunday service was always a highlight of the week for everyone, so they wanted to get home to get a good night's sleep before church in the morning. It was that important to them.

As Elizabeth sat in the kitchen drinking her morning coffee, she began to think about Debbie. Elizabeth was pleased to see the changes in Debbie and felt that in the long run those changes would benefit both Debbie and Josh and even the children they might have someday. She knew that wisdom took time to develop. She was also pleased that Rebecca was present to hear how friends stood shoulder to shoulder to solve problems and forgave one another when mistakes had been made. It was a good lesson for her.

But what Elizabeth didn't know was that as Rebecca grew close to all the wonderful people who had become her new extended family, she felt guilty about Elizabeth. Or that over and over Rebecca would think to herself, *my mom is the light and strength of my life and I won't lose her, I just won't!* and would grit her teeth, and send that thought toward heaven trying to be sure God heard her thoughts.

Elizabeth had come to recognize that something was bothering Rebecca, that she seemed to be angry and seemed to approach her faith with a challenge. She wondered if Rebecca was frightened about what the future might hold. She understood this. She herself was devastated by the thought that she might not be around to help Rebecca reach an age where she could make it on her own. She was afraid that dropping the teacup the other day was a sign that her illness was beginning to encroach upon her and wondered if Rebecca picked up on her fears and reacted to them. She hadn't told anyone about that incident and didn't plan to, but perhaps her stress level showed and Rebecca was reacting instinctively to that. A high stress level wasn't good for her illness either, so she'd have to work on that problem. A catch-22.

Elizabeth felt that it was best for the two of them to spend as much time as possible with Mary and Kevin and their friends, so Rebecca could become an integral part of their lives. Being with the others helped them lay aside their own problems for a while, especially as they watched the reversal of roles between Debbie and Josh and saw everyone do their best to help the young couple.

Josh too was up early that morning thinking that everyone at the party last night could see that he was miserable, but no one knew the turmoil that raged in him as he sensed that Debbie had grown away from him, didn't need him anymore. He realized he'd made a big mistake when he broke off the engagement, but he wasn't going to beg either. He'd been thinking quite a lot about what Caleb had said to him last week when they sat together on Mary and Kevin's hearth. Slowly he was realizing that Caleb was right.

He had also begun to realize that he did want the kind of marriage, the kind of relationship that existed between Caleb and Ann, Sarah and Matt, and Kevin and Mary. He just didn't know what to do right now to make that happen. He doubted his own ability to follow all the rules and bury his ego. He hated the thought that he might be asked to give in to something that didn't go the way he felt it should.

Josh had been reluctant to go to the party last night. He knew Debbie would be there and that had unnerved him. He was torn between his desire to ignore her and to "kiss and makeup." No wonder he was in a bad mood. No wonder everyone could tell. Yesterday afternoon, Josh had spent a lot of time thinking. *Because life seems long, and I'm young, I just feel that I have plenty of time to do things later. Yet time does get away from me. All of a sudden I realize that I've lost something that might be irretrievable, that I might not be able to go back to "fix it." I guess I need to learn what to do with Debbie and how to head off similar problems that I might encounter later in life.*

Maybe because I wouldn't let anyone teach me in my early teen years, it is now impacting on how I'll fare in the future. Caleb and Sarah got more instruction than I did as teens simply because they accepted the help. When Mom died Caleb had been twenty-three already, and Sarah had stayed connected to the youth group, but I rebelled and ran from both Grandma's advice and the youth leader's help when I was most in need of it. I had been only thirteen.

Dad had always been useless as a father because he drank and lived in the bars. He'd never been a role model, and sadly he'd never learned how to hold a real gentle teaching conversation. In fact, I don't ever remember a conversation with him about anything but sports. The opposite of the way Caleb is. I was so angry that Dad was never home all those years and when he was it was chaos and pain. I still sometimes think that his ways was what had made Mom die so young.

Josh remembered the scripture he had once muttered under his breath about his father when one of the ministers was trying to get his father to recognize that his drinking harmed the family. Now Josh understood that the same verse applied to him:

> *You are stiff necked,*
> *resisting the Holy Spirit.*
>
> *—Acts 7:51*

Josh heard the bitterness in his thoughts, the desire to shift blame, and realized that he often did this . . . just like his father. He even did it to Debbie, wanting her to take the blame for his mistakes. He was an adult now. He couldn't blame someone else for his troubles any longer. He had to make things right himself. Josh also wondered if that "sins of the forefathers pass to the kids" thing was his problem. He didn't want to be like his father.

Josh also realized that despite his Dad's lack of guidance, and his mom's early death, God had still provided him with the instruction and background to make these changes in his life, so he shouldn't just sit on his duff and do nothing. Grandma wouldn't like it, and even Caleb can see it. But that's what he was doing to fix it: Nothing! As his mind wandered to a future with Debbie, he thought: *To think that a father can figure that he can address his child's needs later is the grave mistake that many parents make. This completely ignores the urgency of today for kids whose parents make no time for them! That's what my father did and maybe why I'm so messed up right now. Did my father feel that life was so busy that it was difficult for him to make the time to change himself, or teach his kids what God wants of us? This really leaves the kid high and dry. Ultimately, because we are given our free will, all choices are ours. We are responsible for choosing how we spend the time we have, and we must choose correctly. My father didn't do this, and I guess I'd better realize that I don't either.*

Suddenly Josh saw that although he'd been addressing most of his thoughts to his father, they applied to Josh himself, and called for an action that he himself should be taking regardless of what had or had not happened to him as a teenager. His thoughts continued, and he asked himself, *If the parents don't teach their children, who will? If I don't know of or practice God's instructions myself, how can I teach another to do so? If I wanted my child to load and run the dishwasher, I'd need first to teach him how to place the dishes and utensils into the dishwasher, how to add soap, what type, how much, how to properly close the door, and finally what buttons to push to make the machine start. After a while, I could allow the child to wash the dishes alone because I taught him properly. Why did my father do much less when it came to the word of God. Will I do the same?* These thoughts had rolled back and forth through his head for a few days, conflicting with his macho feelings. Without a resolution, he had been miserable at the party.

When Josh entered church this morning, his mind was still in turmoil. He had no idea how he could resolve his conflicts. But when the minister began to speak about the responsibility of a husband and father, Josh was amazed. *How did he know what I needed?* he thought. Then Josh remembered that it was God, not the minister, who was speaking and God knew exactly what he needed and was giving it to him.

In awe, Josh listened as God spoke to him through the minister, "God Himself, throughout scripture, entrusts husbands with the responsibility to care for their wives and their children's spiritual instruction. He demands that both parents meet their responsibility to teach their children about Him and about those things that should guide their life and become their goals.

Husbands must not leave the children's spiritual care to their wives alone, but must take an active role themselves, by word and by example. Theirs is the ultimate responsibility. Not meeting this responsibility is costly to both child and parents. While no parent wants to see their children suffer, some ignore the fact that by not doing what God advises they can be the cause of their children's suffering." He went on to use a Biblical verse that clearly showed that God wants us to pass on to our children all He has revealed to us.

You shall teach them diligently to your children,
and shall talk of them when you sit in your house, when you
walk by the way, when you lie down, and
when you rise up.

—*Deuteronomy 6:7*

The minister also said that parents should speak to their children about the words of God, and indicate how God wants them to live and develop. He admonished parents to take time to sit and teach, and asked, "Where do you sit with them? When do you find the time to walk with them? What do you teach them when they go to bed, and when they rise up. How do you teach them? Do you know God's word yourselves?" Josh remembered the scriptures he used.

Embrace thy children, bring them up with gladness,
like a dove, and make their feet firm and strong like a pillar:
For I have chosen thee.
—2 *Esdras* 2:15 *Apocrypha*

And you Fathers, do not provoke your
children to wrath, but bring them up in the training
and admonition of the Lord.
—*Ephesians* 6:4

Josh felt uncomfortable. It seemed that the minister was looking directly at him most of the time. But the message was getting through. Josh asked himself: *How am I going to do this if I'm angry and unforgiving?* He realized that while he needed to look at what God expects of him as a parent, he also needed to know what God expected of him as a husband.

The minister had gone on to say, "With or without our help, today's children will become the future leaders of our country. They will develop mores, laws, and religious doctrines. They will be the fathers and mothers of children for even more generations in the future. If this generation doesn't teach them properly, how can they teach others, how can they lead in a manner that will bring God's blessings?" Josh thought, *So many people . . . including me . . . are too complacent.*

"The task of teaching our children in today's world can be daunting when you think of what the world is offering them," the minister said. "We live in a world filled with many subtle teaching mechanisms, most of which are harmful to children. From television shows to movies, from video games to the classroom, it is almost impossible to shield our children from violence, hatred, disrespect, foul language, and other ungodly actions. These influences come in the guise of attractive animals, beautiful people, kind words, exciting action figures, and games of skill to name a few. It becomes more and more difficult for parents to see beyond these innocent fronts to the message that is being sent to their children, and even more difficult for parents to shield their children from these elements. Becoming desensitized to violence destroys our ability to be empathic. This ultimately destroys our ability to love. Thus, without a strong foundation in the Word of God, children are easy prey to the evil spirits of the world."

"In truth, the only hope our children have to learn what is right in God's eyes is through us, through our willingness to teach them about God, about His statutes, and about His future plans for us. And they must be taught what to avoid in this world. By our examples, we teach them how to love and act. We need to be a living example to them, not simply someone who talks about it. In today's vernacular, we must walk the talk."

When the service was over, Josh realized he hadn't "walked the talk." Then with that thought, Josh asked his minister if he could set a date to come in for counseling. Unnoticed by Josh, the minister smiled to himself, so pleased because he'd already spoken with Debbie and had prayed that Josh would also ask for help. He sent God a prayer of thanks. *The hand of God was surely moving mountains to bring change,* he thought.

Josh left the church with a more buoyant step and waved hello to John and Elizabeth so exuberantly that they knew something good would soon be happening in Josh's life. They too had heard the words of the minister about the responsibilities of a spouse and a parent and had hoped it would hit home with everyone in attendance. It certainly had with them.

John had invited Elizabeth to church and lunch so they could enjoy one another's company while waiting to pick up Jayden and Rebecca from an after-service youth group meeting where they would have lunch with the other youth and the ministers. Elizabeth had told John about her fateful diagnosis and the fears she was experiencing, so John wanted to speak with her without the children being present.

When they were settled in their booth at the restaurant, and had ordered their lunch, John reminded Elizabeth that he'd been a deacon in his church for a very long time, and had seen more miracles than he could count. He told Elizabeth that they would begin praying for a miracle for her. "As you know, Elizabeth, the Bible is the most published and, to many, the most important book in the world. It is the recorded history of God's relationship with mankind. Its importance is not because it details ancient events, but rather because it records the Word of God that gives us guidance still today. It contains a detailed prophecy of things to come, and teaches us the highest moral standards. Furthermore, medical knowledge, historical facts, practical recommendations for daily living, and beautiful poetry are contained in the Bible. It's the medical part I wanted to talk to you about.

"Although many religious communities as a whole acknowledge that scripture addresses every part of life, few people realize, as Grandma did, and as Sarah and Matt showed us the other day, that scripture contains admonitions and exhortations that are related to the use, the design, and the decorating of our homes. This gives us insight into how much God loves us, how much He wants to teach us.

"But we must remember, our health is important to God too. Amazingly, scripture not only addresses our health, but it also clearly demonstrates that God does not issue arbitrary commands to test us, or make demands of us. Rather, He speaks out of His infinite wisdom and love for us, to protect us in our walk through life. He is truly being our loving Father. Here are two examples, and you may already be aware of them.

"In Genesis, God spoke to Moses, telling him that male babies should be circumcised on the eighth day. The Jews carefully followed this advice. A number of years ago, when hospitals advocated that mother and child stay in their care for three to five days, circumcision was performed on the day, or the day before, the mother and child were to be discharged from the hospital. Today, with stays of a single night at the hospital, male children are returned to the hospital for the circumcision at the parents' convenience, usually within a few weeks of the child's birth. Having this procedure done on a day other than the eighth day is not considered a sin. Why? If it is not a sin, why did God give this instruction to the Israelites?

> *And you shall be circumcised in the flesh of your foreskins, and it*
> *shall be a sign of the covenant between Me and you.*
> *He who is eight days old among you shall be circumcised,*
> *every male child in your generations,*
> *he who is born in your house or bought with money from*
> *any foreigner who is not your descendant.*
>
> *—Genesis 17:11, 12*

"Medical research has shown that antibodies in the mother's milk and the blood clotting mechanism of the child both vary every day after birth. While the antibodies diminish and the clotting mechanism improves, the combination of the two is at the optimal level on the eighth day. Therefore the child is best able to fight infection and manufacture the necessary clotting mechanism on the eighth day. Here it seems that God was not being arbitrary in giving this instruction, or telling us what is sinful here, but rather was simply looking out for the health and well-being of the child as well as of the Jewish nation. God gave this instruction to help His people stay healthy in those primitive times.

"Also, in the Old Testament, God suggests that the Jews not eat certain foods. They were given a list of animals that they were not to eat, which included among many, pork, vultures, and anything that had died on its own.

> *These are the animals which you may eat . . . ,*
> *. . . You shall not eat, such as these . . . ,*
> *Also the swine is unclean for you . . . ,*
> *You shall not eat anything that has died of itself.*
>
> *—Deuteronomy 14:4-21*

"Yet the New Testament suggests that one need not be concerned with what is served or what is eaten in homes where people came together to speak of and worship God.

> *And when Peter came up to Jerusalem, those of the*
> *circumcision contended with him, saying,*
> *"You went in to uncircumcised men and ate with them!"*
> *But Peter explained it to them in order from*
> *the beginning: . . . "for nothing common or unclean*
> *has at any time entered my mouth." But the voice*
> *answered me again from heaven, 'What God has cleansed*
> *you must not call common.*
>
> *—Acts 11:2, 3, 4, 8, 9*

"Which of these two somewhat contradictory passages is right? Could they both be right? Medical research has shown that trichinosis is prevalent in pork and can be deadly if the pork is not properly prepared. Perhaps, in the Deuteronomy verse, God was looking after the health and well-being of His people and not laying down a rule which, if not followed, produced sin.

"I believe the correct answer is that Our Heavenly Father was caring for and protecting His children in words and a manner best suited to their understanding and to the conditions of the world at that time.

"The rules regarding certain foods certainly appear to be less rigid in the New Testament. Could it simply be that while the Old Testament addressed life in the wilderness and under primitive conditions, the New Testament speaks of life in the cities and townships where there might have been better facilities for raising, cleaning, storing, and cooking their meats? Or did this last verse mean that God had actually removed the 'unclean' elements from the food before it was eaten?

"The more important point here is that God is looking out for our natural health and well-being along with our spiritual health when He gives us direction. Additionally, the New Testament verse reminds us that God is in control of all things and can always exercise that control any time and any way He wishes. Here we see God protecting Apostle Peter from harm. Other passages in scripture also show God is always protecting us.

> *Look at the birds of the air, for they neither sow*
> *nor reap nor gather into barns; yet your heavenly Father*
> *feeds them. Are you not of more value than they?*
> —*Matthew 6:26*

> *Are not two sparrows sold for a copper coin?*
> *And not one of them falls to the ground*
> *apart from your Father's will.*
> —*Matthew 10:29*

"These are two of so many examples that show how God has taken an interest in the things affecting our life and general day-to-day well-being. They suggest that through all of scripture a loving God is looking out for us. Moreover, throughout the New Testament are examples of God curing all sorts of illnesses. Some by asking, some by touching the hem of His gown, others through prayer . . . all sorts of ways. Just last night, we looked at areas of scripture where God speaks of the home environment. Now we can assume that He speaks these words for our benefit as well. Similarly, when He instructs us what to do in our homes and daily lives in regard to our children, there too must lie a great benefit to us if we follow His suggestions.

> *Give attention to my words;*
> *incline your ear to my sayings.*
> *Do not let them depart from your eyes;*
> *keep them in the midst of your heart*
> *for they are life to those who find them,*
> *and health to all their flesh.*
> —*Proverbs 4:20, 21, 22*

The waiter brought their lunch and broke John's train of thought. When the waiter left, John apologized to Elizabeth. "Elizabeth, I am sorry to be so long-winded. Many people have complained about it. It probably comes from my many years of preaching and counseling. Also, as an engineer, I always felt the need to provide a thorough background to support what I wanted to say." Elizabeth replied softly, "John, I enjoy very much the way you talk. You present your thoughts very clearly. I always find new insights from what you say. Please go on."

Relieved, John continued, "Let me try to get to the point. Your two major concerns are your health and its effect on Rebecca. The Bible is filled with instructions to parents regarding how to raise their children. As we gather and read these specific verses, we can begin to discern how these instructions might impact our lives. We can see that the parenting instructions in scripture require us as parents to provide the means by which these instructions can be implemented. Excellent as it is, it isn't enough that children attend church or temple or religious classes. God gives parents much instruction regarding home teaching. Consequently, it is of utmost importance to discover what we need to do and how to do it. You have done that . . . and God will bless you for doing that.

"God tells us to pray, so we will begin praying about your health. He also tells us that He will give us the desires of our heart when possible. Therefore, I want you to come with me to see my physician. He is a naturopathic physician who believes that God has provided us with a body that, given the right tools, the right nutrients, can heal itself. God has also told us that He can do anything! Let's see if He will work a miracle for you through my physician.

"All through scripture we read that Christ had incredible healing power, and also that He gave His apostles this power. All these things are ours if God allows it. So it's worth a try, ehh? If we find that God has other plans, then we'll worry about how to get through that tribulation.

"Elizabeth, always remember two things God has told you:

> *Now faith is the substance of things hoped for,*
> *the evidence of things not seen.*
>
> —*Hebrews 11:1*

> *Therefore do not worry about*
> *tomorrow, for tomorrow will worry about*
> *its own things.*
>
> —*Matthew 6:34*

"Okay? Ohh, and one other thing, did you know that over 8 percent of cases of suspected ALS are misdiagnosed?"

Elizabeth couldn't believe how much better she felt from John's loving, inspired words. She was so grateful God had brought him into her life, and she readily and eagerly agreed to see his doctor. She felt her stress level drop when he said he would pray for her. She'd really needed a good talking-to like that! Squeezing John's hands as they rested on the tabletop, Elizabeth smiled, whispered her thanks, and told him he was truly a wonderful friend and brother in Christ. They left to pick up Rebecca and Jayden, grateful that God had given them each a friend to fill the void that their past losses had brought them.

When they arrived back at the church to pick up Rebecca and Jayden, they could see how happy the children were. While Rebecca described the meeting and how wonderful it was to be with the other youth, Jayden contained his inner excitement. A few days earlier, he'd been speaking with one of his favorite ministers who was also his youth leader, telling him of his worries that Rebecca would lose her faith if anything happened to her mother. He explained how hard Rebecca was praying and that he and his grandfather were also praying. Of course, Elizabeth, Rebecca's mother was praying too.

Jayden's minister had told him that when a friend prayed for another friend and asked someone else to join that prayer, God was there with them, actually in their midst, as they prayed. God would hear that prayer and act on it. He had shown Jayden the scripture that gave that promise, then he had called another of the ministers into the sacristy and the three of them prayed fervently for Elizabeth and Rebecca.

Again I say unto you,
That if two of you shall agree on earth as touching any thing that they shall ask,
it shall be done for them of my Father which is in heaven.
For where two or three are gathered in my name, there am I in the midst of them.
—Matthew 18:29, 30

After John dropped them at home, Elizabeth and Rebecca saw Mary and Kevin in the living room and stopped to speak with them for a few minutes before going to their rooms. Mary and Kevin had just been talking and praying about Elizabeth and Rebecca, thanking God for sending Rebecca back into their lives and for the precious gift of Elizabeth. They had asked their Heavenly Father to heal Elizabeth, help them all become a close-knit family, and allow the carriage house to serve as a Bethany for Elizabeth and Rebecca.

They had also been praying for Debbie and Josh. Earlier, they had spoken with Caleb and Ann who asked them to pray that Caleb would be able to touch Josh's heart whenever they spoke together. Caleb had shared his concern for the relationship between Debbie and Josh and told them that Ann, ever-faithful Ann, also prayed with fervor alongside Caleb.

Caleb had done his best to talk to Josh. Everyone saw so much good in Josh. Caleb knew that his attitude really resulted from a lack of trust in his heart and knew that this stemmed from Josh's loss of trust in his own father. But Josh didn't know that. In fact Josh would have been furious had anyone told him this because he loved his father with a passion, despite his father's shortcomings. Josh was angry over this but didn't know it. Caleb could tell from some of things Josh said that he allowed himself to be angry with his mother because she was easy to blame; she had left him and wasn't there to defend herself. But for some reason, he couldn't bring himself to blame his father, though Caleb was sure that deep in his subconscious he knew his father should bear the blame.

How can this be resolved, Caleb wondered, *how can I tell this to Josh when I know he'd be very angry with me and retreat into denial, making me the new scapegoat because he won't face the truth?* Caleb had the same father and had lived through the same pain, but had been able to place the blame where it belonged, then move through blaming to forgiveness and finally into understanding and peace. Maybe it was because Caleb had been older when their mom had died and he'd felt that he'd be doggoned if he'd allow his father's mistakes to affect his future. He knew that until one resolved this stuff, it always festered, waiting to rear its ugly head. He wondered how he could get Josh to acknowledge this. Acknowledging it was the only way to get over it.

But Caleb also knew the power of prayer. He and Ann were going to pray as often and as hard as they could that Josh would come around before it was too late, before he lost Deb completely.

The heavens were bombarded with the prayers of the faithful.

After Elizabeth returned to her room, she worked to complete her drawing of a floor plan for the carriage house using Divine Proportion for the rooms. When she finished, she went back to the kitchen to show Mary and Kevin, but they were not there, so Elizabeth left the plan on the counter.

Later, when Mary and Kevin returned to the kitchen, they saw her plans and realized how hard she must have worked to create those proper proportions. They knew Elizabeth would be blessed in that striving. They were all trying their best, in things small and things great, to learn God's word and gain His incredible blessing and a future so very special.

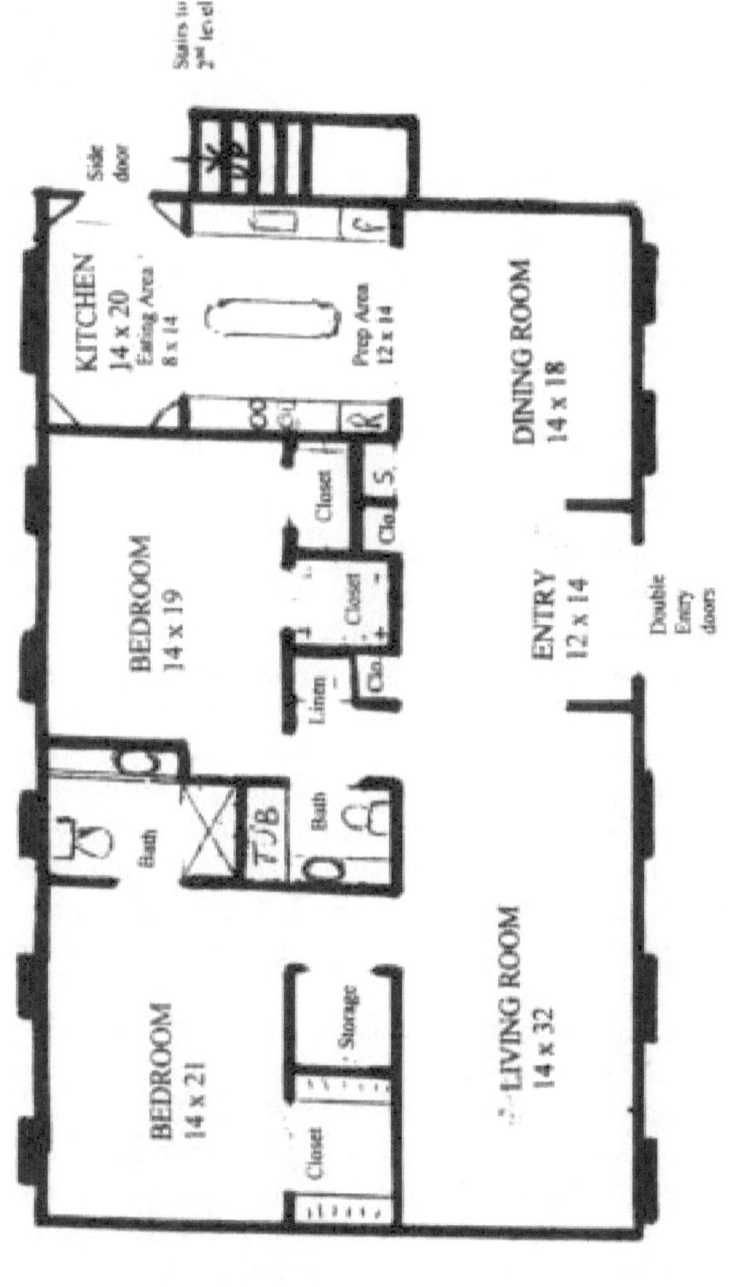

Stairs to 2nd level

Side door

KITCHEN
14 x 20
Eating Area
8 x 14

Prep Area
12 x 14

DINING ROOM
14 x 18

BEDROOM
14 x 19

Closet

Clo. S.

Closet

Linen

Clo.

ENTRY
12 x 14

Double Entry doors

Bath

TUB

Bath

BEDROOM
14 x 21

Storage

Closet

LIVING ROOM
14 x 32

Chapter Twelve

MIRACLES

Now therefore listen to me, my children,
for blessed are those who keep my ways.

—*Proverbs 8:32*

Josh and Caleb were sitting on stools placed in front of the island in Caleb's kitchen. On the counter were the huge sandwiches with crisp Cuban bread that Ann had just made for them, along with side dishes of potato salad, crunchy dill pickles, and sliced tomatoes. After placing a large pitcher on the counter filled with fresh lemonade and a dash of pomegranate juice, Ann walked around the island and stood behind them, gently resting her hands on their shoulders. She tactfully explained that she wanted to go outside and finish some work she had started in the garden. Turning halfway from the counter, with one arm still on the black granite counter, both Caleb and Josh reached around Ann with one arm to embrace her before she left the kitchen.

They both knew that Ann was being diplomatic, that she would really prefer to stay, but she was discreetly leaving the men to their conversation. Ann was wise enough to know that Josh and Caleb would talk more openly by themselves, brother to brother, man to man. When she reached the garden, she quickly prayed that Josh's heart would be receptive to Caleb's words and that everything would work out in a way where everyone would know that God had helped.

When Josh began telling Caleb that he'd prayed with the minister after service this morning and told him he wanted to begin counseling, Caleb had to fight back the strong rush of emotion he felt. So happy was he with this news that a welling up of thankfulness made his eyes water and made him struggle for the moment to find his voice. He reached over to Josh and grasped his shoulder in a brotherly, but bearish hug.

Josh continued by explaining that, after his conversation with Caleb while sitting on the hearth at Mary and Kevin's house on moving day, he had asked God to help him. He wanted to make the right decisions for his life, not only now with Debbie, but always. He said that when Caleb left him, his words began to take effect. He had looked across the room at Debbie and he suddenly realized that what he really wanted out of life was to follow in his brother's footsteps, to do what God expected of him. He wanted to earn Caleb's respect, wanted to be an integral and respected part of the family, and he wanted Debbie beside him.

"I don't know if I can do it, Caleb, but I am sure gonna try. I have to learn how to keep my life in balance . . . God's balance. Like the monkey swing, it won't be easy! I'm not expecting to be perfect, or to never make a mistake. I just want to be able to recognize when I do and have the guts to acknowledge it and correct it."

Caleb told him that no man could accomplish that task alone because they all had sinful natures, but with God's help, they could continue to improve and to overcome their sinful nature. He went on to describe an analogy he'd heard about balancing life correctly: "When you studied chemistry, you learned that there is an attraction between certain elements. The components of table salt and the components of water are two simple examples. Sodium and chlorine atoms in equal quantities are attracted to each other and, when placed together, will grasp one another and bond to form table salt. Hydrogen and oxygen atoms in proper quantities are also attracted to one another and bond together to form water.

"One of the benefits of living as God admonishes us is that when we do, we are providing the proper atmosphere for the Holy Spirit to dwell within us. The Holy Spirit is attracted to, and will thrive in, only the proper setting. Like sodium and chlorine, and hydrogen and oxygen, are attracted to one another, the Holy Spirit can be attracted to a man's heart and bond to him if the right atmosphere is present. The atmosphere we want to provide for the Holy Spirit is a heart that is open, seeking God, and striving to live in accordance with the word of God.

"We, as men, as husbands and fathers, must be sure that we provide an atmosphere in our home, and in ourselves, that will attract the Holy Spirit and allow it to abide in us and with us. We must remember that without the 'occupancy' of the Holy Spirit, that hollow space in us may attract other spirits, those belonging to Satan, to dwell there instead. There will be a price to pay if this happens. As the Bible warns, even more spirits will come at us, worse than the first," Caleb said.

"I'm not sure I have enough self-discipline to do these things, Caleb, but I am going to try my best. I guess I'm a little scared that if I try and fail, I might feel foolish and give up." Caleb replied by telling Josh that he could do it if he asked God to help, because God loved him and didn't call him to fail, but was 100 percent behind him when his heart was right.

> *Now prepare yourself like a man; I will question you*
> *and you shall answer Me:*
> *Would you indeed annul My judgment?*
> *Would you condemn Me that you may be justified?*
> *—Job 40:7, 8*

"Josh," Caleb asked, "do you remember the little games Grandma played with us? Remember when she'd ask us to call out remedies, or Bible verses? Remember when she would ask us to take turns trying to remember the problems or faults and failings of each of God's most beloved? Remember, Josh? Remember how she'd rattle off that Noah was a drunk, Abraham was old, Isaac was a daydreamer, Jacob was a liar, Leah was ugly, Joseph was abused, Moses stuttered, . . . and . . ."

Josh, grinning now, picked up the cue, saying, "Yeah, I remember . . . Gideon was afraid, Samson had long hair and was a womanizer, David was a murderer, Elijah was suicidal, Isaiah preached naked, Naomi was a widow, . . . and . . . uhhh . . . can't remember another."

Caleb filled in once again, and said, "Peter denied Christ, Job went bankrupt, Jeremiah and Timothy were too young, the disciples fell asleep when Christ asked them to watch while he prayed, . . . uhhhh, me too . . . can't remember any more."

"Oh yeah, Martha was a worrier," Josh continued, laughing at the memory of Grandma reciting these names, "Zaccheus was small, the Samaritan woman had been divorced more than once, and . . . I can't remember any more."

Then Caleb said quietly, "There's one who was like you, Josh, . . . remember, Josh? . . . Remember how Jonah ran from God . . . sorta like you were doing. So my question to you is what makes you think you are any different than these people were? You just have to do exactly what you've done . . . make a commitment to try, and God can then step in and help you, like He did with those people in the Bible who also had their failings! And, Josh, you really have to think for a minute what will happen if you don't."

For in those days there will be tribulation,
such as has not been since the beginning like a man; I will question you
of the creation
which God created until this time, nor ever
shall be. And unless the Lord shorten those days, no flesh
would be saved; but for the elect's sake, whom He
chose, He shortened the days.
—Mark 13:19, 20

"Remember, when you ask, God will give you what you need, and then reward you for your striving."

For You will light my lamp;
the Lord my God will enlighten my darkness.
                                                    —Psalm 18:28

Being examples to the flock . . .
. . . when the Chief Shepherd appears,
you will receive the crown of glory that does not fade away.
                                                    —1 Peter 5:3, 4

And it shall be that if you earnestly obey My commandments
which I command you today, to love the Lord your God and serve
Him with all your heart and all your soul, then I
will give you the rain for your land in its season, the early rain
and the latter rain, that you may gather your grain,
your new wine, and your oil.
                                                    —Deuteronomy 11:13, 14

When they finished their lunch, Josh thanked Caleb, telling him he was the best brother a guy could have, and said, "Well, please thank Ann for the great lunch. I'm on my way to Deb's now hoping she will forgive me. I called her and asked her if we could talk. I already prayed with the minister this morning for the outcome. I'll keep you posted." Then a new Josh, one who'd made the decision to walk with God, left his brother to drive to a meeting with the woman he hoped would still want to be his wife. Caleb watched him go and thought, *Thank You, God, thank you that Your miracles still happen!*

Debbie was waiting for Josh. Part of her was excited with the hope that things would work out between them, but another part echoed the patience and caution she was trying so hard to learn. She knew that before she jumped back into the fire, she would follow the minister's advice: "Pray first for guidance, listen patiently to all Josh has to say, then follow your heart."

The first few minutes together were awkward. But as Josh spoke, her heart swelled with joy from his words. She was surprised and pleased by his honest appraisal of his past actions. He asked her to forgive him for putting her down. He said he realized that he'd never covered her little errors of conversation where she'd excitedly described something by saying 'hundreds of times' when in actuality she should have said "many times," or she'd said "a week ago" and should have said "five days ago." He had always corrected her in public in the middle of her story and had blatantly told everyone she exaggerated details. She had been so embarrassed by it that it took the joy from her and she did not want to complete her story or ever tell another in his presence.

Now Josh was promising her that he wouldn't do that anymore, that if he felt something needed correcting, he'd speak with her privately, and she could either correct what she'd said or try to be more precise in the future. Deb always knew that she should try to be more precise in her speech, so she wouldn't take offense at being corrected if it was said in private. She had felt that Josh had been cruel in disagreeing so publicly with what she said and in a way that disparaged her. But now he was acknowledging this.

He told her that he was beginning to understand the anger and insecurities caused by his past, and was trying to recognize the denial he used in his effort to cope. All these contributed to his behaving badly. He thought that this might be why he was so demanding. Josh explained that since he began to recognize some his actions, he was taking steps to overcoming them. He told her about how he was praying that he could be an overcomer and how he had met and prayed with his minister this morning and arranged to begin counseling. He told her that he wanted to spend the rest of his life with her, that he wanted them to follow God's word together so that they would be good examples and role models to their children.

Though the tears streamed down Deb's face as she listened, she stood apart from Josh, wanting to embrace him, but wanting to wait for him to finish speaking. His words tumbled out fast, unrehearsed, honest, filled with regret. Finally, as he finished, he said quietly, "Debbie, I will try my very best to make you happy. I will continue in counseling and try to never disappoint you again if you will give me another chance."

The sincerity she heard in his voice grabbed at her heartstrings, and she did as the minister suggested. She followed her heart. She ran to him, and they embraced, both talking at the same time, laughing, hugging, happy. When they ran out of words, dried their tears, and found their breath, to Debbie's surprise, Josh said, "Can we pray together, Deb? Now?" And when he prayed, Deb knew in the deepest recesses of her heart that they were going to be okay, that God had truly blessed them.

> *You have a few . . . who have not defiled*
> *their garments; and they shall walk with Me in*
> *white, for they are worthy.*
> —*Revelation 3:4*

Later that day, when Josh had left, Debbie telephoned Elizabeth to let her know that she and Josh were back together again. After she thanked Elizabeth for her moral support, her guidance, and her prayers, she also told Elizabeth that she felt a miracle had occurred, not only because of the change in Josh, but also because of the changes within herself which would allow her to be a better support to Josh. "Elizabeth," she said, "isn't it amazing how something we think of as a terrible event in our life can turn out to be such a blessing?"

Elizabeth agreed with Debbie and told her that she was happy for her and Josh and that she would look forward to seeing what God planned for their future. When she hung up the phone, Elizabeth realized that perhaps the same thing was happening in her life. The illness, which she considered such a terrible catastrophe, had brought her to finding Mary and Kevin and all the others, maybe even a new church for her and Rebecca. Maybe her illness would turn out to be a huge blessing to her and Rebecca; that would be another true miracle.

After John mentioned that he had a friend who was a physician who practiced alternative medicine, and Elizabeth had agreed to meet with him, John had phoned him and set up an appointment with him. He'd run some tests and started her on a three times per week regimen of twelve thousand milligrams of intravenous vitamin C in a sodium chloride solution. He also included many of the other nutrients that Elizabeth's body needed to repair itself, especially the B vitamins, selenium, and calcium. Elizabeth was amazed at how quickly she began to feel well. She had only two treatments, but already the numbness and tingling in her hands and feet had disappeared. Her unsteadiness was almost gone, as was her poor manual dexterity. She felt happier too, less confused. Her hope had begun to return. *Maybe I will look back over these months and consider my diagnosis not to have been a tragedy, but to have been the catalyst for an incredible miracle in my life and in Rebecca's life,* she thought.

Elizabeth also noticed that as she felt better and had more energy, Rebecca seemed less worried. Rebecca told her mother that Jayden had enlisted many people at church to pray for them and had shown her the verse in the Bible that said Christ was in the midst of them when two or more prayed together. Rebecca had been touched by Jayden's explanation of why and how he had sought his minister's prayers on her behalf. He had said that they all had been praying on a regular basis.

Elizabeth was pleased when Rebecca also told her that she asked if she could come to all the youth meetings with Jayden and that she had asked if she could join in their prayers too. Elizabeth was also pleased that Rebecca was becoming so comfortable with Mary and Kevin's new church, one that Sarah and Matt had introduced them to only a few months ago.

After attending her second youth meeting on Sunday, Rebecca had admitted to the minister who was now her youth leader that she had challenged God and demanded He cure her mother or she would never go to church again. She explained that she was now worried that she would be punished for saying that. The minister spoke with her and gently explained that God never punished, that He understood her anguish, her reasons for doing what she did, and that He wanted Rebecca to come to Him with a willing heart, and simply . . . trust Him. He explained that just as a natural father would gladly give everything he could to his children, God who is all-good, all-loving, all-powerful, gladly gives so much more. But when things didn't go our way, when we didn't get what we wanted when we wanted it, we still had to trust God, accept His will. He explained that God sees so much farther than we do and does what is best for us in the long run.

Little by little, seeing her mother strengthened each day, learning to trust in what the ministers taught her, and impressed by the faith and conduct of her new friends, Rebecca was beginning to let go of her fear and to grow in her trust in God. She asked forgiveness for her challenge and her anger and felt peace for the first time in a long time. Now, Rebecca wanted to follow God, not just bargain with Him. She wanted to grow up to be as strong and wise as her mom, as expressive as Sarah, as loving as Mary, as supportive as Barbara, and as gentle as Ann.

It had taken Rebecca a while to understand Ann because Ann was always shy and quiet. But as she got to know Ann she saw a gentle heart that was never self seeking, but always unselfishly wanting to see others succeed. Yet Rebecca wished that she could see a little more exuberance and happiness in Ann, and a little less shyness. *Everyone has prayed for me*, Rebecca thought, *so I can surely add Ann to my prayers. Maybe God can bring Ann a miracle too!*

Ann knew she was shy. She also knew that it stemmed from a concern that no one really knew how much she cared about them, or how often she prayed for them. She just wasn't the type to 'blow her own horn' as the saying went. But still, in her heart, she craved just a little recognition that she did love this family and did care so much about them. She wished she could know, really know, that they appreciated her and wanted her in their midst.

As Ann had watched each family member and friend come into the fullness of God's love, she was strengthened too. She understood that her own prayers were of great value even though she prayed quietly behind the scenes, but she also knew that no one really knew how much she did this, and sometimes she wished someone would notice. She knew that she did the right thing when she prayed for her family and loved them, yet she often wished she knew beyond a shadow of a doubt that they loved her back; not because she was Caleb's wife, but because she was, well, just Ann. Sometimes she felt like a wallflower, unnoticed by all except her wonderful, gentle Caleb.

Ann was soon to get her wish and Sarah would be the one to bring it to her. After the men moved Sarah's furniture from her apartment, Sarah was to move in with Ann and Caleb for that last week before the wedding. Sarah was eager for some time alone with Ann.

A few days earlier, Sarah had purchased a gift for Ann, a special gift, which was separate from those she would give everyone who would be in her wedding party. Those she planned to give out on the day of the wedding. This gift was something special; this one was just for Ann. Sarah felt that it was something she really wanted and needed to do.

It wasn't until Thursday evening that Sarah and Ann were alone. Caleb had gone to church to help with something or other, so Sarah knew this was the time and ran to get the gift for Ann. As she gave it to her, she said, "Ann, you have always been the rock of this family, you have always been there for us, always willing to help, always willing to pray, always willing to take second place so the others could take first place." She told Ann that she had noticed the sacrifices Ann made for them, that, actually, everyone noticed what she did and loved her for it. She told Ann that to them she was like a saint, self-sacrificing, the quiet foundation they could all build on, a real role model and friend.

Ann was thrilled by what Sarah said and bent to open her gift. She read the inscription and had to fight back tears of joy. Sarah placed the delicate gold chain with its engraved pendant around Ann's neck and fastened the double clasp. On the front of the pendant was an enamel angel and on the back were engraved the words "We love you Ann, with all our hearts. Matt and Sarah." Ann was speechless and so very, very touched, and slowly tears of happiness slid down her cheeks. She rose to embrace Sarah. Sarah told her that she was thankful, so very thankful to have her for a sister-in-law.

Sarah told Ann of the joy she felt that they were sisters-in-law and friends, and that she had asked God to bless Ann with the desires of her heart. Little did Sarah know that it was a moment like this that Ann had longed for . . . to know she was understood and was loved by them for herself. From Sarah's sweet words, Ann finally experienced how God blesses even those who may not serve Him with a lot of fanfare, but who loyally and lovingly gave of themselves in prayer to others. She was so happy to learn how much Sarah loved her. She knew that while Sarah was completely sincere, God had moved Sarah's heart to express just what Ann had longed to hear. Ann had been given a desire of her heart and she too knew that miracles still happen!

The next morning, Sarah and Ann were able to spend even more time together and spoke about the plans for the day. They were looking forward to the rehearsal at the church that night and were now preparing for the dinner Ann would have at her house for everyone afterward. Ann teased Sarah that tomorrow was the big day, the wedding day, the day that Matt and Sarah thought would never come, and finally here it was!

As they talked, Sarah realized that with the wedding rehearsal, the dinner tonight, then the wedding and the honeymoon, she wouldn't have another period of time alone with Ann. Sarah told Ann to speak up more and encouraged her to let them know when she needed to hear 'I love you'! "I do it all the time!" Sarah told her, "Living with two brothers, I had to! Even with Matt. I'll sometimes say, 'I need to hear it, fella!' and Matt or my brothers, pretending to hate to say it, will pipe up with 'I love you, Sarah!' Now, it's gotten to the point that as soon as I say, 'Hey, guys,' they say, 'Yeah, we know, and yeah we do love ya!' The truth is, that even in jest I do get a lift out of it. I also think they've become more sensitive to my needing to hear it once in a while because I speak up about it."

Ann laughed and said that she'd heard somewhere that sometimes we do have to ask for what we want. Sarah's kind and timely words changed Ann by teaching her she'd been wrong to think she wasn't noticed and wrong to be afraid to speak up and express her concerns. She also learned that God notices every good deed, every prayer, every sacrifice we make for others. Ann was so pleased to feel such a close and special bond with Sarah and Ann's heart was finally content.

After the wedding rehearsal, they all gathered at Ann and Caleb's house for a late supper. Everyone was talking about the big day tomorrow . . . *the wedding day*! Each of them chattered about how fast time had gone and how many things had occurred during the past few months. They all decided to share their experiences of faith with one another.

Mary and Kevin said that they could never have imagined how much joy God could bring into their lives. First Sarah and Matt had entered their lives and shown them how to rid themselves of fear and superstition by loving and trusting God and by understanding who brought the fear to them. Then Elizabeth and Rebecca had been additional gifts from God, which fulfilled years of yearning and hope and wiped away Mary's many years of heartache. And soon, the new baby would also enter their lives. They realized that choosing to give God their devotion miraculously resulted in the most rewarding life that they could ask for. They now believed that even through times of sorrow, if they would exercise patience and trust, God would see them through. They felt that they had been incredibly blessed and wanted to become a blessing to those around them.

Josh and Debbie were back together again, and everyone could see a new maturity and sense of purpose in Josh. They too, spoke of the changes that had come into their lives over such a short period of time. Debbie said, "Miracles are not only those huge, amazing moments when lightning strikes and something extraordinary happens, but they are also those smaller events that often come to guide us and to show us how fully and deeply God cares for us. Josh and I can certainly attest to that, we've been so blessed and the miracles that have occurred for us these past months are those moments of true awakening and understanding where we began not only to recognize the path we wanted and needed to follow, but also to accept the help and guidance God was offering us."

Ann pointed out that sometimes the very smallest things, especially when remembered and added up, show us that slowly, over time, God answers even those prayers where we worry that we are asking for such small and inconsequential things when compared to the greater, serious requests others might be bringing Him. "He answers even these small prayers just because He loves us so much and wants us to know He is with us in everything." She reminded them that miracles were still happening and would always be happening, large and small, day in and day out, if we would be aware of them by counting our blessings.

Elizabeth added that she too could attest to receiving miracles over these past months as she saw the change in her health, the joy in Rebecca from being reunited with Mary and her own delight in meeting so many wonderful people and thus gaining an extended family.

To reiterate how one small incident could become a blessing or a miracle, John recalled something that occurred one day as he was leaving his garage. A shovel fell and hit him in the head. He'd taken a few minutes to pick the shovel up and secure it once again, to look at his head in the mirror to make sure the skin wasn't broken, and then finally, had left. He'd complained and complained as he drove away, wondering just why such a dumb thing had to happen just when he needed to hurry to be on time for an appointment. When he pulled on to the highway a few minutes later, he saw a huge multi-car accident that had occurred just minutes earlier. Suddenly he realized that, if the shovel hadn't fallen, he might have been in the middle of that accident. "So even the smallest mishap may be the greatest miracle; an incredible intervention by Our Heavenly Father for our good," he said.

As the evening was drawing to a close, and the women were putting away the leftovers, the men teased Matt about the pending loss of his freedom. When all was done, Caleb gathered the family around in a circle of love and they prayed together. They thanked God for all He'd brought into their lives, the good events that had increased their faith, the difficult events that shaped their hearts, the little things that showed them God's ever present care, and the huge events that gave them a renewed sense of God's immense power over all things.

As the others were getting ready to leave, Matt asked Caleb and Josh if he could talk to them privately for just a few minutes. Sarah, Debbie, and Ann were in the kitchen, so Caleb asked Josh and Matt to join him in his study and closed the door to prevent any interruptions. Caleb sensed that Matt had something important to say.

Caleb's study was cozy and with its myriad of books lining the shelves adjacent to the fireplace, looked like a comfortable old library. This was the room where he and Ann spent time reading and talking. It was beautifully decorated with dark cherry furniture. Wall-to-wall, floor-to-ceiling, built-in bookshelves lined one wall, except for the break in the center for the entry door. The door, bookcases, and moldings too were stained a deep cherry color. An antique brick fireplace was on the wall adjacent to the bookshelf wall. The fireplace had a raised hearth that extended the entire length of the wall and since it could be used for seating was thus fitted with thick square edged cushions. Caleb's huge kneehole desk was placed a few feet in front of a third wall so the desk chair faced out to the rest of the room. A very large floral antique oil painting in reds, blues, yellows, and greens hung behind the desk chair, giving balance to the architecture of the other walls.

Caleb went to sit behind his desk on the brown leather swivel chair that faced the rest of the room. Matt and Josh gravitated to the two matching traditional-style brown leather recliners on the fourth wall, not too far from the desk, that flanked a round table holding an oversized lamp. These chairs also swiveled making it easy to turn toward Matt. Josh and Caleb waited for Matt to speak.

"I'm not sure how to begin, because I'm about to tell you the big secret everyone's been talking about, but I need to know from you that you will also keep it a secret." Both Caleb and Josh quickly agreed not to say a word and reassured Matt that he could count on them. They could hear in Matt's voice that it was very important for him to know that they would not reveal what he was about to tell them.

"I received a phone call from someone very special who is coming to the wedding from halfway across the country," Matt began. "He is not only coming to the wedding along with his entire family, but he is going to officiate at the wedding. Guys, remember your youth leader, who now heads one of the district church offices?"

Josh and Caleb, almost at the same moment, said, "No, you've got to be kidding! He's coming all that way . . . just for us? He's far too busy, he has so many huge responsibilities!"

Matt grinned, glad that they both knew immediately who he was talking about and recognized the great honor they were to receive.

"Wow, is Sarah going to be surprised!" said Caleb.

"She's gonna flip!" said Josh, "and so will I, he was one of the greatest influences other than Grandma on our lives! He was a rock for all of us and an incredible role model to all the kids he looked after."

Matt's thoughts darted back to his first introduction to the man that Caleb and Josh were now remembering. Matt had met him while they were in college and Sarah had been excited by his return to town for an event that Matt couldn't now recall. Sarah had explained how she knew this man and his family.

Sarah explained that when her mother had died when she was eighteen, she'd blocked her grief and turned to Grandma who became Mom, Dad, Grandma, Godmother, and Aunt to Sarah and Josh. Grandma tried to be everything rolled into one. Josh and Sarah would not speak of their mother because losing her had hurt so much. Caleb had already recently married.

The family had not yet met Matt. Grandma did everything to help Sarah and Josh, but what had also helped was their connection to their youth group at church and the love and respect that they had for the youth leader. This same man had been Caleb's youth leader before he had married Ann. Caleb had for many years looked up to this man who cared for the young people with such enthusiasm and heartfelt love. He'd been a great example to them all. He never found fault, always sought to keep his connection close with every child of God, never exhibited an ego or worried about what his peers would think, always loved, defended and supported the youth groups that he cared for.

Through Caleb's association with the youth group, Josh had known this youth leader and Sarah had also known him and loved him even before she herself had joined the youth group at age fourteen. Josh and Sarah had seen him apologize for things others did and do whatever it took to let those in his care know that he loved them and would always stand by them.

He was a minister, married with two children, and about forty years old when Sarah's mother died. He was tall, slim, athletic, smart, kind, and felt passionately about the importance of role models for young people. He had lost his own mother when he was a teenager and had a great empathy for those who had suffered such a tragic loss. When he had needed it, God had looked after him by providing him with a youth leader who had gone to great lengths to help him understand

God's plan of salvation and to trust God to have made the right decision. It had made such a strong impact on him that he vowed to do the same for other young people when he could.

That day came not too many years later. He became a minister in the church and then, soon after, the leader of the youth group. As youth leader, Caleb was in his care. A few years later, Sarah joined the youth group. When their mother died, he did his best to spend time with Sarah and Joshua, help them accept God's will. They didn't know it at the time, but he had prayed for them two or three times a day and had also put something extra into the offertory at church for them asking God to help them find peace despite their loss.

Josh, being five years younger and new to the youth group, had handled his loss a little differently than Sarah and was outwardly angry, so he did not come to every youth meeting, as did Sarah. But way down deep, Josh respected this man and he admired what he was doing for all the kids. Josh didn't want to talk about his feelings and rather than feel pressured, six months after his mom died, he just stopped coming to the youth meetings, feeling that he needed some alone time. But Josh knew that he was prayed for, he knew he could return whenever he wanted, and that his youth leader would be there for him, if he needed him. He also saw how Sarah was helped by this man's constancy and example.

Sarah bonded with her youth leader and with his wife, and they became close friends. They both became excellent role models for Sarah. Without realizing it at the time, Sarah had fashioned her personal and professional goals on how this couple conducted their lives. Grandma had encouraged her to stay close to this wonderful, loving couple whose main endeavor was to do God's work, which at that time meant doing their best to direct the future spiritual growth of all the youth through loving friendship and gentle teaching. Even though this minister moved to higher offices within the church, he kept on as youth leader because he had such a special love for the youth and a very special understanding of their problems.

Sarah had just entered college when this man had been asked to move to the city where the church had their main offices. From there they conducted church business for their eleven million members, worldwide, so this was a big task and meant coordinating efforts with those heading the Canadian and European districts as well. Now that he had been appointed to a higher ministry he had a great deal more responsibility.

Therefore, other than one previous visit back home, Sarah hadn't seen him for eight years. They exchanged Christmas and birthday cards, and perhaps one or two phone calls each year, but Sarah knew that he traveled extensively to help God's children worldwide, and didn't want to take up his time. However, the impact he had made on her life had been enormous and she'd never forgotten him. His work for the church now placed him in a very high position, and therefore Matt had been totally surprised by the news that he was coming to their wedding and, miracle of miracle, officiating! This was almost unheard of, yet he was doing it for Sarah, for them, for Grandma and for her Mom.

What a boon this would be for all the other members of the congregation, too! And what a blessing!

Caleb and Josh were still stunned; they too remarked about how thrilled everyone would be to have the honor of his visit and to hear him bring them the wedding blessing!

"Matt, when are you going to tell Sarah?" Caleb asked.

"I'm not," Matt replied, "when she gets to the altar, our minister will switch places with him and that will be the first Sarah will know."

"Sarah might faint, Matt, if she doesn't know ahead of time," Josh said.

"I'll just have to hold her up and count on both of you to watch carefully and help if necessary," Matt countered.

"This is big, Matt, really big. Now I know why you were so adamant about us teasing you and asking questions. I'm sorry for bugging you. Gee whiz, can you imagine what the congregation will do? They'll be so happy, so surprised. Will we have a chance to see the family and talk with them, are they staying for the reception?" Josh asked.

"Yep, the whole nine yards," replied Matt. "I need you guys to be on the lookout to help me. We have to keep the secret right up to the last minute. Right now only our minister knows and he's in a total flutter making sure the church looks good, the grounds are manicured, you know, like the women are whenever we have a fellowship! Everyone wants everything perfect for those they love! I need you to keep an eye on everything and just help me make sure that all goes smoothly, okay?"

"You've got it, buddy," Josh replied. "This is incredible, really amazing, and boy am I glad that I can finally tell him how sorry I am for not realizing what a great gift he was offering me at the time and that I'm getting married too and that I turned out, well, not toooooo badly, huh, guys?

"You're a-okay, Josh, we're proud of you. It will really be a treat to see them again and wow, will Sarah ever be thrilled! He will be thrilled to see all of us too. You can count on us, Matt. Well . . . maybe if the three of us look at one another tomorrow, we'll grin from ear to ear and get asked if we have a cat in a bag, but we'll hold on, just another, how long . . . another sixteen hours?" Caleb said.

Matt stood, relieved that he now had support in this monumental secret, and he too felt that Sarah would really be amazed!

List of furniture

Twin bed, coverlet & dust ruffle
2 storage nite stands & lamps
Triple dresser & mirror
Easy chair and footstool
Loveseat sofa bed
2 side tables & lamps
Coffee table
Antique armoire with TV
Tall lightweight chair
Tall antique clothes pole/rack

Ideas for walk-in closet

Double row of poles for blouses, skirts & slacks
Shoe rack built on door wall

Ideas for other closet

Single pole for dresses, coats, bathrobes
Shelves above for storage boxes
Built-in shelves on each side for boxes, shoes

Other ideas

White crown molding, doors & other trim
White chair rail

Paint one color above chair rail and another below
Curtains, shams, chairs & sofabed match/coordinate

REBECCA'S ROOM

14 x 19

BATH

Epilogue

THE WEDDING

Matt and Sarah had met with their minister yesterday, the day before the wedding. He wanted to be sure they understood what their responsibilities were to one another as husband and wife and what the sacrament of marriage would mean to each of them. He also spoke about the commitment they would undertake should they become parents and, most importantly, about their commitment to God. They were excited. This was the final step, the final day before their marriage. Understanding the responsibilities the minister spoke of, they gladly told him that they would support one another all the days of their lives, that they would serve God with all their heart, and that they would do their best to learn and follow His word.

They knew that soon, all the waiting, preparations, and prayers for this special day, their wedding day, would culminate at the foot of the altar. They knew that at the altar they would be encompassed by the love of family and friends, faithful and loving ministers, their supportive congregation, and the immeasurable blessing from above. They knew that their special day was almost here! And they were thankful.

It had rained yesterday, the day before the wedding . . . torrential rains with lightning and thunder accompanying the rain. They had all gone to the church for the wedding rehearsal and then to Caleb and Ann's for a late supper. Everyone teased them about the rain, but they weren't worried . . . it didn't matter. Rain or not, they would be married and God would bless them.

But today, their wedding day, the sun was shining brighter than ever before, and highlighted the exquisite blue of the sky and the undulating marshmallows of white clouds. The foliage of the trees and shrubs danced in unison, wearing their deepest green dress, having blossomed richly from the rain that had fed them just yesterday. Even the flowers seemed fuller, their colors more vibrant, and the normally oppressive heat of an August day turned crisp and clear. As each person who planned to attend the wedding woke to the incredible beauty of the day, they recognized that God had especially blessed this day with these marvels of nature created by His perfect and exquisite design.

The last of Sarah's furniture had been moved from her apartment, the house was ready, the wedding plans seemed in perfect order, and the days she had spent with Caleb and Ann were a special time of bonding where hearts joined in the shared joy of being in a lifetime friendship between like souls. It brought to Sarah, the deep understanding and even greater appreciation of what fine people Ann and her brother were.

The morning brought with it an aura of excitement. Everyone was thinking of what remained to be done, and what would soon be the culmination of so many hopes and dreams and wishes. They'd all packed their little bags of cosmetics, clothing, and personal items. The men would bring theirs to Matt's house, and the women to Caleb's house, where they would dress and chatter away about last minute details and tease one another to lighten the excitement. Both Sarah and Matt were filled with anticipation. So, too, was everyone else.

At 10:00 a.m. all the women converged at the hairdresser's to have manicures, pedicures, and their hair done. When they finished at the hairdresser's, the women planned to gather at Ann and Caleb's house where all the gowns were laid out in the guest rooms. The men were to meet at Sarah and Matt's house where the tuxedo's had been delivered. The wedding was to be at 5:00 p.m. at the church.

When finally coiffed and manicured, the women arrived at Ann's and found that Ann, ever thoughtful, had prepared wonderful little finger sandwiches, bite-sized chocolate-covered cheesecakes, and strawberries dipped in chocolate so they would have something to munch on as they rested and freshened up before getting dressed. The limousine was to arrive at 4:30 p.m. to take the women to the church.

The gowns were an exquisite emerald green color, created in a lightweight satin with princess seams that provided a narrow waist and fuller skirt. A white satin sash completed by the overlay of a sheer, printed georgette with tiny green polka dots fit snugly around the satin waist sash. Both were tied in front, formed into a thick knot, from which a cascade of fabric spilled to reach to the hem of the slightly flared, gored skirts. Along the white satin sash encompassing the waist and falling in a ribbon that cascaded to the toe, the georgette overlay embracing the white satin sash provided the contrast of tiny green polka dots against the white ribbons. The gowns were sleeveless and had wide straps outlining a scooped neck. They would all wear white pearls at their neck and ears, gifts that Matt and Sarah had given them to commemorate their wedding day.

Pinned to the back of their heads, not visible from the front, were slender ribbons created from the white satin and the sheer georgette of the waist sashes, and were tied into the same large knot as on the waist sashes. The knot was pinned to the back of their head near the crown. This allowed the slender ribbons of fabric to spill from the knot and cascade gracefully from the top of the head to the waist and provide interest to the back of the gowns. The green polka dots on the georgette contrasted delicately with the white satin of the slender ribbons and created an elegance of matching fabrics and colors between what fell from waist to floor in front and head to waist in back. The shoes were dyed to match the gowns, and very small bows of the sheer white georgette with the green polka dots were attached to their green shoes, and peeped from under the gown when they walked. They would carry deep red roses set into a bed of dark green ferns with tiny clusters of white baby's breath tucked between the roses and cascading over the edge of the arrangement to contrast against the deep green of the gowns.

Rebecca's gown was a duplicate of the other women's but also had a matching emerald green jacket with long bell sleeves. The jacket was fitted, and the length of it went only to beneath her bust line. It was the perfect touch to set her apart, while still blending perfectly with the others. As flower girl, Rebecca would carry a small white lattice basket, lined with deep green ferns and filled with red rose petals. The basket had ribbons trailing from it in the same sheer polka-dot fabric that encircled the women's waist sashes. At the final fitting, Rebecca had been amazed by how grown-up she looked and how elegant she appeared. Sarah was so pleased with how beautiful they all looked, and how wonderfully matched everything was.

The women dressed first; then together they dressed Sarah. Sarah looked exquisite! Her gown was of white brocade, with a fitted waist and slightly flared skirt. The hem of the skirt was cut quite a bit longer in the back to form a small train. Over the dress was a short jacket that ended just below the bust line curving upward from the back toward the front to a stand-up collar, creating an open V neckline. The long sleeves of the jacket were slightly puffed where the sleeves met the shoulder, and they were cut very long and shaped to create a V below the center of her hand just above her middle finger. This combination created an aura of elegance and formality. The classic simplicity and fine cut of her exquisite dress was perfect for showcasing her beautiful face, her shining demeanor and the incredible joy that emanated with stunning force from her inner being.

On her head, Sarah wore a crown of the same white brocade as the gown. The white brocade encircled a wire frame from which hung two pieces of sheer silk shantung, which formed her veil. The front piece was short and when draped over her face fell only to her bodice. When removed from her face it would form a cape from the crown of her head to the back of her waist to flow over a second piece of silk. The second piece of elegant fabric was much longer in length and draped in soft folds down her back and across her shoulders reaching its end at the hem of her dress, which had formed a graceful, flowing train across the carpet as she walked. The entire veil had white seed pearls sewn across the fabric in carefully calculated abandon.

The brocade frame, which sat atop her head, with one third covering the uppermost area of her French twist, had a second, smaller crown that fit atop the larger frame. This one was covered with seed pearls and had been Sarah's mother's wedding headdress. To wear it made Sarah feel that her mother was with her. Sarah carried a cascading bouquet of white roses upon which had been attached even more seed pearls to give the roses the look of dew on their petals. That had been one of Grandma's tricks, to use little seed pearls on the flowers she placed on her dining room table. She hoped her mother and her grandmother would be able to come from eternity to the church today to witness her wedding and see how she wanted to honor them.

Sarah seldom wore makeup, but today the women had added blush to her cheeks, a fine line to her eyes and eyebrows, and lip liner to enhance her lips. The women had added a long lasting white tinted lip gloss over her lipstick, which added to Sarah's ethereal beauty. She was breathtaking with her flawless skin, radiant smile, and elegant hairstyle.

She wore her hair in an elaborate French twist, and the crown of her headpiece had been shaped to straddle both the top of her head and the top of the twist. Her nails were done in a clear polish with just the tips in a soft white. Her shoes were also white brocade for which Ann and Barbara had fashioned two small silk shantung bows covered with seed pearls that attached to the front of the shoes. She looked like a fairy princess, a Cinderella! All the women were snapping pictures and commenting on the perfection of all their hard work. Sarah hoped that Matt, who hadn't seen her gown, or the bridesmaids' gowns either, would like the way they looked.

Caleb was doing double duty today. He would walk Sarah down the aisle, and he would be best man to Matt, Josh filling in for Caleb until he brought Sarah to the altar. Three limousines were to arrive at Sarah and Matt's house. One would pick up the men to bring them to the church, all except for Caleb. Caleb was to leave Matt and Sarah's house for his own house with the other two limousines, one for him and Sarah, one for the rest of the women. The women would leave ten minutes before he and Sarah would leave.

Caleb prayed with Sarah before they entered the limousine, just as he had done with the women and earlier with the men before any of them had entered their limos. Everything went like clockwork, and suddenly there they were, in the car on their way to the church.

Sarah was suddenly nervous. "Caleb, what if I trip or fall, what if I faint? What if . . . what if . . . ?" and Caleb took her hand, told her to stop worrying, and reassured her that everything would be perfect. Sarah looked into her brother's eyes and knew that he would always be by her side, knew that he had prayed fervently, knew that he would lay down his life to make sure everything went well for Matt and Sarah, and her heart began to slow to its normal beat once again. Caleb smiled at her, squeezed her hand again and told her that she was beautiful inside and out and that he was so very, very proud of her for the woman she had become and for the kind of wife she would be to Matt. Sarah leaned over to kiss her brother, her confidant, her friend, her role model and felt so very blessed.

When Sarah and Caleb arrived at the church, climbed from the car, and entered the large double doors of the church, almost immediately the organist began playing the wedding march. Sarah didn't have time to be nervous. She hardly saw the incredible array of flowers on the altar in white and green, or those attached to the sides of every pew along the center aisle of the church along with their large bows and cascading ribbons, their deep greenery and white flowers. She didn't smell the flowers, or see the people who filled the church, her family, friends, and congregation, or even the deacons and the ministers. All she could see was Matt, up at the altar, looking at her, smiling, waiting. And she smiled, her heart bursting with joy to see Matt, thinking how handsome he was, how blessed she was to have him.

Looking only at Matt, Sarah held on to Caleb as they slowly walked to the altar, Caleb forcing her to keep time to the music, forcing her to walk slowly. Then they were there, at the foot of the altar, and Caleb placed her hand in Matt's and took his place next to Matt as best man.

Matt was stunned when he saw Sarah enter the church. He'd always thought her beautiful, but he wasn't prepared for this elegant princess, this incredibly stunning creature coming toward him. She was perfect, absolutely perfect! He was so very, very blessed. *Please, God,* Matt thought, *let me be all to her that I can be, all you'd want me to be. Thank you for this precious gift of Sarah.*

Then Sarah was standing at the altar with Matt, their eyes locked to one another, and then they both turned to look at their minister and knew that this was it, this was the moment they had waited for. This was the day that the Lord had made for them! This was their beginning! Together they would face life, they would develop their faith, they would stand shoulder to shoulder in adversity, and together they would rejoice every day in prayer for the gift of God's perfect plan!

As their minister spoke, to Sarah it seemed as if he was saying something she couldn't understand, hadn't expected to hear. She wanted to concentrate on all he said so she wouldn't miss this wonderful moment, these precious words! She knew that Matt was listening carefully so he too could take this blessing with him into their lives forever.

But again Sarah was confused by what the minister was saying. Suddenly, as if struck by a bolt of lightning, she understood that something unusual was happening. Her minister had indeed been saying something she hadn't expected. He seemed to be introducing someone. She forced herself to quiet her nerves and concentrate on his words. *What did he say?* she thought. *It can't be, it can't possibly be!*

Then, as the minister spoke, Sarah saw from her peripheral vision that another man was walking toward the altar from a seat on the far right side of the altar. As she looked at him, immediately recognizing him, yet hardly believing what she saw, she gasped. So did those sitting in the congregation.

For a moment Sarah thought her legs wouldn't hold her up; so shocked was she. She leaned against Matt, and he turned to her and put his arm around her waist and looked down at her face seeing tears beginning to roll down her cheeks. *Maybe I should have told her,* Matt worried, *maybe this is too much of a surprise along with everything else going on.*

The minister was still talking when the other man arrived to stand next to him in front of the altar. It had been an introduction after all, and an explanation of who would be officiating. Then Sarah's minister, after kissing Sarah and shaking hands with Matt, went to the seat that had been left unoccupied, and the man who had stepped to the front of the altar looked at Sarah smiling, and whispered, "Surprised?"

Sarah smiled. Then she beamed, and she shook her head up and down to indicate that yes, she was indeed surprised. Now, Matt knew everything was okay again and that Sarah had recovered from the shock. He had already dabbed at her tears with his handkerchief, but she hadn't even known he'd done it, so much enthralled was she with what was happening.

Matt saw that both Caleb and Josh were unabashedly shedding tears. Matt knew that memories of this man's love, of how God had sent them yet another comforter when they needed help, perhaps even memories of their mom and Grandma overflowed their hearts.

Sarah could not believe that he was here. For her wedding. Here, with them. Here, officiating their wedding! This was truly a miracle, truly a moment that they would never forget, a blessing filled with beautiful and poignant moments, memories in the making that were filled with the realization of what God had done for her when her mom had died, how He had looked after her by sending this special man of God to teach her and help her and pray for her. Grandma would be so thrilled.

Sarah was overjoyed. She was humbled too as she recognized that she, along with every other member of their extended family, had had their own incredible miracle occur in the last month. She turned to Matt and saw that he was looking at her. She whispered, "A miracle, just for us." Matt's heart overflowed, knowing exactly what Sarah was thinking and he sent a quick prayer of thanksgiving to His heavenly Father for providing such a gift, for letting them know once again how close He was to them and how He cared for every detail. Matt glanced again at Caleb and Josh, and they too were beaming.

Sarah and Matt listened carefully to what the minister was saying as he started to conduct the marriage service. Soon, their own participation was required as they were to exchange their vows. As they turned to one another to say their vows, their hearts filled with joy, with thankfulness and with love. They dedicated their lives to God not only with their words, but with their whole heart. Then, suddenly, they were married. It was over. They had their whole lives ahead of them . . . together. Matt kissed his beautiful bride, and then they both hugged the man who had traveled so far to bless them, who had kept his love for them alive, and who wanted to give them this surprise.

As they turned to walk back down the aisle, for the first time they saw the faces of all those who had come to be with them and wish them well. They were amazed and overjoyed; they wondered at the number of people who had come to celebrate with them. Though everyone had been there when she came in, Sarah couldn't remember seeing them when she and Caleb walked up the aisle.

What a joy to be surrounded by people who pray for us, love us, and are striving to please God and to learn His words, just as we are. We are so blessed. Oh please, God, help us to always be thankful, Sarah thought.

Matt had similar thoughts as they walked arm and arm back down the aisle and he saw all the people. He was reminded of the many who'd taught them, stood by them, encouraged them and he too sent a prayer of thanksgiving to God for bringing these wonderful people into his life.

Rebecca followed Matt and Sarah as they left the altar, and then Ann and Caleb followed them as they walked toward the entrance to the church to form the reception line. Then Barbara and Jim, Josh and Debbie, and Mary and Kevin followed them to join in greeting all the guests. Matt and Sarah took a moment to look into one another's eyes and saw their own joy reflected in the eyes of the other and knew their love would sustain them in good times and, if necessary, in bad.

Together they would experience the joys and troubles, the excitement and disappointments of life. Together, and with all their beloved family members and friends, with their congregation and ministers, and most of all with their Heavenly Father by their side, they would work toward the day when Christ would come and take them all to His Wedding, a wedding they all longed to be a part of.

For everyone who asks receives, and he who
seeks finds, and to him who knocks it will be opened.
Or what man is there among you who, if his son asks for bread,
will give him a stone? Or if he asks for a fish, will give him a serpent?

If you then, being evil, know how to give good gifts to your
children, how much more will your Father who is in heaven
give good things to those who ask him?
—*Matthew 7:8, 9, 10, 11*

They knew that life would bring some hardships; that not all their prayers would be answered the way they wished them to be. But they also knew that they had learned how to trust God and how to cover themselves in the armour He provided for them. Now, when the enemy did attack, when Satan's forces were at work, they would come through it. They would have true and trusted friends to hold them up when they faltered; love and teach them when they made mistakes.

They understood that in life, troubles were on their way. Their faith would be tested, but they would try to come forth from those trials like gold tried in the fire; strong, beautiful, pure for their Heavenly Father to use for all eternity. They understood that loving one another brought joy not only to them, but also to the heart of God. But most of all, loving God with all their heart would bring them, together, to a future far more magnificent than anyone could ever imagine.

And thou shalt love the Lord thy God with all thy heart,
and with all thy soul, and with all thy mind,
and with all thy strength, this is the first commandment.
And the second is this, thou shalt love thy neighbor as thyself.
There is none other commandment greater than these.
—*Mark 12:30, 31*

Bibliography

The Holy Bible, King James Version, published by The New Apostolic Church, Canada, Thomas Nelson, Inc., Camden, NJ, 1972

The Holy Bible, New Kings James Version, published by The New Apostolic Church, North America, Thomas Nelson Publishers, Nashville, copyright 1994

James Strong, LLD, STD, *Strong's Exhaustive Concordance of the Bible*, Abington, Nashville, thirty fourth printing 1996, copyright 1890

CIBA Review, *Textiles in Biblical Times*, Basle, Switzerland: CIBA-GEIGY, 1968/2

Timothy Roland Roberts, *The Celts in Myth and Legend*, Friedman/Fairfax Publishers, New York, New York, 1995

Internet: www.ucsfhealth.org/adult/medical_services/neuro/lou_gehrigs_disease/conditions/als/p . . . UCSF Medical Center. Lou Gehrig's Disease (ALS)

Internet:

Emedicine from WebMD: Vitamin B-12 Associated Neurological Diseases, Updated January 29th, 2008. Niranjan N Singh, MD, DNB. Fellow in Neurophysiology, Department of Neurology, St. Louis University School of Medicine.

Grandma's Little Book of Poetry, Helen Gumienny Glowacki, Xlibris Publishing, To be released in 2009.

Endnotes

For those readers who would like to utilize the Greek method for obtaining the room ratios of their personal decorating project, following are additional examples of room sizes, their ratios and common denominator, and the solutions for correcting ratios that do not meet the proper proportions recommended by this mathematical procedure.

The solution for improperly proportioned walls is to create the illusion that you have either elongated or shortened the two opposing walls that do not meet the proper specification. To create the illusion of elongating a wall, use furnishings on those two walls that are long and low, such as a pedestal desk, a buffet, or a series of low bookcases.

To create the illusion of shortening the walls that do not meet the proper specification for good proportion, use furnishings on those two opposing walls such as a secretary desk, grandfather clock, tall bookcases, or an armoire.

Sometimes a long and narrow room that does not meet the ratios of proper proportion should be divided into two areas of proper proportion. One area can be treated as a living room and another an area of study. See drawing at the bottom of the endnotes.

10 x 12 = 5 x 6 using 2 as the common denominator. Solution: shorten the two 10' walls

10 x 14 = 5 x 7 has no common denominator, but is closest to 10 x 15 so elongate the 14' walls

10 x 15 = 2 x 3 using 5 as the common denominator, reflects a perfect proportion of 2 to 3

10 x 16 = 5 x 8 using 2 as the common denominator, reflects a perfect proportion of 5 to 8

12 x 8 = 3 x 2 using 4 as the common denominator, reflects perfect proportion of 2 to 3

12 x 12 = 2 x 2 using 6 as the common denominator, elongate two opposing walls

12 x 14 = 6 x 7 using 2 as the common denominator, elongate the two 14' walls

12 x 16 = 2 x 4 using 4 as the common denominator, elongate the two 16' walls

12 x 18 = 2 x 3 using 6 as the common denominator, reflects a perfect proportion of 2 to 3

12 x 20 = 3 x 5 using 4 as the common denominator, reflects a perfect proportion of 3 to 5

12 x 22 = 6 x 11 using 2 as the common denominator, shorten the two 22' walls

12 x 24 = 1 x 2 using 12 as the common denominator, shorten the two 24' walls

12 x 26 = 6 x 13 using 2 as the common denominator, divide room into 12 x 18 and 12 x 8

12 x 28 = 3 x 7 using 4 as the common denominator, divide as above to 12 x 20 and 12 x 8

14 x 21 = 2 x 3 using 7 as the common denominator, reflects perfect proportion of 2 to 3

14 x 30 = 7 x 15 using 2 as the common denominator, divide into 14 x 21 & 14 (elongate) x 9

15 x 24 = 5 x 8 using 3 as the common denominator, reflects perfect proportion of 5 to 8

16 x 24 = 2 x 3 using 8 as the common denominator, reflects perfect proportion of 2 to 3

14 x 30 Room

NOT IN

PLEASING PROPORTIONS

14 x 9 (5x3 RATIO)

14 x 21   (2x3 RATIO)

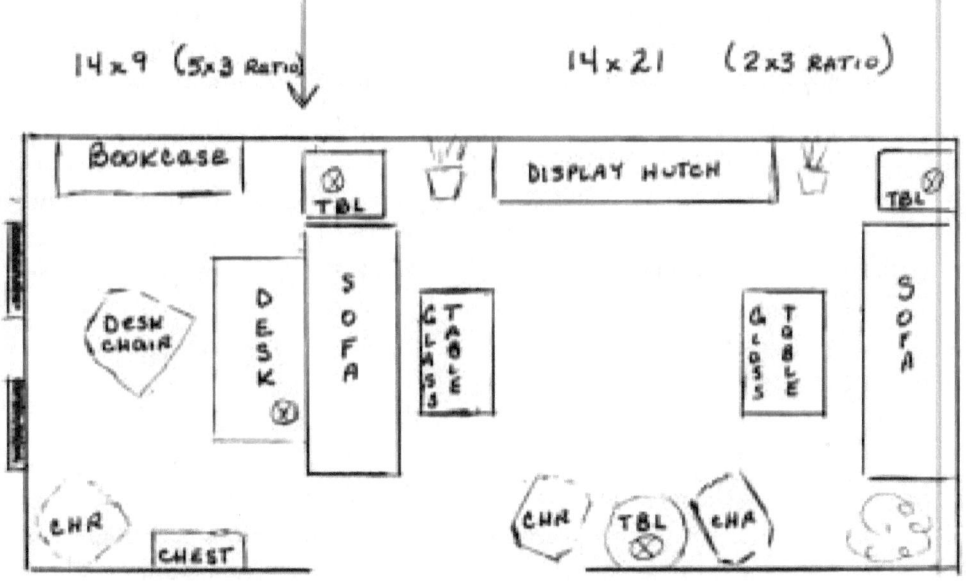

Scriptural Index

Satans abilities

Teachings we should provide

Understanding scripture

Warnings God gives us

Excerpt from:
Grandma's Little Book of Poetry

DESCRIPTION:

The Grandma Series of novels include poems written by the author. These address the questions that the characters of the story bring to God during their greatest heartache. The poems try to demonstrate that no matter how difficult our burden seems, God will see us through it. *Grandma's Little Book of Poetry* is a collection of many of these poems and is meant to inspire, uplift, and reassure those coping with a loss of hope, a disappointment, or a personal heartache. It does this by making us more aware of the joy of knowing God, the traps laid by an enemy seeking the destruction of those God loves, and the triumph God will ultimately give us.

Throughout these poems is a story. At first, the story appears to be whimsical, perhaps somewhat like a fairy tale. But as it unfolds, an incredible plan comes to light, one laid into place eons ago as a part of the physics of our universe. It is the story of God's plan of salvation, the perfecting of the Bride of Christ through great trials and tribulations and in spite of an enemy who works day and night to hinder it's completion. This story shows us what our ultimate goal is and the incredible feat of engineering that God placed into His plan of salvation, a plan for every soul that was ever born, ever died, or was ever conceived.

It is the story of how God's love and His patience is manifested in a plan so incredibly conceived that it covers every contingency of life and provides for every soul. It is the story of how love is perfected in our hearts and the power that love has to cripple evil. It is the story of the greatest gift ever given. It is a story to be shared with everyone.

Chapter One

The Birth of Prayer

Once upon a time, in a land of marshmallow clouds and skies of the most beautiful azure blue, where gentle music played and everyone sang, the angels watched and waited. All across this land flowers grew everywhere one looked, always blooming full and perfect and filling the soft warm breeze with the fragrance of their perfume. A light so bright that it caused everything to shine vibrantly clothed this lush and lovely land, enhancing the beauty of all it touched. The clouds were the whitest white imaginable and the grass the greenest green. Even the trees were exquisite, symmetrically formed with perfect bark and beautifully shaped leaves in graduated colors of gold, green, and rust. An all-encompassing aura of love permeated every living thing and filled the soul with warmth and with a great sense of peace and comfort. Pure love lived everywhere in this beautiful land in the heavens and it ruled in every heart.

This verdant place of peace was high in the heavens, far above a spinning planet that was slowly, insidiously dying. The cold bleak planet below the land of the angels seemed as if it harbored a hidden cancer gnawing its way through everything good. Yet, none of the inhabitants of the dying planet recognized that their planet was anything less than perfect, or that its life was so limited. The people who occupied this planet thought that everything would always go on as it had in the past. Sadly, many of them became complacent, egocentric in their thinking and narcissistic in their actions.

But the angels could see the cancer, growing, eating at the planet from the inside, determined to destroy it. The cancer was evil and its goal was not only to destroy the planet but also to destroy its inhabitants before God could claim them. The evil had been born of disobedience and jealousy, which had then given birth to hate. It was on these three activities that the cancer thrived. This is why the planet was doomed.

The angels knew why the planet would die, and they knew when it would die. They also knew why the planet had been created, when it was created, and what its replacement would be. But this was a great secret. The angels were held to strict secrecy about the future, and could not share their knowledge with the inhabitants of the planet far below them. They could only watch. And wait. And never breathe a word about what they knew.

Despite the concern the angels felt as they watched the evil devour the planet below them, they weren't distressed by what they saw or what they knew. They weren't distressed about the planet's inevitable death, or about the future of its inhabitants. This was because they knew the great secret, they knew about the incredible plan, and they knew what the outcome would be. They understood that the inhabitants who lived far below them were in the midst of a great battle, in the midst of a struggle between good and evil, in the midst of the potential development of pure love in the heart of man, which was the only weapon that could overcome the evil.

The angels rejoiced when some of the inhabitants began to understand and to respond to what was offered to them. The angels knew that those who did respond could have their names written in the great white book that lay open on a table made of marble and gold. The book could only be filled with the names of the righteous and thus it was a book of great importance and was revered by the angels. It was called "The Lamb's Book of Life."

The angels knew how very important it was that the inhabitants of the cold bleak planet below them develop in such a way that they could have their names entered into this book for then they could escape the destruction. They also knew that another book had been provided, one that could teach the inhabitants how to overcome the evil by learning how to love. This book was called The Holy Bible.

In the pages of this Holy Bible were wonderful words that God provided for the inhabitants to help them in their struggle. It was important for the inhabitants to learn to use this gift to overcome evil and thus allow them to have their names written in the Lamb's Book of Life. In the Holy Bible in Revelation 21:27 God described who would be allowed to enter heaven, saying "And there shall in no wise enter into it any thing that defileth, neither whatsoever worketh abomination, or maketh a lie: but they which are written in the Lamb's book of life."

Those whose names would be entered in the Lamb's book of life were those who were willing to learn from the Holy Bible, those who learned of and practiced love toward their fellow man, those who weren't complacent but sought to overcome. Those who were always thankful for what they had been given and demonstrated their thankfulness brought joy to God's heart. These were the people who were becoming "different"; they were becoming the "peculiar" people God spoke of in 1 Peter 2:9 saying: "But ye are a chosen generation, a royal priesthood, an holy nation, a peculiar people . . . . . .". The inhabitants didn't know it yet, but they were searching for a way to fill the void in their hearts that could only come from love, the pure self-sacrificing kind of love that living by God's words could provide.

The angels who watched the planet below and who waited in patience were, in reality, watching God's great and magnificent plan unfold. The plan was called "God's Plan of Salvation" and had been created by the Father, the Son and the Holy Spirit to help men overcome evil and eventually choose for themselves whether they would live under hate or under love.

When the plan had been completed and the Father, the Son and the Holy Spirit deemed it perfect, they merged the plan with the natural law of the universe, the physics of things, so it would help the inhabitants of the spinning planet far below the heavens. The plan was a part of everything and was unchangeable. The plan was righteous and gave everyone the same opportunity for success.

One element of the great plan that had been built into the natural law of the universe, the physics of things, allowed the angels the privilege of hearing the conversations of the inhabitants. The angels understood how these conversations would be used and why they were so important, but the inhabitants of the cold bleak planet did not yet understand. It would take time for them to comprehend the importance of their conversations, but eventually they would.

Unbeknownst to those inhabitants, the natural law of the universe, the physics of things, caused their conversations to be carried to a certain point high above the planet, where the ether picked them up and converted them into radio waves of binary code. The ether currents grasped and transported the coded conversations up to the land of the angels. The inhabitants did not understand this concept, because they did not yet know of the great and magnificent plan that God had developed for them.

Nevertheless, through the natural law of the universe, the physics of things, the conversations were coded and then were converted into digital streams as they moved into the different atmosphere surrounding the beautiful and verdant land of the angels. When these coded conversations arrived at the heavens where the angels lived, they were recorded and categorized. Most of them were then locked into a great computer where they would remain until the new world was in place. These archived conversations would be used to separate the goats from the lambs on judgment day. The goats were those whose names had never been written in the Lamb's book of life.

One type of conversation was recognized as a very special conversation. They were conversations directed to God rather than to other inhabitants. They were called prayers. These prayers blossomed from the thankful hearts of the inhabitants who found great peace when they spoke directly to God. These conversations were separated from all the other conversations and went directly to the glittering palace that sat high on a majestic mountain. The palace was surrounded by a light so beautiful that its' multitude of crystal prisms reflected what appeared to be a million rainbows, bouncing a sparkling tapestry of color across the huge edifice. Because the conversations called prayers were considered very special, they were handled with great and loving care.

Counterfeit prayers of repetition or those spoken for show were easily recognized for their lack of sincerity and were not accepted.

Only genuine prayers would pass on to the glittering palace. Prayers were judged genuine if, and only if they contained a certain element that identified them as coming from a pure heart. Again, through the natural law of the universe, the physics of things, only those prayers coming from a seeking heart that held no guile could pass to the palace. Counterfeit prayers would be caught and recorded and categorized like the other conversations. Only pure prayers with no falsity went to the palace. The angels knew that in the Holy Bible in Luke 18:11,14 God had warned the people by explaining that everyone who exalted himself in prayer as the Pharisee had would be abased.

Prayers that passed to the great palace made the angels happy. They knew these prayers were cherished and knew that the inhabitants who sent these prayers were loved very much by those in the palace. Most often, these prayers came from those whose names were written in the great white book, the Lamb's book of life, that lay open on the table made of marble and gold.

So the angels watched and waited, happy when they saw these special prayers, knowing they were of utmost importance to those who engineered the natural law of the universe, the physics of things. These prayers always got a response. An immediate response. For God had said of these prayers in the Holy Bible: "And the publican . . . saying, God be merciful to me a sinner. I tell you, this man went down to his house justified . . . he that humbleth himself shall be exalted" (Luke 18:13,14).

The learning process came easily to the inhabitants who had an open heart and desired a loving nature. But still, it took time. Before they first began to recognize that they were loved and cared for, they thought that the good things that came their way were just a coincidence. They didn't understand that God was working in their lives to draw them to Him. But as they experienced more and more of what they thought were coincidences, they learned that these things came from God and they were then able to pray differently.

Coincidence

I knelt in reverence to send a prayer
to my Heavenly Father above,
but the answer seemed a coincidence,
not a sign of the Father's love.

Yes, while I asked on bended knee,
in prayer, with folded hands,
I doubted that I had been heard,
and entered in God's plans.

At first, it seemed coincidence,
this answer to my plea,
this is truly how I saw it,
for what else could it be?

And so it went the first time,
the second, and the third,
until one day I realized
my prayers were being heard.

And thus I came to listen,
to God's plan for my life,
and I learned the awesome power
that prayer has over strife.

When God heard these prayers, God smiled. His great and magnificent plan was beginning to take effect. The natural law of the universe, the physics of things that He had instituted to protect and teach the people was progressing. It was bringing about the development of His peculiar people who would understand the nature of evil and seek love instead. And the angels smiled too, and there was singing and rejoicing in the heavens. The first of God's peculiar people had understood. And now the plan could move to the next phase.

Excerpt From:
Grandma's Hidden Treasure

Mary sat in her garden looking out toward the carriage house, watching Rebecca play with six-month-old Teddie. He had Mary's coal black hair and pale blue eyes, but he had Kevin's contagious smile and outgoing personality. He was a happy child who brought so much joy to everyone, and being the only baby in their circle of family and friends, he always had someone to hold him and meet his every need.

They'd chosen the name Theodore because it meant "gift of God," and that was exactly what Teddie was. *How happy my life is now!* Mary thought. *I can understand that living through those terribly difficult times had been the means by which God could reach me and change me.* Mary was so grateful . . . grateful now for the experiences she once thought would destroy her. *It made me ready for this moment,* she thought, *prepared me so I could accept what God wanted to offer us.*

Her mind flew back over how her life had changed since Matt and Sarah had bought the house across the street sixteen months ago. She had been so fearful then. She'd searched for any means that would bring her good luck. She had suffered from panic attacks and sleepless nights and had felt alone and isolated, unable to relate well to others. She had also become obsessed with trying to find peace, harmony, and good fortune through the use of the ancient decorating art of Feng Shui. She'd almost lost Kevin over it. When she'd refused to allow Kevin to bring the beautiful hand-painted chest his sister had sent them into their house fearing bad luck from "poisoned arrows" purported to emanate from all sharp corners, he'd balked. She was glad now that he had. How foolish she had been!

As Mary thought back to life just sixteen months earlier, she realized that her life had been like Grandma's monkey swing; everything she encountered, every effort she made, tipped the foundation of her life, causing it to slip away and fall apart. She'd tried to build a life on the wrong type of foundation and hadn't recognized what would bring balance into her life. But now, thanks to the help of Matt and Sarah, she and Kevin had been able to find that one precious commodity that could change their life and bring them the protection she had longed for.

It had been a slow and painful process, but when she and Kevin finally turned to God, one by one their prayers were answered, and their understanding was opened. Her courage to trust God brought her a miracle of faith by reuniting her with Rebecca. God had also given her Elizabeth as part of that wonderful package. Elizabeth became a sister, a friend, and a mother all rolled into one.

At last, with Matt and Sarah, Ann and Caleb, Debbie and Josh, Barbara and Jim, John and Jayden, her own small family of Kevin, Rebecca, and Elizabeth she was surrounded by the "extended family" she'd always longed for. All of these wonderful and loving friends had become aunts and uncles for Rebecca and Teddie, sisters and brothers for her, Kevin, and Elizabeth. They filled what had been such a terrible void in her own life, and their fellowships together were precious gifts from God. *It is wonderful to share my faith with others and to strive shoulder to shoulder with them toward the same goal.* This thought still brought tears of thankfulness to her eyes. These wonderful people were truly children of God who not only came under God's blessing themselves but taught her every day how to seek His blessing for her and her family in everything she did.

As Mary looked past the children and down the path to the carriage house and saw the last stack of materials awaiting installation, she understood that even in decorating, God had provided them with direction. This still amazed her. *Who would have thought,* Mary wondered, *that God would even teach us what to do in our homes to gain His blessing and protection? Who would have thought that even this would be in scripture?* Now she knew that here was yet another way to touch God's heart.

How wonderful that Sarah found her grandmother's decorating manuscript at just the right moment. *Grandma's journals were a legacy of love, a gift from a heart that had sought God and found Him, a gift that she desired to pass on to all she loved. Grandma would be so happy if she could see how many people she had reached, and to see that her precious Sarah was the instrument God used to do it,* Mary thought.

Mary and Sarah had spoken just yesterday about their many blessings, but they also spoke of the trials and tribulations they may yet face as they walked their path of life. They spoke of the journey ahead of them to reach the goal of becoming the Bride of Christ. Sarah also mentioned the poem she loved so much that showed how God would help them on this journey. Sarah had explained that the poem was based on the story of how footprints in the sand indicated that God carried us through our difficulties. She'd brought Mary a copy. Mary had carried this poem into the garden with her so she could read it a few times and keep it in her heart. She decided to read it again, and read it aloud so Rebecca and Teddie would hear it too.

WHERE ARE YOU?

Lord, I saw some footprints impressed upon the ground,
And recognized a pair was mine, the others, Yours I found.
I saw then that You walked so close, and shared my joyous days.
I felt assured of kinship, and of all Your loving ways.
But then, there came another day, one filled with great despair,
And I asked, "Oh God, where are You?" for the footprints were one pair.
"Must I walk this path alone? Where are You in my pain?
What did I do to make You leave? How can my soul make gain?"
And gently then, the Lord said, "I never left you child,
I carried you safely in My arms; those are My prints through the wild."

—Helen Gumienny Glowacki

As she finished reading, Mary's eyes filled with tears as her thankful heart spilled over, too full to be contained. She sent a silent prayer to God to let Him know how much she appreciated the treasures he placed in her life. Rebecca, Elizabeth, Matt and Sarah, and their family and friends were treasures to nurture and protect.

Mary suddenly recalled something that Sarah had told her about miracles. She'd said, "You know, Mary, we are so spoiled, like the child who asks for a doll for her birthday then sees roller skates and wants them too, never satisfied. We ask God to answer our prayers, and He does, even provides little miracles to prove to us that He answers us. Yet the sly devil comes to us, like he did with Eve, and says, 'Did that *really* mean God heard your prayer? Better ask for confirmation.' And so we ask for more, then more again, as doubt begins its insidious quest to overwhelm us. But it is the little everyday miracles that we should listen to, believe in, even write down so we can stay thankful, stay in the assurance that God is with us every minute."

Mary was thankful for that advice from Sarah. It helped her remember all the little things as well as the big things that God had done for her. So she prayed and asked God to never let any of them stray from Him, to help them remain faithful always, to allow them to keep in their minds all He had done for them.

And God heard, and He gave Mary the promise that He would never let them go. But there would be tests ahead, trials, and cares, and worries, and they were not for Mary alone. But God would be there with them and for them, and He had already provided that Grandma's Hidden Treasure would also be there for them.

About The Author

Helen Gumienny Glowacki is an interior designer, writer, teacher, and motivational speaker. She was the host, writer, and producer of the television series *The Contemporary Woman*, broadcast by UA-Columbia Cablevision, which addressed interior design and the health, relationship, parenting, and life issues of interest to women.

Helen also co-hosted a number of twenty-four-hour telethons featuring celebrity guests to raise funds for various community projects and was a guest co-host for a cable television game show.

Helen's writing credentials include an extensive background as a freelance feature writer and a staff writer for four newspapers; author of newsletter articles; developer of marketing manuals, most notably for the INOVA Hospital System; and designer and editor of a newsletter for the Martin/St. Lucie Chapter of the United States Amateur Ballroom Dancers Association.

A graduate of William Paterson University, Helen received her Bachelor of Arts degree in communications, magna cum laude. Helen also has an associate of science degree with honors and is a registered nurse. She has served on the boards of directors for two associations and taught interior design for adult school programs. Some of her larger design projects include Avon Headquarters in Morton Grove, Illinois, and Chilton Hospital in Pequannock, New Jersey and was listed in *Who's Who of American Women* and *Who's Who of Women Executives* in 1992.

As a popular speaker at ease with an audience, Helen addresses aspects of interior design and addresses the work of God and His word through scripture. Her venues have included women's groups, church groups, community service and religious organizations, high schools and colleges, libraries, cruise ships, and large adult—and assisted-living condominium complexes.

Helen appeared as a guest on a radio show and performed dance routines for theater groups, television, army camps, and veteran's hospitals. She held the title Mrs. Packanack Lake for five years and has received a number of community service awards.

Helen has donated her *"Grandmother Series"* novels and her *"Why God Why Series"* of non-fiction books to cancer centers, drug and alcohol rehabilitation centers, prisons and mission schools, most notably to *The Henwood Foundation* in Zambia, Africa to bring testimony. She also posts articles on her Facebook wall which address our relationship with God,

Helens greatest joys are her husband, two children, and four grandchildren, and singing in the choir of the New Apostolic Church. She and her husband enjoy ballroom dancing and have performed for various charitable functions. Her heart's desire is to help others find the love and comforting presence of God through her writing.

To learn more about Helen's novels and her non-fiction books, visit her website at www.helenglowacki.com.

To become a distributor or to purchase in quantity for a fund raising project or to provide testimony, please send an email to helen@helenglowacki.com.

Helen's readers can also visit the author on Face Book at http://www.facebook.com/pages/The-Grandmother-Series/155300907853909?ref=ts.

𝒩𝑜𝑣𝑒𝓁𝓈 (Book Size 6 x 9)

by Helen Glowacki

When God Broke Grandma's Heart: (208 pages) Rising from sorrow to become a beacon of faith Grandma struggles in an abusive marriage until God moves her from unequally yoked and broken to the healing of His love and forgiveness. Her granddaughter Sarah learns where to find answers to her problems and carries that legacy to those she loves. **Paperback: ISBN 978-1-9847-2110-8**

When God Took Grandma Home: (268 pages) About the heartache of drug addiction, of the enemy who destroys children through drugs, why God allows righteous anger, why we should pray for those in eternity and a description an incredible experience of faith for Matt and Sarah about why God allowed such heartache to occur.
Paperback: ISBN 978-1-9847-2111-5

When Grandma Chased the Spirits: (216 Pages) The magnetism of idolatry, it's invisible power, and the heartache of bearing a child out of wedlock brings debilitating panic attacks to Mary and affects her husband Kevin. When Matt and Sarah tell them about their faith, God engineers a miracle to solve what that they thought impossible to resolve. **Paperback: ISBN 978-1-0847-2112-2**

The Granddaughter and the Monkey Swing: (292 pages) A wedding, a broken engagement, renovating and decorating a home through Divine Proportion, the truth about Halloween, and the gift of role models create a tender story of friendship. Helping through the planning and problems of a wedding culminates in the unveiling of a secret. **Paperback: ISBN 978-1-9847-2113-9**

Grandma's Little Book of Poetry: The Story of God's Plan of Salvation: (285 pages) This beautiful whimsical story for all ages, begins when Sarah finds a manuscript in Grandma's desk and recognizes the story Grandma read to her and Josh and Caleb when they were children. Angels watch the inhabitants below them struggle to find God. **Paperback: ISBN 978-1-9847-2114-6**

Abiding Faith, Hidden Treasure: (270 pages) Serving in Iraq, Jim loses his faith to see a loving God allow so much heartache. Barbara invites him to dinner where Grandma shows him why creation and evolution co-exist and God's enemy creates the injustices Jim blames on God. Letters from the grave bring an incredible experience of faith. **Paperback: ISBN 978-1-9847-2115-3**

And Then They Asked God: (295 Pages) When Rebecca and Jayden arrive at their college campus they are overwhelmed by betrayal. Losing the values Rebecca once cherished fills her with guilt so monumental that she cannot forgive herself. Chaldeth the evil angel is defeated when God's grace frees Jayden and brings Rebecca's recovery. **Paperback: ISBN 978-1-9847-2116-0**

Non-Fiction Books (5 ½ x 8)

by Helen Glowacki

A Politically Incorrect Bible Study: The Get Some Gumption Handbook when Enough is Enough: (297 pages) Fifty timely and controversial issues are examined under the politically correct approach along with a description of what scripture says is the approach that He wants his children to take. **Paperback: ISBN 978-1-4507-9074-1**

The Many Faces o Depression: How To Be Happy: (220 pages) We all face heartache, and all feel sad from time to time. But depression comes from a satanic attack that robs us of hope and our relationship with God. Thus our Heavenly Father tells us through scripture how we can tap into His blessing and find joy even in tribulation. **Paperback: ISBN 978-1-4507-9077-2**

What No One Tells You About Addictions: (220 Pages) Discussing the merits of tough love, the selfish co-dependency of the enabler, what scripture tells us about spiritual warfare and invasion, and generational sin, make this book a must read. **Paperback: ISBN 978-1- 4507--9075-8**

To What Purpose?: (126 pages) The first book of the *Why God Why* series is written to provide answers to questions about why we are here and what we need to learn. It is

written in an easy to read and easy to understand manner and one you will want to share.
Paperback: ISBN 978-1-4507-7580-9

__Why God, Why?__: (126 pages) This second book in the *Why God Why* Series describes why we experience heartache, its purpose, and how to face it. It answers questions about God's plan for us and what we need to do to be found worthy. **Paperback: ISBN 978-1-4507-7581-6**

__Why Trust Scripture?__: (126 pages) This third book in the *Why God, Why* Series addresses the challenges against scripture, who wrote the Bible, the importance of the sacraments, what role Satan plays, and how health and the Bible are related. **Paperback: ISBN 978-1-4507-7582-3**

__What Should I Know about Life after Death and the Coming Tribulation__?: (126 pages) What occurs following death, what will happen during the tribulation, and what the seven seals could mean to us are explained in this fourth book of the series. **Paperback: ISBN 978-1-4507-7583-0**

__What Does God Want Me to do Right Now__?: (126 pages) A concise explanation of what God asks of us, how we can live up to His expectations what is required to become a part of the Bride of Christ, and what God plans for the future with or without us. **Paperback: ISBN 978-1 4507-9076-5**

__Do The Little Sins REALLY Count?__: (126 pages) Most of us believe that the little sins we commit each day are not important on the grander scale, but what does scripture tell us? And interesting look at the Bride of Christ. **Paperback: ISBN 978-9847-2117-7**

Book Reviews

Rev. Richard C. Freund, President, New Apostolic Church USA, Sea Cliff, New York: Magnificent writer, a story that makes the reader become emotionally involved, a joy to read, strong Christian values. *"When God Broke Grandma's Heart",* best seller quality.

Rev. Fred Krueger, (Ret.) Lutheran Minister 12 yrs and Clinical Social Worker 26 yrs, Dallas, Texas: "Inspiring, grabs the heart, author headed to the bestseller list, a pleasure to read, masterful. *"When God Took Grandma Home"* filled with insight into God's plan!

Rev. Richard C. Freund, President, New Apostolic Church USA, Sea Cliff, New York: *"When God Took Grandma Home"* "Delights, brings comfort to those who grieve. Inspires, gives insight into the after-life, masterful portrayal.

Priest Derryck Beukes, Montana-De Aar Congregation, Northern Cape, South Africa: Dear Helen, I personally often use your articles in my soul care visits, especially where youth are involved. I can assure you that your articles made a difference to my way of thinking, and I am busy encouraging fellow priests to read your works, as they are so factual and insightful! Thank you for your hard work. II thank God for you, and the wisdom He gave you! Please continue with the excellent work.

Deacon Shadreck Wilima, Overspill Congregation, Ndola, Zambia: Your articles prompt realistic examples which New Apostolic Christians need for their everyday living.

Youth Chairperson, Sunday School teacher, Mulenga Ernest, Lusaka Central Congregation, Lusaka, Zambia: Through your writing I am constantly reminded of what to be aware of. I pray that God keeps you in the hollow of His hand, guards you and guides you to reach your brethren as you do me. Thanks for caring for the souls of many.

Priest Aurelio Cerullo, Atripalda Congregation, Campania, Southern Italy: Your books and articles, and even your social networking are a means to bring brothers and sisters the words of our faith and to touch the hearts of those who do not know our faith. Our goal can still be found through the grace of the apostolate and in this sense, the word's from 1 Corinthians 15:58 assumes an important meaning: *"Therefore, my beloved brethren, be steadfast, immovable, always abounding in the work of the Lord, Knowing That your labor is not in vain in the Lord"*. Now that I am a minister of God for about a year I too am grateful to our beloved Father in Heaven for having opened the eyes of my soul, for having removed the plugs from my ears of my heart to hear and listen to His will in connection and communion with those who precede us, guided by the light of the Holy Spirit. God's work always evolves and adapts to the times and even via computers, cell phones and smart phones. I Thank God for having been able to know you, you're a very valuable pearl. God bless you richly.

NOTE: The articles which are referred to in these reviews are excerpts from Helen Glowacki's non-fiction books. Not shown are reviews by the ministers who oversee *The Henwood Foundation*'s New Apostolic Mission Schools in Zambia and review all reading materials prior to distribution.

Priest Andrew Muliokela, Alexandria Virginia congregation: *The Granddaughter and the Monkey Swing* and this series of books is awesome! A journey unlike another, read a great novel, learn about confidence, love and support but also learning Bible verses at the same time! Helen Glowacki teaches through her books and I recommend them 100%. You'll enjoy the journey!

Priest Kevin Speranza, Palm Beach Gardens Congregation, Florida: *And Then They Asked God* so happy I read this, weaves and documents biblical precepts, addresses political correctness, moral & political corruption, biased teaching, the insidious growth of socialism renamed progressivism, self-importance, guilt and its debilitating power. WELL DONE! Identifies danger, artfully shows Biblically how to address them.

Frederick Rothe, Retired NAC Minister, Fort Pierce, Florida: Retired minister spending 48 years serving God another 30 in the congregation. These books contain an accurate account of what God wants of us, why we suffer. The application of scripture and the people in the stories stand for the principles God wants in all of us.

Patricia Robinson, wife of a Ret. Rector, Indiana 5 star rating: *When God Broke Grandma's Heart*: WONDERFUL INSPIRATIONAL NOVEL, enjoyed this book, well written, Bible references , how to achieve peace of mind and soul .

Colette van Loggerenberg, wife of a Priest, Scottsville Congregation of Pietermaritzberg, South Africa: *Grandma's Little Book of Poetry: The Story of God's Plan of Salvation:* This has to be one of the BEST EVER books that I have read....If you ever get the chance to get one of Helen's novels...READ IT. It's like a fairytale but a TRUE fairytale.....Close your eyes and picture this: Grandma with her hair in a bun, glasses perched delicately on her nose, sitting delicately on her nose, sitting in a rockying chair with her grandchildren sitting on the floor with BIG eyes hanging onto her every word.....but with a twist!!!!! If you have doubts about PRAYERS...read this book. I LOVED IT...thank you Helen Glowacki in a rocking chair and her grandchildren sitting on the floor with BIG eyes hanging onto her every word.....but with a twist!!!!! If you have doubts about PRAYER...read this book. I LOVED IT...thank you!

Debbie Espeland, wife of a Rector, Palm Beach Gardens Congregation, Florida: 5 star rating: **When God Took Grandma Home** is so HEARTWARMING! This book touched my heart. It is both heartwarming and very spiritual.

Aletta Venter, wife of a Deacon, Scottsville Congregation, Pietermaritzburg, South Africa: *"Grandma's Little Book of Poetry: The Story of God's Plan of Salvation".* What a learning process for me. Oooh I just **love** the way the angels are telling the story, **very original!** When is mankind ever going to learn? The inhabitant's lesson was to learn of good and evil. And they failed miserably each time. The devil has his agenda, and the inhabitants are the target. They call upon God for help, the angels rejoiced. Great....!!!

Priest Luke Jansen, Sr. V. P., Medical Connections, Boca Raton, Florida: "To Ms. Glowacki, author of **The Grandma Series**: grateful for your books, refreshing to find a Christian author who sees the *difference* between religion and spirituality AND that the two can and should be used in the same sentence."

292

Aletta Venter, wife of a Deacon, Pietermaritzburg, South Africa: *"Abiding Faith, Hidden Treasure"* is the deepest and most rewarding novel I have ever read, touched my soul, made me cry, author's understanding of God's work is astounding, opens the mysteries

Katharina Leipp, Schopfheim, Germany: This is the first time I have ever heard of a female New Apostolic author and I am very impressed by your articles. I have sent your link to my Shepherd and German friends and would like you to consider advertising in our German *Our Family Magazine.*

Rosemarie Schaal, wife of a retired Evangelist, Palm City, Florida: *Abiding Faith, Hidden Treasure:* Reader develops empathy, feels emotion, hears a battle between scientific and spiritual knowledge. Skillful, detailed, brilliant, vivid, teaches nothing happens that is not planned by Him.

Claudine Visagie, South Africa: I'm trying to think of a way to introduce Helen's books and articles to others... especially to our youth. They are life changing!

Rabecca Mukuta Mukato, Lusaka, Zambia, Africa: Speaking on behalf of my Dad, District Elder Mulako, your articles are brilliant because they have changed me! Because of your articles my Dad has less headaches!

Edith Stier, 32 Years as the wife of a Minister, (Ret. Dist. Ev), Clifton, New Jersey: *The Grandma Series* helps those in need, inspirational, heartwarming, ends with a beautiful example of how God explains our pain, renews hope, shows us the way, creates miracles. I love this series.

Tammera Shelton, M.S. Psychology, Odenton, Maryland: I find *"When God Broke Grandma's Heart"* inspirational, beautifully portrays need to let go of negative events and that despite injustice, no pain is for naught.

Robert W. Rothe, USMC 1970-1976, Nevada: 5 star rating: *When God Broke Grandma's Heart:* Outstanding writer, kept me riveted, an angel sent to help through trying days. Thank you for helping me find peace.

Frank Geores, from Port St. Lucie, Florida: *"When Grandma Chased The Spirits:* beautiful spiritual experience, can see caring nature and loving heart of author, eloquently reveals her love for God and search for truth. Worthy of the Star of Bethlehem rating. Thank you for sharing your magnificent gift.

Ben Lodwick, Avid Reader., from Brookfield, Wisconsin: Wow! An eye opener about God's plan of salvation, and why bad things happen to good people. Reminds me of Jim LaHaye and Jerry B. Jenkins "Left Behind Series". MUST READ!"

Dr. Walter Forman From North Palm Beach, Florida: *Grandma's Little Book of Poetry: The Story of God's Plan of Salvation:* a "wonderful book about success and failure in life. All Helen's novels are wonderful, a balm for the soul and an education to the seeker."

Susan Day, From Jupiter, Florida: *Abiding Faith, Hidden Treasure* : I hated to put it down, couldn't wait to pick it up, read all Helen's books, proves every point, shows what to do through God's words. I am 90 and Helen's books have helped me call on God.

Georgette Rothe, From Fort Piece, Florida: *Abiding Faith, Hidden Treasure* was more than I expected, like a Biblical course making you re-evaluate your beliefs, enjoyed the journey very much.

Fred D'Alauro, from Palm Beach Shores, Florida: Internet 5 star rating: **When God Took Grandma Home:** Remarkable! Inspirational and moving. A fascinating storyteller with a real message.

Debra Forman, Chester, New York. Internet 5 star rating: *When God Broke Grandma's Heart:* Written from the heart, shares the strong beliefs that shelters us in times of need, courage captivates the reader. Thank you.

Anonymous: Internet 5 star rating: *When God Broke Grandma's Heart:* WHEN LIFE GETS YOU DOWN, PICK THIS BOOK UP, it wrapped its arms around me. A wonderful read. Congratulations on an inspiring work.

A reviewer, a reader in Kentucky: Internet 5 star rating: *When God Broke Grandma's Heart:* Well written, heartwarming, overcoming heartbreak through God, touches your heart. A worthwhile read for all generations.

A reader: Internet 5 star rating: *When God Broke Grandma's Heart:* a must read for all generations. FANTASTIC!

A reviewer Internet 5 star rating: *When God Took Grandma Home:* Moves you, captivating.

A reviewer, a Kentucky reader: Internet 5 star rating: *When God Took Grandma Home:* MUST READ! Touching story of life's tragedies and how lessons learned from these heartbreaking events can turn into blessings.

Novel Characters

Grandma: Grandma's life was filled with sibling betrayal and marital abuse. Her love of God, home remedies and famous boxing stance touches the heart.

Sarah: Sarah helps Grandma write her journal, learns about God's plan of salvation and the enemy who wants to harm her. She carries on Grandma's legacy of faith.

Matt: Matt, Sarah's husband, has a rock-like faith but when he loses a loved one, struggles with his anger with God, until he has a miraculous experience of faith.

Paul: Paul is Matt's older brother who earned a Captain's license for a seagoing tugboat. His faith sustains him despite enduring terrible circumstances.

Mary and Kevin: Mary and Kevin become Matt and Sarah's neighbors and friends. Mary's panic attacks end when God brings a miracle they never thought possible.

Elizabeth: Elizabeth adopts Rebecca, loses her husband twelve years later, is confronted with a potentially deadly illness and searches for Rebecca's birth mother.

Rebecca: Rebecca is Elizabeth daughter and Jayden's friend. Her father's death, the illness her mother faces, and a series of challenges at college almost destroy her.

John: John, a deacon, lost his wife to a debilitating disease, becomes Elizabeth's friend, and helps his daughter and grandson through a difficult divorce.

Jayden: Jayden is John's grandson and becomes Rebecca's friend. He has learned that prayer helps solve problems and he and Rebecca begin to share their faith.

Wade and Ruth: Wade is Jim's boss and friend who adopts two children from Iraq. Ruth is Jayden's mother and John's daughter who struggles to let go of the past.

Joshua and Debbie: Joshua, Sarah's younger brother, was demanding and judgmental until Caleb stepped in. Debbie looks to Joshua's family to be her role models.

Caleb and Ann: Caleb is Sarah and Josh's older brother and the family looks to him as they once looked to Grandma. Ann, Caleb's wife harbors a secret sadness.

Barbara and Jim: Barbara, Matt's sister is also Sarah's close friend. Her husband Jim plays devil's advocate in family debates, and matchmaker for his friend Wade.

Heza and Bara: Heza and Bara endured a suicide bomber attack when Bara was one and one half years old and Heza as she was born. They are adopted by Wade.

Chaldeth: Chaldeth is a fallen angel sent to destroy Grandma's family. He plots to bring great heartache to Rebecca and Jayden and their family to break their faith.

Durk: Durk, abused by a cruel father, is a sophomore at the college Rebecca and Jayden attend. He brings great harm to Rebecca and Jayden but Jim gives him a second chance and Jayden and Rebecca offer him forgiveness.

Professsor T. Nagorra, and Emils, and Dean Peerca: These tenured professors befriend Durk and engage in activities which brings harm to the students and the campus.

Professors Doog and Sendnik, and President Legna: These three share a faith in God, a love for their country, and desire to be role models. They help save the campus.